Praise for *Spilling Clarence*

"Anne Ursu's interesting and offbeat debut novel . . . raises essential questions: Is it only the easing of pain over time that keeps us willing to face the future? Are we able to keep on living only because, blessedly, we forget how hard life really is?"

—*Minneapolis Star Tribune*

"Total recall stirs up differing emotions for these characters, and is the ideal vehicle for Ursu's descriptive skill; like Proust, she understands the link between our recollections and our five senses."

—*San Diego Union Tribune*

"Oh, what a book! Haunting, heartbreaking and, at turns, very, very funny, Ursu's *Spilling Clarence* is about regret, loss, love and, most particularly, the power of our memories—the ones we desperately cling to, and the ones we'd give our very souls to be able to forget. Peopled with a cast of characters as indelible as a waking dream, and written in pitch-perfect prose, *Spilling Clarence* is a profoundly original exploration of what it means to be human."

—Caroline Leavitt, author of *Coming Back to Me*

SpillingClarence

Spilling Clarence

anne ursu

An Imprint of Hyperion
New York

Library of Congress Cataloging-in-Publication Data

Ursu, Anne.
    Spilling Clarence / by Anne Ursu.—1st ed.
      p.   cm.
    ISBN 0-7868-6778-7
    1. Pharmaceutical industry—Fiction. 2. Industrial accidents—Fiction. 3. City and town
life—Fiction. 4. Reminiscing—Fiction. 5. Minnesota—Fiction. 6. Regret—
Fiction. I. Title
PS3621.R78 S65 2002
813'.6—dc21   2001024097

Paperback ISBN 0-7868-8662-5

FIRST PAPERBACK EDITION

10 9 8 7 6 5 4 3 2 1

to my mother and father

act one   spill

one.

Clarence, before spill

THE BREAK ROOM microwave is dead, to begin with. There is no doubt whatever about that. It has been in the process of dying for a great many years; for the psychopharmaceutical factory employees, the chunky box has always acted as an orangy-brown reminder of bygone decades.

Through the years, the appliance's failure to shuffle off this mortal coil (never mind the management's refusal to replace the thing) has slowly changed from seeming absurd to downright inspirational. As a result, people have been using it less and less, and recently the brave factory workers who have attempted to cook food in it have done so surreptitiously, lest they be identified as the one whose ultra-lite popcorn finally did in their Saiushi EZWave 4000.

So, now, with the break room empty and the hallways clear, one of the secretaries turns the primeval knobs to the appropriate settings, then scurries out the door. Thus, nobody is in the room to hear the prophetic crackle crackle pop as the magnetron tube bursts, or to notice the smoke rising, or to see sparks come out of the thick black umbilical cord. The microwave sighs its last sigh and the break room quickly transforms into a funeral pyre.

The fire alarm shrieks and wails, and as workers begin to proceed in a calm and orderly fashion out the door, the sprinklers activate throughout the Harris Jones psychopharmaceutical factory. It does not take long for the old old sprinkler system to short out the old old electrical wiring. Just as the plant safety engineer takes the massive Emergency Procedures binder off the shelf, a red light on his operations panel begins to flash, foretelling the demise of the refrigeration system. As he skims the index of the manual, the blue light that monitors the supercooled chemical tanks begins to blink frantically. As he flips to page 34, the molecules of the liquid chemicals in the refrigerated tanks begin to excite and expand, ready to transform into a new state of matter and reach a higher plane. The safety engineer finds the appropriate code, and as the tanks swell, he turns to his old old computer and punches in Code 121: *Fire in the Factory. Likely Airborne Dispersal.*

Then he calls his wife and tells her to get out of Clarence, pronto. And take the cats.

IT WILL BE a few more minutes before the sound of the civil defense sirens startles the customers flipping through books and sipping lattes in the town of Clarence's new Davis and Dean superstore. For now, though, it is commerce that is airborne. Through the currency of bright smiles and swooshes of credit cards and thank-you-for-shopping-have-a-nice-days, capitalism foams and bubbles over like frothed milk. Booksellers beam at bookbuyers, cash registers pop open, receipts churn and coil, bags blouse, doors revolve—the people of Clarence enter and leave inexorably, accompanied by noncontroversial jazz and humming air-conditioning. It is a perfect sixty-eight degrees in the store, and Clarence wants to buy.

Bennie and Sophie Singer sit in the bookstore's café today, as they have every Friday since the Davis and Dean was built. Friday has been Bookstore Day for the two of them ever since Sophie learned to read. Lizzie, actually, started the tradition, back before there was a Sophie. Bookstores with cafés were a rare and wondrous phenomenon back then, and the newly wedded Ben and Elizabeth McCourt Singer would sit at a table every Friday afternoon reading the magazines they couldn't afford to subscribe to. Lizzie would pore over women's magazines—her secret obsession—gleefully searching for tropes, discourse, and dogma, and Bennie would read newsweeklies searching for nothing in particular. One Friday, he reading *The New Yorker*, she studying advertisements in *Elle*, he picked up her hand, almost knocking over her coffee.

When we have a child, we will take her to the bookstore every Friday.

Lizzie looked up from her magazine and beamed.

Bennie blinks the memory away.

Bennie and Sophie Singer sit in the café today, as they do every Friday. Bennie will schedule no students, attend no meetings, allow no exceptions. I have a standing date, he explains to the sputtering cognitive behaviorist as he shuts his office door and scurries out of the psych building to pick Sophie up from school. We'll do it on Monday. I'm here late on Mondays.

It's not as if the department could like him any less.

Bennie is the token Personality professor at Mansfield University, and is thus looked upon with some derision by those who think an understanding of the human psyche is best achieved through close interaction with rodents and computer simulations. Bennie, in turn, despises the notion that human behavior can be explained through the interplay of impulses and neurons, chemicals and electricity, mice and mazes. If humanity is really so base, what is the point of living? What is the point of experience? What is the point of the mind? At Mansfield, psychology students dissect and experiment. They will be excellent researchers, yes, but who will treat the patients?

Sophie can buy one book a week. She always knows what she will buy as they enter the store; she spends her time amongst the stacks categorizing and prioritizing for weeks to come. Then, after Sophie has finished crawling through the kids' section, the two retire to the café. Sophie has an Italian soda. The first Friday of the month she has cherry, the second orange, the third raspberry, and the fourth lime. If there are five Fridays in a month, then she has strawberry kiwi, which is her favorite. Bennie has the coffee of the day with three to four packets of artificial sweetener.

Now, Sophie sips her raspberry soda and flips through books from children's reference while Bennie wishes thoughts away. Sophie eats these books up every week, washing facts down with neon soda. She will remember them all. Sophie remembers everything. She knows countries and capitals, states and dates. She knows wars and treaties, tribes and tributaries. She knows Greek gods and Roman hills. She knows Tippecanoe and Tyler too; she can list First Pets, First Ladies, and even some of the mistresses.

It awes Bennie. Did he ever know this much? Could he reel off the posts of the Cabinet and the ranks of the British peerage system fueled only by childhood alacrity and a sugar high?

I don't know, sweetie, he smiles as she quizzes him. You tell me. I'm getting old, sweetie. Bennie gave up on history long ago, but when did it give up on him? When did all the facts leave him? Where did they go? Sure, there are remnants. Mnemonic devices still linger. Every good boy deserves favor. Please excuse my dear Aunt Sally. My very earnest mother judiciously served us nine potatoes. King Peter came over from Germany seeking fortune. The phrases rattle in his head, but Bennie can't remember what they are for—random keys cluttering a drawer and he has no idea what doors they unlock. Stripped of their meaning they become surrealist mantras. His own Dada manifesto. Art for Art's sake. Meaning is dead. Facts are a lie. His little girl can list off Great Lakes, types of rock, and geological eras, while he struggles every night to recall the smell of his wife's hair.

He would have killed himself if it hadn't been for Sophie. There's no doubt about that.

Sacred Fridays with Sophie give respite from real life days of blue books and department meetings and nights of clammy sheets and irrevocable dreams. He has given his life to his daughter, and now there is no going back. The agreement is unspoken, unconfirmed, but six years ago when Bennie chose Sophie's nascent life over his much desired death, he made a bargain with his toddler daughter: I, Benjamin, will live for you. In turn, you, Sophia Madeline, must never leave me.

Couldn't the world freeze, and he always be sitting here with Sophie with eyes as bright as her soda, so full of Lizzie? It is absurd, impossible, he knows, but why not?

"Hey, Soph . . ."

"Hmm?"

"Do you remember that story I used to read to you? About the magic watch?"

She sighs and looks up from her encyclopedia. "Which story?"

"You know, the watch that controlled time. There were trolls and they had this watch and they would speed time up, stop it, send it back, stop the world."

"Dad, they weren't trolls, they were elves. The girl elf made a wish. The genie heard. She got this watch."

"Elves. Yes, that was it. That was one of my favorites."

Sophie tosses her thin blond hair. "Yeah, it was okay."

Bennie leans in. "Wouldn't it be nice if it were true? If we could wish a genie down here, if he could give us a magic watch. We could just sit here and you could read your books and drink your sodas as long as you wanted."

Sophie sighs again in the way she sees on TV and closes her book. "Dad, you should know better than that."

"Oh, Soph, it's just pretend."

"Yeah, but didn't you learn anything from the story? Don't you remember what happened to that girl elf? That's the way it always happens in stories—wishes seem like a really good idea but then you get your wish and things get all messed up. That's what wishes do. That's the way stories go. That's the whole point."

Sophie smiles at her father compassionately and opens her big white book back to "Flags of the World."

The civil defense sirens will go off in another two minutes. For now, Bennie Singer sits in the café and stares at the wall and wonders at how still the world has become.

THE DAVIS AND Dean superstore sits equidistant from the psycho-pharmaceutical factory and Mansfield University. Walk outside the bookstore's revolving doors. Stand on the sidewalk. Turn your head to the right, and you'll see the three smokestacks on the horizon. Turn to the left and you see photo-perfect towers and spires. The effect is off-putting, the dissonance dizzying. Look again. And again. And again. The factory and the university face each other warily, and you, caught in the middle, do not know which way to turn.

Harris Jones Pharmaceuticals is owned by HJ Medical Systems down in the Cities. The company's particular specialty, and the Clarence factory's niche, is the mind. Harris Jones dedicates itself essentially to treating the modern condition; their medications attack such ailments as anxiety, distraction, depression. Their stock is on its way up, and you might consider making a small investment.

Occasionally there is some grumbling among the factory workers of Clarence about the nature of the drugs made at their plant. After all, the economy of the town is based on the factory, but anxiety, sleep, fear, depression, and despair are not the town's problems. (At lunch, a worker points at the photo-perfect towers and spires to indicate just whose problems these are.) The people of Clarence make drugs for outsiders to take. They work day and night making drugs for rich people. What kind of medications are these anyway? Medications are for sickness. For life and death. Not for mood. What kind of people have the need and resources to medicate their mind?

Shouldn't their livelihoods be based on something they can use? Harris Jones worries about insurance, losses, reputation. Who will take care of Clarence? What if something should happen? All those chemicals . . .

If there were any poetry at all in Clarence, there would be a great river running through the town. The river would bisect Clarence perfectly; factory on one side, college on the other. Time card punchers on one side, dentists on the other; American cars on one side, foreign on the other. If there were any poetry in Clarence, the river would divide the town's two worlds with a deft blue stroke manifesting the bifurcation in perpetual motion. If Clarence had poetry, there would at least be some good old railroad tracks to give the town its proverbial right and wrong side (which is which would be depending on your point of view, of course).

Clarence has no poetry, though. Clarence has Bargain Barrels, Krazy Savers, Dollar Hutz, and Pizza Domes. The division, then,

must remain invisible. Theoretical. Philosophical. Literary. Like
the international date line or the boundaries of good taste.

The best anyone can do is invite you to take a tour. Visit some restaurants and compare—say Vinnie's, then Tandoori Jewel. Bob's
Bar, then Strange Brew Café. Susie's Secondhands and The Closet.
Contrast the crowds, the clothes, the conversation. Hairstyles. Ac-
cents and accessories. Study. Use what you have learned. Go to the
common grounds—gas stations, grocery stores, fast food restaurants.
Guess who is from which world. There. You are able to begin drawing the line yourself. A deft stroke in perpetual motion.

The Davis and Dean superstore has tried valiantly to bridge the
gap. The Clarence store is an experiment after all, and harmony is
essential to the experiment's success.

A few years ago, the Davis and Dean muckety-mucks met to
discuss the next phase of the war between D&D and its nemesis,
Vanguard Books. The combatants had already consumed and exhausted the cities and suburbs and exurbs; there needed to be a
new battleground. Thus was born Operation Hinterland. D&D
would strike in the less populated areas. Where men wear flannel
shirts and smell like a hard day's work. Real People. America's
heartland. Mom, Pop, Apple Pie, Bait and Tackle, and the Good
Lord. Research teams and focus groups led Davis and Dean straight
to Clarence—home of Mom and Pop, and of Mansfield University. Thus, there would be deportees from the city—with their
proven able brand recognition—to lead the way through the
store's doors.

Clarence's mayor has a strong sense of capitalistic duty, and
the experiment, to be sure, would be talked about in all the
trades and business weeklies. People would be watching closely.
Other progressively minded nationally sanctioned companies
might come. The economy would soar. Clarence would soar. So
when Davis and Dean officials came to the mayor carrying pro-

posals and compensations and all kinds of charts with towering majestic columns and bright happy graphs with arrows going up, up, up, the mayor in turn said, Yes. Please. Come. What shall we knock down for you?

There were a few protests of course. A Chamber of Commerce splinter group called Stop National Chains in Clarence (SNCC) held a Breaking the Chain rally on the front lawn of the city hall steps with folksingers and a bad sound system. The rally was small; many of the Clarence elders thought that they could not possibly support anything that involved folksingers. Those who did march on the town hall spoke passionately of a desire to keep Clarence *Clarence* without those nasty big city chain influences coming in to homogenize and desensitize. What would separate Clarence from any other city, now? What good are these corporations? Who will watch out for Clarence?

But in a few weeks everyone stopped caring, as is the general way of things. Hands were shook, documents signed, announcements made, ground broken, espresso imported, and Bingo! Clarence joined the Davis and Dean empire well before Vanguard could move their troops into the hinterlands.

And the experiment is working. D&D has become a community center. A piazza. The factory worker and the college professor sip coffee side by side. And since the store was built, no aimless Mansfield humanities graduate has ever been in want of a job. You know this place. You may be there now. And we have a good place to begin our story.

AS BENNIE FINISHES the last gulp of his coffee, the safety engineer's wife and her two cats get on the freeway leading straight out of Dodge. Police sirens sound quietly in the distance. Add fire trucks. Ambulances. One screech after another joins the chorus and the sirens crescendo, grow more immediate. The emergency is close. And getting closer. One after another, people in the store look up, look out the windows, joke nervously and laugh like choking.

Is the store on fire? *Heh heh. Heh. Heh . . .*

Heh.

Then the cacophony passes by and fades off into the distance. Someone else's emergency. The bookstore exhales and the air returns to normal—

—and then the emergency alert sirens go off.

There is silence in the bookstore. Customers and employees look at each other. Nobody moves.

Is it a test?

It's not the right time of the month.

A tornado this late in the year?

A man peeks out of the window. The sky is smoky and yellow. "Look at that!" he yells. Everyone looks.

The stillness grows. The sirens blare on. Everyone watches each other watch everyone else. Bennie is frozen. His mind flashes to his yearly freshman psych lecture on the bystander effect; after Kitty Genovese was killed on the streets of New York while an entire neighborhood watched and did nothing, a group of psychologists ran an experiment: In a room where students are taking a test, smoke pours through the vents. If a person is by himself, he will pull an alarm, call someone, leave the room. If the person is in a group, smoke will fill the room and he will glance around, cough, wait for someone else to act.

Bennie has always given this lecture with a degree of arrogance, of reassurance. I am a psychologist. I know the urges. I understand the nature. I will be better than this.

But in the face of all this stillness he finds himself frozen. His lungs constrict. The sirens burst in his ear.

It is not until Sophie looks at him, big eyed, her body shrinking into the chair. "Daddy—?"

"It's okay, sweetheart," he whispers, and smiles, then announces to everyone, "Perhaps we should turn on the radio?"

The black-haired girl behind the café counter emerges from the back room with a small radio. Sophie smiles at her father worshipfully. The sirens continue to wail and with a twist and click, the radio begins to harmonize.

This is the emergency broadcast system. This is not a test. All residents of Clarence are asked to stay where they are. Repeat, stay where you are. This is not a test. All residents of Clarence, stay inside. Stay tuned to this station for further instructions.

Davis and Dean employees begin to bring other customers to the café. A man in a cartoon bird tie introduces himself as the manager. "We'd like to ask everyone to stay in the store. We're bringing down more radios."

He smiles nonthreateningly, and the relief among the customers is palpable: *It is all right. Someone is in charge here. We have a manager. He will tell us what to do.*

Outside of the window of the store, creatures covered in yellow billowy plastic begin to appear, carting road blocks.

The customers in the bookstore start.

What the—

Yellow guys do not just happen. Yellow guys are not in my life. Yellow guys do not just emerge out of thin air. Yellow guys are in the movies. Yellow guys are not real. Yellow guys are for Chernobyl, not Clarence. Why don't I have a yellow suit? I do not have a yellow suit. Where the hell is my yellow suit? I quite clearly need a yellow suit.

People begin to stare at each other more frankly. They appraise obviously, guiltlessly. Their eyes ask, Who are these people? Is one of them responsible? Are they all bystanders too, hostages in a movie, trapped in an elevator, on a bus with a bomb? Will we be huddled here, days later, on the floor, dirty and thin? One person always dies. One is always afraid. One is brave and sneaks through the vents and frees us all. The rest are extras, with muddy, panicked faces, providing occasional squeals and moans.

And through the room, the thought passes: I am an extra. The time has come, and I am just an extra.

This is the emergency broadcast system. This is not a test. All residents of Clarence are asked to stay where they are. Chemical accident. Possible toxic exposure. Stay inside. If you are in your car, park, close the vents, and stay where you are. Stay tuned to this station for further instructions.

"It's the factory."

People nod their heads.

"Goddamn chemicals."

"What's going to happen to us?"

The room is as close and shrill as the sirens.

Bennie turns and glares. Be quiet. Everyone. Can't you see there's a little girl here. Can't you see my daughter is young. Can't you see my Sophie is scared. Take a deep breath, everyone. Remain calm. Panicking is human instinct but we can overcome it. Mind over matter.

Bennie cares about three people in Clarence. There is his accidental friend, Phil, Contemporary Studies professor. Phil will be at the university, working. Phil will be all right. There is his mother, Madeline, in Sunny Shadows, Clarence's retirement community. She will be there, in her apartment. They will have procedures for this sort of thing. They have people in charge. Fire exits, tornado cellars, bottled water and canned food. Mother will be all right. There is Sophie, shrinking, withering, here. Sophie has only him.

The manager fingers his tie nervously. He whispers to the café worker, Lilith, who begins to cut up scones and muffins from the café. The radio blares on.

There has been a fire at the Harris Jones pharmaceutical factory. Barrels of chemicals have exploded. There has been a deletrium leak, repeat, deletrium leak. Possible harmful exposure. Chemical spill. Stay inside and await further instructions.

"What the bloody fuck is deletrium?" a bookseller mutters. The manager glares at her. But nobody minds. Everyone shares the sentiment.

Sophie says in a small voice, "My dad will know. He's a professor. Don't you know, Dad?"

Heads turn. Bennie blushes and shakes his head. Sophie looks down at the table. Bennie grabs her hand.

Susannah Korbet sits in the café tugging at her brown ringlets, absorbing other people's panic, and thinking about her fiancé, Todd. Todd will be working at the school lab. Todd wouldn't leave anyway. Todd may not even hear the sirens. But Todd would know what deletrium is. Todd would know exactly what this does. Todd would look it up on his computer, print out fact sheets, conduct his own experiments. Todd would have multicolored easy-to-read charts printed up. Todd would stand in the center of the room humbly stating his graduate student credentials and would make a presentation that would both soothe and edify. Half the girls in the room would develop a crush on him. The men would cede the title of alpha male without complaint.

There was a time when Susannah would think about this with pride. Now she feels nothing but blame. If something happens, it is because Todd brought her here. If something happens, he will probably be immune.

Before the sirens, Susannah Korbet sat in the bookstore café twirling her masses of curls in her fingers, trying to discern any differences between the mural on the wall here and the one in the D&D café by her home one thousand miles away. She thought she could almost be there. If you added diversity, urbanity, and fashion sense to this small-town bookstore crowd, Susannah could have pretended she was back home.

Now, sirens blaring, things become more urgent for her. If she closes her eyes and concentrates on the mural, she could be transported back to that D&D. Holes in the stores should open up, and she should be able to move through them effortlessly, one to another in a blink and a click of the heels. Away from sirens and away from Clarence.

The radio continues to proclaim, the manager continues to smile, and everyone's thoughts continue to run on the same current: Is this the moment when everything changes? Will my life thus far be thought of as Before the Spill? Ah yes, that was Clarence, Before Spill. You're referring to Clarence, B.S.? Will we be those people, those people on the news and on miniseries who lose all of life as they know it? Will our children have six heads and bad dispositions? Are we living a disaster movie? Where is the ominous music? Where are the heartfelt declarations? There must be more than the radio, pieces of currant scones, and these billowy yellow men.

A dozen lives flash before a dozen pairs of eyes, and the reckoning begins: Nothing. I've done nothing. I am nothing. I am a waste. It has all been wasted. I could have done so much. I would have done it all differently. Now I become a cancerous blob with a tail and too many toes, a living hideous monument to failure and regret.

But our heroes do not reckon. Reckoning is for people whose lives have motion. Susannah Korbet and Bennie Singer look at their lives at the same moment and find that they feel nothing.

Of course, they look at the present. They stalwartly refuse to awaken what lies in memory.

two.

All these things are locked away.

SUSANNAH KORBET HAS spent a lot of time finding just the right words to describe the backwater podunk one-horse hole-in-the-ground that is Clarence. Susannah has always been very interested in precision of language.

Clarence, she says, seems to consist of five police officers, four country music stations, three family-style restaurants, two lesbians, and one Lutheran way of life. Down the street from the apartment she and Todd share is Nelson's Redemption Center, which Susannah naturally assumed was for Jesus but she has discovered is really for bottles and cans.

And there is the factory. The revolting stink that emanates from it permeates Clarence's every corner. When she and Todd moved in, Susannah thought something had rotted in their apartment. She checked the refrigerator, the sink, the bathroom, she left a message with the landlord, then she went outside to buy some air freshener and she realized the whole world had rotted.

In her daily life, Susannah Korbet has always spent a lot of time pandering to her olfactory glands. It is a basic courtesy; in a world full of chaos, the least we can do is smell pleasant. Susannah uses room deodorizers, scented bath gels, talcs, moisturizers, candles. She washes her clothes carefully. She has developed an attachment to a certain kind of dryer sheet. To Susannah, poor hygiene in an individual is a sure sign either of a lack of self-respect or of a rebellious, antisocial nature—both good reasons to keep your distance. She has never before encountered these problems on an incorporated scale.

At first sniff, Todd smelled like artificial pine additives.

Susannah has spent a lot of time contemplating the precise nature of the factory smell in Clarence. This is what she has come up with:

The air here has a carrion-after-one-thousand-noontime-suns quality; an eau de rotted flesh rubbed with rancid milk; a perfume of fusty armpits, melted skunk, and old bananas; an aura of the leftover lard of fat-fried death. The wind carries the smell of the place Chinese food goes to die.

Things weren't like this in the city. The whiff of car exhaust still summons recollections of heartskip glances and breathless afternoons. A Mansfield student drives by, windows down, music blaring, and Susannah is back on the streets of the city, drinking cappuccinos and twirling with love.

Now, pine-scented fiancé Todd is in his first year of Mansfield University's Memory Studies Ph.D. program. Getting into Mansfield is a coup, but Todd specializes in coups. He could have gone anywhere he wanted to, and because of Memory Studies, he wanted to go to Mansfield.

"Come with me. Please. Susannah. You are the energy to my

potential energy, the e to my MC squared, the principle to my uncertainty. Marry me."

(That was when he was into physics. There was a point when his language had a biological deterministic slant to it, another when it was specifically Darwinian, and now he fills her evenings with talk of memory. Tonight, Susannah, you are dining at Memory's Restaurant. We are pleased to serve you. We'd like to start you off with some of our crunchy capacitator noodles. Our entree this evening will be a fresh cut of cerebral cortex with a sauce of serotonin and julienned dendrites on the side. Watch for firing neurons, and enjoy your meal.)

Superstar Todd could go anywhere and she would go anywhere with him—she would go, she would figure it all out, she would be with Todd. Susannah had not realized that anywhere would lead to nowhere and nowhere would smell so damn bad.

The first three principles of love: Location, location, location.

This is Susannah's vision of the future:

Thirty years from now, they are married, and Dr. Todd Lewis gives his Nobel Prize acceptance speech. He smiles off into the audience, he waves to Susannah, and says, I want you all to meet somebody. I couldn't have done it without. Behind every man. Stand up, honey. And Susannah stands, pudgy, frizzy, gray, in a flowered dress and dark panty hose that mask varicose veins. The audience applauds politely.

Afterward, reporters crowd around, *And what do you do?* Microphones point in her face. The world is listening.

She clears her throat. *Nothing. I do nothing.*

While the sirens and the radios sound their alarms, Susannah sits in the back corner of the café framed by the gigantic author mural. In the newfound community comprised of the Davis and Dean refugees, she has gone largely unnoticed. Like placelessness, anonymity is part of the essence of the bookstore. She goes to Davis and Dean because it is the only place in Clarence that does not smell. In fact, the store smells like every other Davis and Dean she's ever been to and she wonders if they manufacture the scent. Somewhere, is there a little town with a factory that makes bookstore smell? And does that whole town smell like this Davis and Dean or does it smell like the waste from bookstore smell chemicals? Maybe Davis and Dean execs are too savvy for that. Maybe gigantic helicopters come and spray that town with Davis and Dean smell to make the people support the factory and instill in them a sense of pride in their part in the sweet bouquet of commerce.

So run Susannah's thoughts. Time has bored panic away, and now everyone just waits. Susannah has found herself feeling calm the entire time, as if she is in the mural, rendered in flat paint with dark heavy strokes, sipping tea at a table with John Keats and Virginia Woolf, watching the people go by.

Next to her is a thin man with round glasses and a full head of dark wavy hair who has pulled his chair next to his daughter, a little girl with prodigious eyes. He puts his arm around the girl and they lean in over big white glossy pages of children's books and politely send booksellers up to the children's section from time to time. ("We'd appreciate it if you would all stay in the café," the manager says to the customers. "Our booksellers would be happy to get you any books or magazines. Right?" The booksellers smile wanly and trot back and forth between the café and the shelves.)

The father squeezes his daughter's shoulder and gradually the little girl's eyes stop showing fear. Susannah's heart swells for the girl. Susannah's father would do that. He would gather Susannah and Sara in his arms and pick out books and they would flip through the pages together. He would explain to them why they did not have to be afraid.

Susannah watches the little girl at the next table as she points out different dog breeds to her father who listens attentively and nods solemnly. Susannah's father is not there—he has other people to take care of now, and Susannah is on her own, painted on a bookstore wall in a mural with dead poets sipping tea and frozen in time.

THE LINE BETWEEN accident and anecdote is a fine one. The temporal distance between the two fates is only a breath, a reflex, a slip. You feel the plane plunge toward the ground and you think, Please let me live to tell the tale. And then the plane rights itself, the passengers groan reflexively, and you have your very own survivor story—an anecdote of facing death head-on and coming through unscathed.

The stories live on. You narrate your near-doom slightly flushed, hands waving. Your audience leans in, mouths open, readying to counter with the tale of the time they, too, saw Death and promptly told him where he could go.

. . . And then the boat . . . and the car swerved . . . and I was so frightened . . . I could see the ground coming toward us . . . time slowed down . . . there was this horrible noise . . . I actually thought we were going to die . . . the tiger bared his fangs . . . the bomb was set to go off in ten seconds . . . and we were trapped in the bookstore and there was this noxious brown cloud heading our way . . .

Fear should at least give you a good story in return for your emotional investment. But, for the people of Clarence, it is not to be.

After five hours in the Davis and Dean café, when the quarantined bookbuyers had consumed their fill of small chunks of muffin and decaf house blend, the sirens stopped and the men on the radio told them they could go home. The fire had been contained. Air samples had been taken, tested. There was still some work to be done, of course. So Clarence should stay inside for the next twenty-four hours. All Clarence businesses will be closed tomorrow. And don't drink the water. Until further notice.

How *typical*. An event that would seem to portend something exciting ends up just being a tremendous inconvenience. This never happens in the movies. No one ever says: Actually, it's going to be all right. You can go home now. But, oh, stay in your stuffy boring houses for a day. You don't mind, do you?

No, it's not supposed to be like this. There needs to be action, adventure, explosions, personal revelations, soul searching, interpersonal growth, and life change. Plot, theme, character, setting, tone. Rising action, climax, falling action. Exposition, catastrophe, denouement. Catharsis. Reversal of fortune and recognition. Hamartia. Hubris. Deus ex machina. A few people might die, but the ones who live will learn a thing or two about the value of family and community. None of them will ever be the same again in *The Spill,* soon coming to a theater near you.

But no. Stalling their lives is simply a step in somebody's Toxin Emergency Response Protocol. Billowy yellow men are just a set piece in a dreadful bureaucratic play. You can go home now.

And, by the way, all the bars will be closed.

BENNIE'S FIRST CALL when he and Sophie get home is to his mother. Madeline Singer lives in an apartment up at Sunny Shadows Estates Elegant Living Retirement Community, where the crisis has been handled much the way Bennie expected. The resident leaders went door-to-door. People met in various community rooms. Radios were brought in. Panic was kept to a minimum.

"Nobody likes it, of course," Bennie's mother says. "These things make us a little nervous."

"Us, too, Mom."

"Oh, yes, is dear Sophie all right?"

"Well . . . yeah. I've had to keep reassuring her that she isn't going to get cancer from this. That girl sees too many movies."

"I was thinking, I might write a novel about a chemical spill and a small town."

"I guess that's one you haven't done yet."

"Yes. The chemical causes something, some disease or ailment, mass hallucinations and the like. And the whole town gets sick. And of course everyone learns something about himself along the way."

"Or herself, Mom."

"Thank you, Benjamin." She laughs. "Or herself. And of course there's a scientist who tries to work for the cure, but he himself needs the most curing."

"Make him a psychologist. I can give you tips. Then put me in the acknowledgments."

"Of course, Benjamin. I always do, my dear. . . . And he'll save the whole town, of course."

"Naturally."

"It's practically written," she says. "Let me talk to Sophie?"

Bennie's daughter climbs over him toward the phone and Bennie settles back in his chair. He thinks of calling Phil (the good thing about there being only three people that matter to you in the world is it really saves on your phone bills) but suddenly doesn't feel like dealing with his friend's situational exuberance. Phil has a take on everything. It's his job, certainly, as a Contemporary Studies prof. (Lizzie was like that too.) Any man who wrote a much ballyhooed Ph.D. dissertation on sexual longing in contemporary architecture would surely be able to provide an interpretation of the cultural meaning of this accident with pith and aplomb. Bennie is not in the mood for either.

Bennie pops some popcorn and he and Sophie settle down on their overstuffed couch and flip the remote control back and forth looking for coverage of the fire. Sophie's big white cat, Eleanor Roosevelt, sits at their feet. Father and daughter compare the graphics the stations have put together—FIRE AT THE FACTORY and CRISIS IN CLARENCE and DRUGS IN THE AIR? but the best in both of their opinions is Channel 8, which proclaims in large block letters: THE SPILL.

No one is sure how the fire started—

While emergency alert sirens blared through the streets—

—the factory will be shut down for several weeks.

—tried to contain the blaze—

—arson is not suspected.

—Coming up, hear from Clarence citizens about where they were during the quarantine—

—Coming up, meet some of the four-legged friends helping the government teams—

—Coming up, meet our local athletes of the week.

—Coming up, find out which Halloween costumes your child will want most this year.

"Jeez." Sophie sighs heavily. "News sucks."

"Sophie." Bennie tries to turn it into a teaching moment. "Your word choice?"

"Sorry, Dad."

"You have a point, though. I suppose the *Clarence Chronicle* isn't going to do much better for us," Bennie says, ruffling her hair. Sophie merely sighs again.

"Well." She looks up at her father, resigned. "I guess I'll have to look on the Internet."

"Tomorrow, sweetie." Bennie turns off the television. "Bedtime, huh?"

Sophie scurries upstairs and Bennie stares at the blank television, stroking Eleanor Roosevelt with his foot.

SUSANNAH GETS HOME at about nine to find an empty apartment and a blinking answering machine. She hears her own message first.

Hi, Todd. I'm at Davis and Dean. You can call here if you want. I'm fine, so, uh, don't worry.

The message is unnecessary. Todd does not worry. Worry is not in the nature of Todd. Worry is not very practical. There is no scientific point to worrying. Worrying impedes the natural processes of the mind. Did he even bother to check the messages to find out where she was? It amazes Susannah. She never met anyone before with such equilibrium. Does he know despair? Fear? Does he even know what it is like to long for something? Susannah used to think that longing is the fuel that makes us all go—then she met Todd and discovered he ran on something else entirely. She is still not sure what his fuel is, but the mystery has become less interesting to her. And now, she does not have the vivacity to find things to long for—now that her life is so motionless, Susannah finds herself longing for longing itself.

The tape plays on. There is a message from her sister, Sara, and then, finally, Todd. Susannah is surprised he bothered to call at all.

I'm going to be at the lab late tonight, Zana. I hope you're trapped somewhere interesting. I'm going to stay here and do some research. This could be huge, Zana, huge. Love you!

Susannah surveys the empty apartment, as she does by habit almost every night. The stillness itself has become her companion. She thinks of telling Todd they should get an animal—a dog, a cat, even a fish for God's sake—something for her to talk to when she gets home from Sunny Shadows and Todd will not be home for hours. The television can only provide so much companionship.

When we are married, we will get a dog, she thinks. When we are married, Todd will like a dog. It will be more like a home, he will think, and I will agree. We will not be having children anytime soon, so we will get a dog.

At the retirement community where Susannah works every day, some eccentric somebody left a grant providing the place with pets from the local humane society—and food and health care—for any resident who wanted one. Susannah's maintenance duties include chasing cats away from the duck pond and keeping dogs from barking too loudly—especially those basset hounds in Building A—but she doesn't mind. They make her want to retire early.

Susannah sighs and looks around for something approximating dinner. The kitchen is papered in sprawling flowers representing the entire array of colors in the bile spectrum. The cream of the background has yellowed and dulled over the years. A few splatters announce the ghosts of previous tenants. *We were here. We left our mark. We cooked chili.*

For the first few months that Susannah and Todd lived in Clarence, both of them were fastidious, for the sake of Todd's studying and Susannah's sanity. The wood floors of the living room and bedroom steadfastly refused to gather dust bunnies, the books on each shelf stood upright like little soldiers, the stove sparkled as if it were auditioning for a TV commercial.

Todd has begun to shirk his duties a bit, but Susannah still tries. Her first priority is her shelves, which she dusts every night. Susannah needs shelves because she has things in glass cases. Dollhouse things. Miniature things, old things, collectible things, intricate things, lush things, beautiful things. Tiny mahogany rocking chairs, little coffee tables with lace doilies, velvet cushions and brass bed frames, and porcelain babies with red rosy cheeks in maple cribs snuggling tiny fuzzy bears, and even a little bead-eyed basset hound that she likes to keep on top of the ball-and-claw couch. She would not move to Clarence without her things in glass cases. Todd does not pretend to understand, but he does not complain. Susannah tells him, "They were my mother's," and he smiles offhandedly and lets the subject drop, as he usually does whenever Susannah mentions her mother.

Despite Susannah's efforts the study has fallen into disarray. Todd is taking a design class as part of his course of study (and a further attempt to be seen as a Renaissance man), working on a series of art projects designed to express the nature of memory. Todd has a manifesto. He gets up in the middle of the night and writes down the phrases that come to him:

Memory induces pleasure. Memory induces pain. Is memory a drug?

It all seems pretty strange to Susannah, who is used to Todd carrying around heavy tomes filled with equations and diagrams topped with a graphing calculator and finely sharpened pencils. She cannot quite comprehend the room filled with lumps of clay, types of glue, scattered paints, and strips of newspaper. And manifestos. This does not belong to her world. Or Todd's, for that matter.

Lately, Todd has been trying to paint neurons. A series of canvases line one wall, paintings of splotches with tails. They are neurons like sea creatures, their tentacles reaching out out out beyond the scope of the canvas, trying to grasp something no one can see.

She is at least glad he is not taking performance art.

He has been designing a board game. Some kind of model. Some sort of interactive art piece for the Art of Science/Science of Art festival in November. He comes home at night with brightly colored BBs and unloads them on her lap. "Susannah Korbet, meet the plastic nuggets of your mind."

Pieces laid out on the floor. Diagrams and decorations. Plastic bits and wood bits and bits of junk. He takes her hand and sits her down on a pillow on their wood floor, sticking a slingshot in her hand.

"Now in the real game, that will be more of a catapult, but I suppose the slingshot is more representative, don't you think? Now, we'll set up a target, over here, filled with all kinds of different colors. Each turn is an experience."

"What?"

"An experience. Your turn! Grab the slingshot. Bam! Neuron fires." He shoots a red BB across the room. "If the 'neuron' hits its own color on the target, Bam! Ten points. You've successfully remembered." He kisses Susannah on the forehead. "But if you hit blue, well, the experience has encoded in the wrong place."

"Oh . . ."

"Pick a card." Todd brings out a selection of multicolored note cards and fans them out before Susannah's eyes. "Go ahead." He smiles encouragingly. "Pick one. Choose carefully."

She does. "It's blank."

"Yeah. I haven't written on them yet. I'm thinking of calling the deck the 'Oops' pile. It's your memory miscue. You see. So your card says, 'Oops. You can't find your keys. Lose three points,' or 'Oops, forget to get off highway at right exit. Lose five points.' or 'Oops, confabulate your life with episode of *Love Boat*, lose ten points.' "

"Todd, I don't think—"

"Listen, Zana, this isn't for toy stores. I'm trying to get at something here. We guide our lives by what we think our histories are. But sometimes we cannot remember. We forget our pasts. We create our pasts and forget we've created them. We encode a dream with a stamp of reality. We encode fiction with fact. We lose the game. And it's all biology. Lives are ruined because a neuron has bad aim."

Susannah stares at the series of note cards in front of her. She turns another over, and another, and another. The cards begin to take on a life of their own, their blankness masking a secret destiny, written in invisible ink. Invisible and indelible. She flips through the whole stack. One after another, the note cards confront her blankly.

"I don't know, Todd, people might think—"

He holds up his hand. "I know. But see, Zana, it's a game. The fact that it's a game is part of the art. Games are random, based on chance, fortunes told by numbers on a die, the luck of the draw, the spin of a wheel. The sling of a shot."

Todd gives the slingshot back to her. "Thousands of these inside your brain, creating what you perceive as reality. Here's your neuron. Do you feel it?" The chilly plastic of the slingshot weighs Susannah's hands down. Todd wraps his own hands around hers. "Scary, huh?" He tightens his grip around hers, then leans in closer to her ear and kisses it. Once. Twice. He grabs the slingshot and starts to slowly move it back and forth in her hand, whispering, "Here is the base. Axon. Here's the top. Dendrite. Axon. Dendrite. Axon. Dendrite. Axon. Dendrite."

A neuron fires and hits its target. A red square. Axons stand on alert and dendrites reach out out out beyond the scope of the canvas. The science building. A pencil in seventeen-year-old freshman Susannah's hand, Todd the poet-physicist enveloping her in mahogany eyes. A blush forms, starting at her neck. Is this how he tutors all the girls? Uncomfortable pauses over gravitational constants. A pencil drops, eyes meet, a smile forms. A giggle and a fiercer blush. She liked his chin. He liked her variables. She passed physics, although she would drop out of school midway through the next year.

Of course, that is history. Ancient history. Over three years ago.

Susannah transfers some canned spaghetti into a dish and puts it into the microwave—this is the depth to which their pantry has sunk. The clock ticks on and there is no sign of Todd, so Susannah curls up on the couch with the remote control and looks for some kind of entertainment. Neurons fire and fire.

Later, Susannah has fallen asleep, and the red spaghetti sauce has hardened in the bowl. The phone trills. Susannah opens her eyes to find some old movie flickering on the TV.

"Sweetie, how are you? Did I wake you?"

"Uh . . . no." Susannah blinks at the clock. "Todd, it's really late. What are you doing there?"

"Research. I'm looking at all the psychopharmaceutical stuff I can find. Really, Zana, I'm surprised they lifted the quarantine. This stuff is a little funny."

"The, uh, deletrium? Funny? Funny how?"

"Are you sure I didn't wake you?"

"Yes."

"Listen, sweetie, I should have called earlier. Be careful, okay? Drink bottled water. Stay inside."

"Todd, what have you found out? What's this stuff do?"

"Well, deletrium isn't really a drug. It's more like a transportation system. No, it's a key. An access code. Psychoactive drugs need a way to get in." His voice carries the authority of a hundred invisible charts and graphs. "See. Your mind is a neighborhood, a network of roads, a planned community. Behind doors, lurking in garages, tucked away in houses are systems. Hormones, memory, mood, pain, creativity, fear, sleep. All these things are locked away. Deletrium opens the doors."

"Oh." Susannah thinks for a minute. "How does it know what to unlock?"

"Well, the chemical that's combined with it to create the drug. The serotonin inhibitor, or whatever it is. That acts as a compass, a navigator, a magnet."

Susannah sits up straight. "What if there's no other chemical? No guide? How does it know what doors to open then?"

"Well . . . then, I don't think it does know."

"Todd . . ." At times like these, Susannah wishes other people shared her appreciation of precision. "What's going to happen?"

"I'm not sure."

three.

I am working toward my goal.

THE CLARENCE CHRONICLE has tried valiantly to cover the factory fire from every possible angle. Unfortunately, after the initial fact of the fire and the spill, there are not really any angles left. Neither Harris Jones officials nor scientists nor environmental experts nor state officials have any pertinent information to add, nor can they assuage the fears of the populace, so the pages are filled with quotes from the governor saying things like, "Our thoughts are with the people of Clarence during this difficult time," and the like. Mostly the *Chronicle* interviews the Person on the Street, Citizen Clarence, to get the Word About Town, the Buzz. Nobody, of course, manages to say anything of any substance and all these tidbits and opinions and factoids and sound bites and odds & ends merely manage to beat any last bit of life out of Clarence.

Many of the students at Mansfield have been on the drugs that the factory makes, and they don't understand the general deflation. What could be better than psychopharmaceuticals leaking into the air, affecting the whole town? Imagine that, everyone's problems cured. Everyone pays very good attention and sleeps through the night and feels comfortable with their station in life and wakes up in the morning ready to face the day head-on! All the little campers buck up! Imagine a whole town happy, happy, happy.

(Side effects may include dry mouth, stomach irritation, headache, sleeplessness, drowsiness, dizzy spells, loose bowels, constipation, nausea, loss of appetite, weight gain, sensitivity to light, mood swings, sweaty palms, numbness in the extremities, heart palpitations, dehydration, night sweats, loss of balance, and sexual dysfunction.)

But no one is happy. The air goes out of the collective psychic balloon with a languid hsssssss. Never before have everyone's simple average-Joe everyday common humble workaday lives seemed so darned ordinary. It will be this way forever. Clarence will never be a movie of the week. Clarence will simply go on, breathing in toxic fumes, dying slowly, while the indifferent world continues to turn.

Phones begin to ring off the hook for travel agents, psychologists, realtors, continuing education officers, career counselors. Citizen Clarence even lines up outside of Madame Z's Fortunes and Futures to see Zelda, the mystic and stockbroker. *What will the deletrium do? Please, what does my life hold? Will I ever make my mark on this world before I die?*

Since the deletrium leak, people have begun to sense small changes in their physical conditions. Ever so slight. Nearly imperceptible. A minor headache. A stitch in the side. A spot of indigestion. A sniffle. Restlessness at night. Languor in the day.

Pockets of illnesses seem to be developing. One Sunday school class is overrun with bowel problems. The entire second grade class of Walter Mondale Elementary has a tummy ache. A great malaise sweeps the junior high.

Clarence dutifully goes to the doctor. It is best to get these things checked out early. Because you never know. Early detection. An ounce of prevention. Better safe.

The hallways beep and buzz with the machinations of MRIs, CAT scans, and EKGs. Laboratories carefully process blood, urine, semen, stool. Patient Clarence—prodded, poked, and pricked— sits in the doctor's office and waits.

There is a knock on the door. The doctor enters and sits down. *I have your results here. I am sorry. I can find nothing wrong with you.*

So for now, people simply go on with their lives.

DR. CALVIN WOODHOUSE, for instance, has decided this is a good time to try out his best hat. In his small apartment on the first floor of Building B in the state's premier retirement community, Calvin is looking in the mirror, experimenting with different angles. Calvin has not gone courting in many years, since the death of his Alice, God rest her beautiful soul, but there is a woman like sunshine and strawberries in Building E and today is the day for his best hat.

It is Tuesday afternoon and the woman's son should be coming by in an hour or so, as he does every Tuesday, and the two should be watching the ducks by the pond as they so often do—Calvin's room just happens to overlook the pond, he has a great affection for ducks—and should a certain gentleman with a dapper hat be walking by at just that moment, well . . .

Calvin tips his hat and smiles at his own reflection. He takes a deep breath. He says, "There is a Hitchcock double bill tomorrow night and I might get scared—"

Calvin stops and clears his throat. "—and I might become frightened—" Calvin licks his lips. "*Unduly* frightened." He looks himself directly in the eyes. "Unduly frightened. I wonder if you might accompany me?" He practices one more time, whispers, "unduly frightened," to himself, smiles, and then he brushes his hair and puts on an ever-so-small dash of cologne. He looks at his cat, Bacall, for approval and she rubs up against his leg. He pulls a chair up to the window and then stops a moment. He goes over to the bedside and picks up the picture of Alice, God rest her angelic soul, kisses it gently, and puts her back down by the bedstead. He brushes the cat fur off his ankle, whispers, "No offense," to Bacall. Then he takes a seat and waits, hat in his lap.

TODD LEWIS, MEMORY Studies graduate student at Mansfield University, is also wearing a hat. When he got into Mansfield, his mother sent away for a sweatshirt, T-shirt, and baseball cap in honor of the occasion. Todd has never been much of a baseball hat guy, but he likes the reddish hat with the bold, sturdy *M*—it certainly beats his alma mater's self-effacing brown and white. He'd been working at the lab without rest most of the weekend since the spill—nothing at all has been published about deletrium, after all, and if he could publish something, well—and, naturally, his hair is a bit out of whack.

It's a special occasion, anyway; Todd is leaving the lab. Today, while Susannah works, Todd is going to search out and purchase a present for her. A Just Because kind of thing. He has no idea what to get, but he needs to get something, because, frankly, his Susannah has not really been the same since they moved to Clarence. She works, she comes home, she rearranges all those things she has, she cleans the kitchen, she makes dinner from some kind

of package, she watches television, she goes to sleep. She sits on
the couch reading. She talks on the phone to her sister. She plays
with her hair, staring off at nothing. She looks through him, about
him, around him, anywhere but at him. And when she does look
at him, it is with such distance, such curiosity, like he is a molecule
whose formula she cannot place.

He should buy her a present.

If he could, he would buy her something a little more intan-
gible. He feels a little goofy thinking this way, but he would like
to give her a little happiness, in a pretty box all wrapped up in a
big beautiful bow—or at least contentment. Or something more
concrete: If he could, he would like to buy her a good job, a sense
of purpose, a reason to get out of bed in the morning. . . .

If he had known what this would be like for her, he would have
looked at other cities. He didn't need Mansfield. They are leaders
in the field, of course, but he could have gone anywhere. He
would come home tonight and tell her he'll apply to transfer, he'll
start all over again, he'll study something else, somewhere else, if it
would make her happy. But she would just shrug and say she
doesn't mind so much, here's as good as anywhere. He suspects
that Clarence isn't really the problem, that all she really wants is to
be close to home. When he asked her to come with him, he was
really asking her to leave home; he knew that, he was happy about
that. The engagement ring was supposed to be a liberation for her.

Todd is not an idiot. He can tell something is wrong, though
she never talks to him about it. It is not him—is it? She knows he
loves her, he tells her whenever he can. And despite his little, um,
problem, she must know that all he really wants to do is sit next
to her and curl up her hair in his hands and say, Zana Zana Zana
Zana. He just wants her to look at him again. He wants her to
bounce in step with her curls. He worries about her, this change,
this listlessness, this endless hair twirling. Something is wrong,

maybe chemically. Maybe not. Maybe it is just him. This is not like the dizzy heartskip Zana he used to know, but they were other people then.

And he cannot help but wonder—he hates to think it, but—well—is this how her mother started out?

And then what will he do?

The problem is simply that Susannah needs a mission. Missions are the fuel of life, the reason for getting out of bed in the morning. When he uprooted her, she was between missions. She never had a chance to get back on track. Clarence is not a good place to find oneself. Unless you go to Mansfield, that is.

Todd has a mission. He always has; sometimes the nature of the mission has altered, but never the ultimate goal. This very fact of a mission has kept him in a constant state of contentment. I have a goal, I am working toward my goal, I am moving toward it all the time, therefore I am happy. It is simple logic. Susannah used to have a mission. She was going to be a doctor. They would be Dr. and Dr. Lewis, and he would be so proud. He doesn't care, now, if she is never anything more than Mrs. Lewis (if she still wants to be that) as long as she is content. She has vague ideas for her future—she talks about nursing now, she says that would be a better fit for her—but she refuses to do anything about it. She has so many excuses—money, time, uncertainty, location—but Todd thinks that mostly her reason is inertia.

Todd cannot buy her a mission, or a nursing certification, or anything really useful like that, so he goes to Davis and Dean instead. He pokes around in cards and bookmarks and staff recommendations and new fiction and new nonfiction and audio books and has worked his way over to the doodads and knick-knacks that are in the café when he notices the black-haired sallow girl working behind the café counter.

"Need something?" she says.

Todd cannot help but notice that this girl is pretty, despite her vaguely mortuary-like appearance, because that is the nature of Todd. She—Lilith her name tag says—lifts one eyebrow and Todd happens to find it extra cool when girls can do that.

Todd says, "Depth charge, please," because Davis and Dean makes the best depth charges of any coffee-making chain in the country—and they all know what it is, they don't look at him and say, "Huh?" like so many do. Lilith nods and turns around and Todd can't help but notice how nice her—

Todd. Susannah Susannah Susannah Susannah Susannah Susannah Susannah Susannah Susannah . . . (This is the short version of his mantra. The long version has to do with reminding himself that Susannah and other girls are mutually exclusive, and how life without Susannah would be no life at all, etc. etc. etc.) Todd goes through this mantra just about every day. It has never failed him, and never will.

"That will be two seventy-five. Thank you and have a nice day."

The café worker turns away and Todd takes a deep breath into his espresso-charged coffee and rubs the brim of his hat.

Oh yes. A present.

THE ROLLING ACRES of Sunny Shadows Estates Elegant Living Retirement Community are home to one of the best independent libraries in the state. It is an agreement among the tenants—almost 20 percent of whom are retired Mansfield professors—that once you are accepted into Sunny Shadows, after the applications and interviews are said and done and you receive your coveted letter of acceptance, once all that has happened, you will donate your life's collection of books to the Sunny Shadows Estates library for the use of the entire community. Exceptions are made, of course.

A beloved volume to be kept by the bedside. A family Bible. A nineteenth-century novel or two. (After all, they don't need another copy of *To the Lighthouse* or *Middlemarch*, for the love of God.) As the residents pass on to the Home or to the Other Realm, they leave their collections behind for the world. The goal is to house a collection of books second only to the Library of Congress. They are many deaths away from that. But the goal is aggressively pursued; Eastern philosophy may be quite bare, but there is an Asian Studies professor at Mansfield who is really getting on in years, and a Buddhism professor over at MSU, and the council is sure both will make a lovely addition to the Sunny Shadows community.

Every resident, too, has a special shelf. Ten or so books that most define their lives' pursuits to be left on for posterity. Surveys have shown that as the residents get on in years their number one regret is that they have not left enough behind. Sunny Shadows does its best to ensure that none of its valued residents suffers from anything at all, especially not from regret.

Bennie's mother changes her ten books every few weeks. Lately, she has forgone her traditional favorites for the books of her youth, tattered volumes of *Little Women* and *Anne of Green Gables*, series selections from *Betsy-Tacy* and *Little House on the Prairie*. (Dr. Calvin Woodhouse recently has been sighted flipping through the books on Madeline's shelf with some amusement.) "These are what I grew up with," she told Bennie. "These formed me. These define me. These taught me to write. This is my legacy."

Bennie pleaded with her, his mother, the author of eight novels and two short-story collections and a few scattered poems. "Your own books, Mother. Lots of the professors do it. What better way to define yourself?"

She would only smile and say, "Benjamin, dear, I have already left those behind."

It does not matter, he reassures himself. Plenty of time to change her mind. His mother is not going to any Homes or Other Realms anytime soon. She had moved to Clarence to be near him and Sophie, after the accident. Sunny Shadows was the best alternative for her. "A clean, well-lighted place," she pronounced it at the time. "There is a pool. There is a community. There is that library. I will move in there, I will put my typewriter by the window, and I will write," she told Bennie. "And I will help you with Sophia." She kissed her son on the forehead, and that was that.

At the time Madeline Singer was Sunny Shadows' youngest tenant. This is no longer true (residents are getting younger as the council gets more aggressive). But she is still more young than old, and can rearrange her shelf for years and years. She cannot die; as she told a sniffling Sophie one day, "I have too many novels left to write."

One person has not objected to her bookshelf selections. Sophie comes every few days and plops down on the floor with a book from Gramma's shelf. Residents sitting at the heavy maple tables put down their dusty tomes and watch Madeline Singer's little round-eyed grandchild reading these books; they crave their own grandchildren and silently make plans to put kids' books on their shelves, too.

The recent events in Clarence have caused a bit of a run on the books in the neuro and biochem sections—unfortunately the library's texts tend to be a little outdated (read: nary a mention of deletrium). This problem was brought to the attention of the council, who instantly put their procedures in motion—goals have been defined, intelligence gathered, inquiries made. The first and second perimeters have thus far proved fruitless, though just today they have found some very exciting candidates in Iowa and Wisconsin.

Bennie and Madeline sit near the Sunny Shadows pond feeding the ducks. It has been unseasonably warm this year. (Because of the o-zone, Sophie explains solemnly.) October is fading, and the birds have not even started to pack their bags for Florida.

"People are scared," Bennie's mother is telling him. "They don't trust chemicals like this. As science passes farther and farther beyond the point of your comprehension you begin to believe that soon it is bound to destroy us all."

"I know the feeling."

"No you don't," Madeline says gently. "You will, but you don't. And it's not only that. We are old. We are moving closer to death all the time." Bennie leans in to protest and she holds up her hand. "Slowly, quietly, maybe, but that is our direction nonetheless. Our lives are finite. We have all had to acknowledge our own mortality. Science has never had to do that. Science is a perpetual child, like Sophie, a wonder which grows and blossoms each day. We have grown old while science has stayed young, and for that, we can never forgive it."

Bennie watches his mother rip off a piece of stale bread, her hands thin and dry. Dead leaves kick up at their feet.

No, Bennie thinks. You are not old, Ma. You will never be old. You are younger than I am. You cannot die. You cannot do that to me.

"How's Sophie?"

"Good. She just won a couple events at a gymnastics meet."

"Good for her."

"Yes, well. The other teams didn't show up. Nobody wants to come to Clarence today, I guess."

"Where is she?"

"Team dinner. They're going to have cherry pie. She's very excited."

"She hasn't been . . . ah . . . bed-wetting?"

Bennie's first instinct is to look around and make sure nobody heard. "No, no, Mom. It seems to be over."

"Good."

"Yes."

"Tell her to go by my section. I've got some new books in there for her."

Bennie pauses. "Last week she told me she wanted to be a writer, just like Gramma."

Madeline smiles. "Lord help her."

"Or a vet."

"Better . . ."

Just then, the garden gate creaks and the small form of Dr. Calvin Woodhouse appears in their line of sight. The gentleman walks closer, his bright gray eyes light on the pair, and he tips his bowler hat.

"Why, Master Singer. Hello, son."

Calvin approaches the two, taking off the bowler, bowing stiffly but gallantly in front of Bennie's mother. "Ms. Madeline. You are looking lovely today."

Madeline looks up at Calvin and giggles. Bennie's eyes widen. His mother does not notice; she is smiling at Calvin.

Bennie has met Calvin a few times, all in the vicinity of his mother, and he is starting to catch on. His mother turns a specific shade of happy whenever she sees him. Bennie has known of Calvin for some time, of course; everyone in Clarence does. Calvin is one of Clarence's last World War II vets. He was something of a war hero in his day, apparently, and is rumored to have been part of the regiment that discovered and liberated Dachau. No one has ever asked him, though, if this is true. How do you ask that sort of thing? How do you make someone call something like that up?

On every Veterans Day the *Clarence Chronicle* features a picture of Calvin in full parade regalia standing against a flag, or leaning back in a chair, looking wistfully off into the distance, his chin raised to a patriotic angle. The first time, the photographer won some kind of state award for this photo. Since then, she has put Calvin in the same pose, year after year, getting the light to surround his head just so. She does not understand why she has not won again.

A few years ago, Calvin had to call Clarence High and politely ask that they work out an arrangement about the sophomore class's WW II oral history assignment. He was a bit old, he explained, to be getting calls from so many nice young ladies; people were starting to talk. The school principal giggled, and from then on Calvin has gone to the school every year and spoken to the entire class.

There are, though, things he will never discuss.

Calvin smiles at Bennie's mother. All of a sudden, Bennie feels like he is intruding. "Madame Madeline, might I request your company at the cinema tomorrow night? There's a Hitchcock double bill on and I may become unduly frightened."

Bennie's mother smiles. "Calvin, that would be lovely."

There are few sensations in the world like watching your nearly seventy-year-old mother being flirted with. Not that Bennie feels any familial defensiveness; Bennie's father died of lung cancer when Bennie was eighteen and while Bennie may never forgive his dad for choosing smoking over living, a good twenty-one years of mourning on his mother's part seemed to honor her husband's memory, frankly, more than enough. But there is something so private about flirting, such vulnerability expressed in the blush. Should he be privy to this interaction? It is bad enough that in several years Sophie will be dating. He has time with her at least before that happens, but really, mothers in retirement communities do not giggle.

Bennie eyes Calvin, who perhaps senses Bennie's discomfort and grins gregariously, gray eyes flickering. "That is, if I may have your permission, Master Benjamin."

Now it is Bennie's turn to blush. The feel of flush against his face startles him. He blinks and something alters in his mind. His face is flushing across a decade and a half. He is with Lizzie. Or rather, he sees Lizzie, sitting at the next table, bathed in fluorescent light. His mouth opens, and words choke up in his throat. His cheeks grow hot. What is this feeling? This girl has the power to heat skin and he cannot even remember how to form words.

He shakes off the moment and Calvin and his mother are staring kindly at him.

"Still with us?" asks Calvin.

"Yes. It's fine. Just don't keep her out too late." Bennie feels the awkwardness of his smile.

Bennie has frequently wondered what it would be like to be charming. What would happen if wherever he went, people were seduced by the light in his eye, the warmth of his smile? What if he always had the most perfect phrase on his tongue for every occasion, the wittiest joke, the most incisive comment? What if he could put people at ease by just the tilt of his head? What if he could pull off a bowler hat? He used to be like that. Didn't he? Wasn't he like that once? He remembers. But that was Before.

He doesn't care. He still wears his wedding ring.

four.

I've had a great time tonight.

SUSANNAH KORBET SITS in Madeline Singer's room drinking tea. She is done cleaning the Sunny Shadows library for the day—the plants are watered, the library cats fed, the tables polished, the hallways swept, the books straightened, the chairs pushed in, the shelves dusted. Susannah has been working at Sunny Shadows for about seven weeks. Todd found her the job—first he'd dropped Mansfield continuing-ed brochures in strategic locations around the house, but when she never picked them up, he came home with listings from the Career Center instead. "This will be good on your résumé," he said, "if you decide you do want to go into nursing."

She and a few Mansfield students take care of things around the campus—general cleaning, groundskeeping, library work. Susannah suspects this maintenance crew is mostly intended to spice things up for the residents—that is, whenever she lingers talking to somebody, no one exactly orders her to get back to work. All it means for her is she has somewhere to be five days a week (other than the bookstore), and some people to talk to. She comes early, spends her lunch break here, and usually stays late. Tea with the author Madeline Singer after work means she can stay there even later.

Susannah has read all of Madeline Singer's books. She has even read *The Road to Miranda* and *Soothsayer* twice. When Susannah finds an author she likes, she will make every effort to read her well. Susannah likes to savor sentences, because if anyone took that much trouble to write them, she should at the very least take care with the reading. When Sara came home one day a few years ago brandishing *Forty Thieves*, Susannah picked it up, spent most of the week with it, then read the Madeline Singer collection, one by one. When she moved here, Susannah had heard the author lived in Clarence, but did not really believe it, for why would anybody who is clearly possessed of all those delicate thoughts, all that beautiful longing, ever live in a place like this?

But there, in the Sunny Shadows library—which is a pretty fabulous library, Susannah thinks—there was this woman with excellent posture and thick brown-gray hair who looks so much like the jacket shots, and Susannah scurried over to the fiction section to check for sure.

"I'm sorry. Madeline Singer?"

And the woman with the excellent posture and the brown-gray hair smiles and says, "Yes?"

"I'm sorry for bothering you. I just—I love your books. I've read them all."

Susannah blushes and pulls on her curls. She is not prone to stopping people. She is more likely to run in the opposite direction. But after careful consideration, Susannah decided that it would not be an intrusion, that she would be very glad if someone

said something like that to her one day, she would not be bothered
one bit—if she ever did anything worthwhile, that is.

The well-postured woman smiles and says, "I am delighted to
hear that. Thank you, Ms.—?"

"Susannah. Uh, Susannah Korbet. But, uh, Susannah . . ."

And she got invited for tea. ("Are you sure? I would hate to—")
*Whenever you want, just stop by, please, I would love your company,
Ms. Susannah.* Mrs. Singer has a way of smiling like it is an embrace.

Now she is there, again drinking tea—it has almost become
routine now—while Madeline Singer, the author, giggles over a
date she has tonight. Susannah is glad she is here to see this, because
now the world is a different place than she thought.

"Are you nervous?" Susannah asks.

"Of course I'm nervous, Ms. Susannah. Do you have any idea
how long it's been since I've been on a date?"

Susannah bites her lip. She does not think that it is polite to
discuss people's ages in front of them.

"When is he picking you up?"

"Two hours."

"Do you want me to go so you can get ready?" Susannah
quickly thinks of who else she could visit. Todd won't be home
for hours.

"No! No, stay, don't leave me!" Madeline laughs and Susannah
sinks back into the soft blue chair. "Besides, you must help me
figure out what to wear."

Madeline treats Susannah like an equal. Most of the residents
do, of course, but Madeline never asks her those questions that
everyone else asks her. She never says, "So, do you go to Mansfield?" or "What do you study?" or "What do you want to do
with your life?" or "Tell me about your fiancé," or "When are
you going to set a date for your wedding?"

Mrs. Singer asks her instead about books and news and her

thoughts on things, she asks her opinion on flavors and smells and colors and textures and the tenor of someone's voice. And every day, she asks:

"Do you have anything for me today?"

Madeline has given Susannah a job of sorts. She is working on a new novel, a small-town novel, but, she says, she is a city girl at heart, and she needs some help.

"I want you to keep your ears open. Listen to people gossip. Report back to me."

"But I'm a city girl, too," Susannah stammers. "I don't know anybody in Clarence at all."

"That's okay. Just pay attention around here. We're all a bunch of gossips. Except nobody tells me anything good, they are always afraid I am going to stick it in some novel."

(Today, of course, Madeline knows the gossip is her. There is not a lot of dating at Sunny Shadows, but when it happens, Buildings A through F are set abuzz. And this date is special. Since Calvin moved in, every woman in the place has been whispering about him. They all think of him as a dapper sparkly-eyed enigma, and they are waiting breathlessly to find out what goes on underneath all those hats. Madeline does not tell them that she is curious, too.)

"But nobody talks about those kinds of things with me," Susannah says. "They just ask me what I want to be when I grow up."

"And what do you tell them?"

Susannah shrugs. "I don't know. . . . Did you know you were going to write when you were my age? When did you figure it all out?"

Madeline smiles. She looks like she wants to brush Susannah's hair, and for a moment, Susannah is somewhere else. "My dear Susannah, what makes you think I have it figured out?"

So Susannah does listen, and she reports back faithfully, and

Madeline nods thoughtfully. Susannah has never had a game quite like this.

The only times Susannah gets nervous are when Madeline leans back, sips her tea, and fixes her eyes on her. She then, invariably, asks her something vague but probing, such as, "So, Ms. Susannah, what is your story?"

Susannah will just shrug and say, "I have no story." There is only one interesting thing about Susannah's life, and she does not share it with anyone. Susannah will then turn the conversation around, as quickly as possible, and Madeline smiles an odd smile and dutifully answers her questions.

"I have one son. Benjamin. He teaches at Mansfield. That's why I'm here, actually."

"Ohhhh!" Susannah nods.

Madeline laughs. "It's not a bad little town. It can be tough on a city girl. But I love where I live. And I am close to my son. And I have a granddaughter. . . . I always wanted a girl."

Susannah thinks for a minute. "Is that why you write about daughters?"

Madeline blinks a moment. "I don't know. Maybe it is. . . ."

She stares at Susannah and smiles. A pause floats between them.

"I'm sorry, I was somewhere else for a minute," Madeline says.

"That's all right. Me too."

MADELINE HAS A game with herself. She used to play it, even before she ever wrote anything—although she never really knew she was doing it at the time. When Madeline talks to people, she tries to decide how to best convey their character, to give a sense of them, in the fewest of all possible words. With some people, it's easy. Susannah Korbet did not take long. Her entire personality is wrapped up in that hair. She spends all their conversations with her hands in it, pulling on those curls, shaking it in front of her face and secretly gazing through the forest of locks. Madeline could watch it endlessly. She wonders if she would even want to make a character of this girl. Her novels are all about journeys; she has never written one about standing still.

Madeline was so much different than Susannah at that age. This girl eyes life through the veil of her mane, hiding from and ever watchful for whatever feral surprise is ready to jump out of the bush. Young Madeline thrust her chin out and set her eyes straight ahead.

She reserves her game for nonrelatives. She cannot reduce Bennie, or even Sophie, to looks, gestures, phrases. They are too close to her, and, in truth, she must always fight the urge to treat those she loves like fictional characters. Her gentleman caller, Calvin, is the first person she has met in a long time whom she cannot turn into words on a page. When she first met him, she could not get the proper distance between herself and him; every time she tried he seemed to draw her closer in. And when she concentrates on picking out the pieces that make Calvin *Calvin*, her mind wanders and her brain instead begins to search for the words that describe the effect he has on her. And, for all her ten books, for her nearly twenty years of writing, for all the indescribable feelings she has ever put words to, all she can come up with is "Happy."

She is still working on it.

Calvin moved into Sunny Shadows six months ago. Madeline met him by the duck pond on one of her morning walks not long afterward. And then he met her again, and again. He began to pay attention to her—such attention!—with his blue eyes and soft voice and ready smile. He would sit next to her at the library, read books she suggested, and she would find him sometimes in an easy chair reading one of her own books. And then, something inside of her would begin to flutter.

There is a specific kind of hope that comes before love. Madeline has not felt it in so long. It came upon her gradually with Calvin; one day, after another meeting by the pond, she noticed that the taste of their conversation would linger with her as she walked home. She found each morning she was excited to see him. She increased the frequency of her walks. He always came. Then she found she was thinking of him as she went to sleep. And then she was thinking of him all the time. And then, there—there is the hope. It comes upon her whenever she is near him. It begins in her stomach and travels up through her chest and catches in her throat. She tries to ignore it, but the feeling will not go away. It whispers to her quietly, *You will learn about him more each day. You will love him for everything he is, and he you. You will fall asleep with him every night. He will touch your face and you will feel such kindness.*

But for now, there is this, this arm's-length friendship, with an undercurrent of a promise. There has been a hesitancy there; Madeline does not know what it is—the memories of a much-beloved wife, certainly, but something else, too. Lately, Calvin has been quieter with her—still dapper, still charming, but more subdued—as if he is conducting a conversation inside his head. He gazes at her as if to say, *Not yet. Give me time. Let me think this through, and then—and then we may begin. We have only just met.* So they have been friends, and Calvin encompasses her with his smile, and the hope swells again.

But they have stalled. There is a natural progression to these things, and it has been time to take the next step for quite a while. It has been at this level for too long. She would like him to grab her by the hand and look deeply into her eyes and declare his undying love, but he is not the type. He is too sweetly traditional, too formal, too nervous. Once the decision is made, he would instead put on a dapper hat and ask her to a dinner and a double bill.

Susannah leaves, and Madeline cleans up the tea and begins to survey her closet. Madeline has not been on a date in at least forty-three years. The first date with Morrie was a walk by the river in the afternoon. He was so quiet and stiff when he asked her, looking at the ground and scratching his thigh. She wondered what could possibly itch so much. When they walked together, she tripped over a branch and he grabbed her arm, and he did it so abruptly that at the time she believed that he must have the soul of a poet, for she had just read Blake and knew about such things.

Madeline was twenty-one. Home from college to be with her mother, who was sick. She was supposed to go back, she had less than a year left, but her mother did not get better. And there was Morrie Singer, twenty-eight years old, waiting on her doorstep with itchy legs and shy eyes that she assumed betrayed a soul that spun music—a heart drumming to the songs of innocence and experience.

Then, as now, Madeline ran her fingers across the clothes hanging in her closet. Who does she want to be? Soft? Tidy? Cute? Vaguely alluring? She can remember the feel of her polished cotton dresses and light sweaters and the crinolines, the waxy smooth taste of the lipstick as she wondered whether to be more Doris Day or Sophia Loren.

Now, with Calvin, she chooses to be herself.

Calvin, who looked straight at her to ask her on this date, twinkled with kindness and something else . . . was it mischief? (Let it be mischief. . . .)

She ironed around the gathers on her skirt for an hour. She saw Morrie—Morris she called him then—approach the porch and rap loudly on the front door. Little Isaac let him in, and her father grunted vaguely at him as Madeline came down the stairs. She walked up to him erect in the new high heels she bought just for the occasion and said, "Hello, Morris." He smiled with half his mouth and then looked at the ground. There was a moment of silence.

"Can you walk in those?" He motioned to her shoes.

Madeline blinked. His voice was so rushed and direct she took a moment to understand the words. Isaac giggled wildly. Madeline glared at her brother, then smiled as graciously as she knew how. "Yes, yes, it won't be a problem."

"Oh. Good."

"Well. Shall we go?"

Madeline hasn't thought of this in years, and suddenly is back on that river path with Morrie and snapping twigs and honking geese. She is sensing that peculiar way he was with her, rough and unpracticed but strangely sweet, too—either he was rude or just awkward, and Madeline chose to believe the latter. They talked about—she thinks—they talked about nothing really. They talked about weather and her family's health and his plans to take over his father's business. She was going to ask him about his family, but she did not, because her friend in the neighborhood told her that one should never ask Morris about his family and she would not figure out why for years. He did mention he was planning on building a house someday and she did not realize at the time that he already had every intention of building it for her.

"There is mystery beneath that thick skin," Madeline whispered to her mother when she got home.

Madeline stroked her mother's hair, greasy against the starched white pillow. Her mother smiled up at her and murmured throatily, "I bet you will not stop till you solve it."

Suddenly, Madeline's fingers are full of grease and starch and her lips are touched with wax. Twigs snap and geese call and a rough arm grabs her and her hands fall across polished cotton. Voices long gone—one rushed and husky, one throatily dying— whisper in her ear. She rubs her forehead and from the corner of the room her typewriter beckons to her.

"Not now," she says sternly. The typewriter stares. "I have a date."

CALVIN IS IN her hallway. He is holding the flowers up to the peephole and she sees his small head poking out behind a blur of color. She opens the door—no heels this time, just loafers and loose pants. Calvin kisses her hand and she knows he is being silly but she also knows her hand has never been kissed before. "Madame. You look lovely."

He looks up from her hand and gazes at her, still twinkling, and she knows then that it is mischief, and that there is something else there too—a bit like affection, or is it attraction?—and something inside of her ripples. She might as well be wearing bright lipstick and pink cotton, fingering the roller curls in her hair.

THEY HAVE DINNER before the movie and Madeline finds herself talking like she has never talked before. Calvin asks her about her life, and she tells him, from kindergarten on, it seems. Calvin says, "I must admit, Madeline, I have not read all your books. Just five of them," and she finds herself giggling, and they go to the theater and he whispers to her and she giggles some more and she half expects him to pretend to stretch and put his arm around her, and maybe he is just about to, but then the movie gets to the part where Cary Grant is running through a field and the plane starts to chase him down, there are gunshots, and then more—propeller sound and gunfire reverberates through the theater, Cary Grant tries to get away, and in the dark next to her, Calvin changes. Something inside of him seems to explode, and then slowly die away, and he twinkles no more.

THEY WALK HOME and Calvin says nothing, nothing at all, and Madeline wonders/hopes if maybe he is nervous, too. Maybe he is wondering whether to kiss her outside her door. (Yes, yes . . .) Maybe he is wondering whether or not she will ask him in. (Yes, yes, yes . . .) Maybe he, too, is worried about how dry and rough his lips must be, how wiry his hair is, how aged and desiccated his face must feel when held against the hand's memory of another face. Maybe he, too, has found himself thinking of the most ridiculous things to say, like, "I've had a great time tonight," or, "You know, I haven't felt this way about someone since," or, "I've been thinking about you for some time," or, "Do you want to see an old geezer's room?" Maybe he had hoped that after multiple decades of life experience, one stopped feeling like a thirteen-year-old schoolboy with a crush.

But Calvin unlocks the Sunny Shadows gates and heads off toward his building with barely a word to her. Madeline stands still, thinking of thousands of things she might have said. She watches him go, looking so much older than he did at the beginning of the evening.

And suddenly, she feels the same way.

five.

A memory stirs.

IMAGINE FOR A moment that you are the chemical deletrium.

It's not as difficult as you may think.

Just close your eyes. Reduce yourself down to your basic parts. Smaller. That's it. Get right down to the molecules.

Now, just change the composition a little bit. Switch around the elements, who needs that much carbon anyway?

Imagine for a moment you are the chemical deletrium and you have seeped into the atmosphere. You have been unleashed. Feels good, doesn't it? You drink up your freedom, dive into water, dance through the air, do the backstroke in some chocolate pudding. You are deletrium. You are free.

But you are getting restless. All this R&R becomes tiresome. You have a purpose after all. The realization strikes you: "I am deletrium, and I am not meant for a life of leisure. I am deletrium,

I have a mission. I am deletrium, I have doors to open." Ah yes, you are invigorated and now with your newfound lust for life you set to work. You find your way into saliva, blood, brain.

Knock, knock.

Who's there?

Deletrium.

Oh, yes! Come in!

Oh, how the other psychopharmaceutical compounds envy you! Such charm, such resourcefulness! They are all bound by the intractable will of the creator. One (you there!) must go to the serotonin. Another (you!) must curl up inside the norepinephrine. But to be free! To be one's own master! To control one's destiny! To give nature and nurture the finger! To be deletrium! The human mind is your playground, and you, frankly, want to play. Uninhibited by commands, if given any choice in the matter at all, if the biochemical gods free your will, you will forsake the passageways of mood, attention, what have you, and head directly to the doors that lead into the very messy back rooms in which live memory.

Knock, knock.

Who's there?

Deletrium. Can I come in and play?

SOMETHING IS OFF at Sunny Shadows Estates today. The place has transformed; you would think it was a nursing home. But that's not right. This is no old folks home. This is not the place where people fade out in midsentence or stare off into space or lose control of their emotions or ramble inappropriately. This is not that place. And yet . . .

The staff runs around picking up the pieces of the tenants.

Everywhere, there is someone who needs help, someone who is shaking, someone who is alone. The doctors will be coming in. Something is happening. Everyone is ill.

In the garden, a man turns his wedding ring around and around and around and around and around and around on his finger. He rocks back and forth quietly. He hums to himself. He does not take his gaze from his ring. No one can get him to speak.

In the library, a woman bursts out crying in the middle of her sentence. She was just looking for a book, that's all, and then something overtook her, some kind of smell in the air. The librarian sits her down, brings her water, strokes her shoulders. The woman cries and cries.

Near the pond, a man sits and talks for three hours. He tells stories about his childhood, his old neighborhood, his brothers and sisters. He talks about his school days and his alley games and the one time he knew true love. No one is next to him.

In the doctor's office, a woman complains of the terrible dreams she's been having. She cannot sleep well. She shakes awake, like earthquakes. Her dreams linger and haunt her. She cannot take it. She asks for a pill. She begs.

In one lounge, people congregate, telling stories to anyone who might listen. Sentences fly through the air and then change course abruptly and crash and burn on the floor. In another lounge, six adults sit perfectly silently, staring at the television screen as black-and-white images flicker before their eyes.

In one of the bedrooms, a woman reaches out to her husband. He shrugs her hand away. He is crying. "How could you? How could you do that to me?"

In rooms all over the campus, people find themselves distracted, confused, consumed. A woman crawls into bed and pulls the covers up over her eyes and refuses to come out. A man takes old family pictures and crumples them in his hands, one by one. Another woman sits shaking—she turns up the heat again and again but she cannot stop shaking.

In her room in Building E, Madeline Singer takes three aspirins. Her head throbs. She tries to type, but the book she is working on is gone from her fingers. In its place are one dozen of Madeline's own stories, filling her hands, urging her fingers on, ready to burst on the page in a frenzy of typing. The thought occurs: Does my body know something I do not? Is it time to write these things down? Will it soon be too late?

In his room in Building B, Dr. Calvin Woodhouse sits on his bed, wordless, colorless. His jaw is set, his brow is wrinkled, his eyes are absolutely focused on his project of ripping apart his war uniform with his hands. He takes it apart, piece by piece.

AFTER WORK, SUSANNAH flops down on the couch and stares up at the ceiling. Her head throbs. Maybe it's the deletrium, she thinks. Brain tumor. Fast Acting. Ready Kwik. Rapid-Gro. Super Solvent.

"Everyone has been crazy," she says to Todd on the phone. "I couldn't get anything done today. People were crying all over the place. It was awful. It was too much like—"

"Must be something in the air," Todd says meaningfully, and tells her he has to work late. In the back of his mind, he notes the wavering in her voice and decides that he should step up the present hunting a little bit.

"Wait, Todd—"

"What?"

"Is it the deletrium? I mean, shouldn't it be making everybody all Prozac-y? Or something? Do they have chemicals that make people sad? Or mentally ill? Is it like some secret weapon they are developing just in Clarence, instead of the flu it gives everyone

major depression? Or just all the side effects of all those drugs,
those are bad enough—"

"Susannah?"

"What?"

"Are you okay?"

Pause.

"Yeah. I'm fine."

"Do you want me to come home?"

"No, no. I'm just going to make dinner."

"I'm perfectly happy to come home."

"No. No. I'm fine. And it's Wednesday—"

Todd laughs. "So you should be occupied. I'll be home before
bedtime. . . ."

"Okay. See you later."

She calls home. It's not the best idea when she has a headache.
It requires too much preparation, too much decompression afterward. She must prepare herself; she is always sure she can detect
the small quiver behind her father's voice, the one that trembles,
Come back home, Susannah, I cannot do this without you. . . .

"Hello?"

"Uh . . . Mom?"

"Susannah! How are you, darling?" The voice sings, bright and
cheery.

"Mom. I'm great. Um, how are you?"

For the last few months, her mother has refused to talk on the
phone. She says she likes to see people when she talks to them, to
be able to look into their eyes. She says when you are on the phone
you have to sit there and carefully keep up your end of the conversation, and you can't just be quiet like she likes to do. She says
when you are on the phone you are more likely to say things you
don't mean. She says you can very easily lose control of yourself,
or at least embarrass yourself, and besides you never have any idea

what the person on the other end is thinking, and that is very frightening. She says she wishes Susannah and Sara wouldn't use the phone so much, that things happen, that she has heard of people getting electrocuted through the phone wires—yes, it's an accident, a freak accident, but she doesn't know what she would do if something were to happen to them. Be careful, sweet girls, promise your mom you will be careful. . . .

When Susannah was living at home—and suddenly Susannah is seeing this behind her eyes—the phone would ring and her mother would stare at it and seem to wither away until she was just two big brown eyes. Susannah or Sara or their father would run to the phone—*Hello, Hello?*—just to stop the ringing so her mother wouldn't even have to think about answering it and all the bad things that might happen if she did. And sometimes, the very worst times, her mother would shout, *No. No. Don't get it! Please!* And then they would stand there, perfectly still, barely breathing, and the phone would ring on. Her father would come over to her mother and put his hands on her shoulder and say, *Shhh, Sharon, it's stopped. It's okay now.*

"I'm terrific, Soos. Never better. How is that dear Todd of yours?"

Now, presented for the first time in months with her mother's phone voice, Susannah does not know whether to ask her about her renewed ability to communicate by the telephone—maybe she forgot she is scared of it, sometimes she does that, and Susannah certainly does not want to be the one who reminds her.

"He's great, Mom. Um, what are you doing?"

Her enthusiasm is itself a cause for alarm. Susannah remembers one time when her mother was "terrific" they had to pick her up from the next state. She had walked. Susannah had forgotten—how could she forget? Her father had that look, like little pieces of his insides were being slowly chipped away, and Susannah wanted to crawl under the seat of the car and hide. The sensation comes back. to her abruptly, is regurgitated and fills her mouth. Susannah wants to crawl under something, anything—the couch, the table, the carpet, to protect herself from the stray splinters of her shattering father.

Susannah takes a deep breath and tries to reacquaint herself with the present moment.

Her mother's voice booms through. "Nothing. Just watching television. Knitting. You know. Keeping busy." She laughs oddly, loudly, gleefully.

Oh. Good. Well. Knitting is good. "Is Dad home?"

"He's taking a nap. I'm making him a blanket. Don't tell."

"I won't."

"Promise?"

"Yeah . . ."

"I'll make you a blanket if you'd like."

"That would be great, Mom."

"I'll have your father call you. Is there any message you would like me to convey?"

"No. No. Thanks, Mom. Just have him call."

"Will do!" And then she hangs up.

Okay. Great. 'Bye. I love you, Mom.

Susannah's sister, Sara—only two hours away from home as the car flies—comes home every weekend as a good girl should. Sara will give her the updates later. Susannah is too tired to think about it right now.

She thinks about calling in sick tomorrow. She is not sure if she can handle whatever mass depressive episode is plaguing her place of work. Too many tears today, too many sentences that trailed off to nowhere, too many random thoughts confusing speech, too many fast talkers and silent rockers, too many tears.

Susannah sinks farther into the couch and checks her watch.

Wednesday night at least. Susannah would not admit it if you asked her but she has become quite addicted to the show *Innocence Falls*. They get you with those commercials. Shots from the pedestrian insides of Innocence Falls High, looking just like your own high school, like this was almost your life if your life were a TV soap. Susannah observes Wednesday nights like the Sabbath.

Will newcomer twins Twilight and Trevor be able to fit in? Will Twilight be able to lose her bad-girl reputation? Can she win the heart of sensitive loner Jander or will the beautiful, rich, misunderstood Mickey get to him first? Can class hunk Wilson date orphan Caitlin without bringing down his social status? Will they Do It? What about Mickey's alcoholic mom and Caitlin's evangelical grandmother? What about rumors of football star Kelvin's homosexuality? Will aspiring filmmaker Fox ever realize Enid's love for him? Will Enid date Kelvin instead? Find out on next week's episode of *Innocence Falls*. Lie back. Relax. For one hour you have no cares.

Imagine Clarence High a prime-time TV series! All those toothsome boys and girls, all that import given to turmoil! Here's the episode where Jack Johnson tries to decide whether to work for the factory or the lumberyard, where Billy Olsen fails auto shop, where Sally Larson asphyxiates from the factory smell. Here's the one where the students learn to use the sewing machine in Home Ec. Where hockey-haired boys spend the afternoon hanging out in the Shop n' Shop parking lot. Where the children of technicians ostracize children of assembly line workers. Where the factory blows up, horribly disfiguring them all. Where Todd, a handsome Ph.D. student from Mansfield, lectures in AP physics, and has a torrid affair with a sixteen-year-old. Here's the one where frizzy-haired guest star Susannah dies of inoperable despair.

. . .

"I AM GOING to secede from the union," sniffles Sophie. "I'm like India. I'm going to break away and make my own country."

"Now, now . . ." Bennie strokes Sophie's hair, and fights the urge to say, "That's Pakistan." Sophie sits on his lap on their sofa, crying into Eleanor Roosevelt's fluffy white fur. The cat is too sleepy to care.

"I want to be Gandhi. I'm gonna go on a hunger strike until they let me be free. The newspapers will run big dark headlines, the people will pray. I'm gonna go on a hunger strike and I'm gonna be my own country. Sophia. Independence for Sophie."

Bennie instantly wishes he hadn't shown her that movie. She wipes her nose on Ellie's back. Bennie hands his daughter a tissue and sinks back into the couch. What can he do? Call the teacher? Call the parents? Bring in a child psychologist? Bring in a hit man? He hasn't quite been able to get the story out between Sophie's sniffling and her talk of self-rule, but somebody has hurt his daughter, that is clear. Is it overreacting to want to hurt them back?

It has happened before. His baby gets off the school bus, crying. The hurt is overt—a cruel word. Oblique—a slight by her friends. Or psychic—an oversight by the teacher, a funny look a bigger kid gave her, a mistake in class.

Which ones are worse? Which bother him more? The internal?—the early signs of perfectionism, excessive desire to please, oversensitivity perhaps. Or the external—the bullies on the school bus, the cliquey girls with the right brand of jeans. One is a quirk of her psyche, the other of the world at large. And beneath her tears he sees more than just hurt. Sophie is a child. All her life, Sophie has operated from the sincere belief that the rest of the people in the world mean her nothing but good. This is a rite of passage he never wanted to see her have to make.

People will be cruel. This of course is part of being a kid. A horrid truth, but nonetheless . . . Bennie remembers. He is remembering now like a cut. There was a bully when he was this age. A sixth grader in the neighborhood. Who would make him and the other boys say Uncle. Who would throw mud and shout, "Jew." The bully didn't even know what it meant. He mouthed the words of his father. Under Madeline's disapproving gaze, Bennie's father taught him to fight back, a cigarette dangling from his paternal hand.

Girls. Here he is lost. If Sophie were a boy, Bennie would teach her to fight. The three ways to survive childhood: toughness, a quick wit, and a good left hook.

Girls. What defense do they have against the schoolyard boys who prey on the smaller because they can. In Clarence, the children of university people pick on factory kids, factory kids pick on university children. The older pick on the younger, stronger on the weaker, cruel on the kind—Darwin on the playground.

A memory stirs. A vein opens. Young Bennie helping the bully play keep-away with a ratty teddy bear, next-door neighbor Steffie jumping and screaming and crying.

Then: Mr. Schwartz holding him up by his ear on his own front steps. Mr. Schwartz gesturing to his crying daughter, brandishing the muddy stuffed bear, and pulling young Bennie's ear up up up! Mother Madeline on the porch shaking her head, the dull disappointment in her eyes pushing a hole through Bennie's stomach.

That night. In the dark, Bennie's pillow salty and wet, his mother sat down on his bed, stroked his forehead, and whispered in his ear, "We are made up of equal parts light and dark. Kind and cruel. This is the great battle of life. Every day we must struggle against the dark. The only way to win the battle, Benjamin, is compassion. You may fall victim to the cruelty of others, but in the long run, you will have won."

His mother stayed there, smelling of baby powder and lotion, stroking his hair while he cried himself to sleep.

The memory dies and Bennie feels his heart spill over as he rubs his baby girl's head and wipes away her tears. "Sophie. Soph, baby. What happened? Shhhh . . . Shhhh . . . I'm here, my girl. My little Gandhi. My little civil disobeyer."

Sophie will never tell. She cries until she is dry. Her father strokes her hair, while the cat bathes Sophie's tears off her fur.

six.

Dirt flies everywhere.

I**N HIS LECTURE** hall the next day, Bennie finds himself staring his students down. This group, in the back. Were they cruel? Would they beget bullies later? Could they be sterilized? These girls, in the front, did they whisper and gossip? Did they discard friendships like old shoes?

The bell tolls and Bennie clears his throat.

"How many of you remember where you were when you heard that the *Challenger* exploded?" Most of the students raise their hands, as always, year after year. (He has realized that pretty soon he will not be able to use this one anymore. Will the world provide another archetypical event for a new generation? Always a mass collective flashbulb moment, every twenty-three years?)

"All right. Now, for those of you whose hands are raised, how many of you would say you are absolutely sure?"

Again, as always, no hands fall.

"Right after the *Challenger* exploded, a university professor asked his students to write down exactly what they were doing when they heard the news. A few years later, he found the same group of students and asked them again where they had been. Almost every student responded that they were 'absolutely confident' as to where they had been, just like you." He always stresses that part, year after year. Absolutely confident.

"Yet many of these 'absolutely confident' students were wrong. They had mixed up details, time, even written down another memory entirely. The students refused to believe it, of course, but the evidence was there. This week, you will read about some related experiments—people who were given a false memory of having been lost in a shopping mall when they were a child, and became convinced, absolutely convinced, that the incident really happened to them. Of course, you've all heard of the controversy over recovered memories. I, personally, do not believe there is a right or wrong to this debate; for each documented case of an implanted memory of abuse, there is a confirmed recovered memory, and vice versa. The only thing we can take from this debate is that when it comes to memory, no absolute statements can be made. Not every memory is true nor is it false. Which leaves us in a bit of a quandary."

He pauses to smile at this point. Most of the students are scribbling furiously in their notebooks. The ones sleeping in the back are still sleeping. Of the two hundred students in the class, about six people look up to meet his smile. Bennie sighs inwardly.

"There's nothing new in the fallibility of memory, of course. You'll read what our buddy Freud has to say on the matter in your packets this week. For Freud, for every forgotten or mispronounced word, name, or deed, there is a reason behind the forgetting. Like a magician at a carnival booth, Freud would have an analysand free-associate on a forgotten word—and each time, presto—he would always uncover some hidden uncomfortable association—a death, lie, a cruelty, whatever. Something that the mind wishes to suppress. Freud has it that we set up screens in front of our past. We replace traumatic events with slips of the tongue, confabulated memories—all to prevent anxiety."

Bennie takes off his blazer and folds it on top of his chair. He rubs his hands together.

"What we can infer from Freud's theories is there is something innate about the tricks our mind plays. Perhaps we are biologically programmed to distort the past. Memory is associative, and we are surrounded by its cues all the time—smell, sensation, word, place—without these screens, perhaps, we would be constantly wallowing in trauma. Forgetfulness is not a sign of disease. It is natural, and may even be biologically positive. Perhaps the mind's ability to make the past malleable is essential for our survival."

Bennie begins to pace back and forth on the stage, as he usually does at the half-hour point.

"Because we've all made horrendous mistakes, suffered trauma, committed troubling acts in our lives. What would happen if we could remember them all, call them up with just a smell or a word? What would it do to us if we remembered our childhoods, our whole lives, every day?"

He thinks again of sniffling Sophie. He thinks of how many times the scene replays itself. How many times for his child, for everyone's children. These wounds for Sophie will go away. They have to go away, that is the way of childhood. But what if they didn't? What if someday, she remembered everything? This is why we forget. Sophie crying on the couch every other week is why we forget.

"Because our bodies and our minds are designed to survive. To protect us. How much do we gain and how much do we lose by living under a screen? Does it keep us free or does it keep us naive? What a delicate balance our minds must maintain to keep us sane. And of course, sometimes the screen absolutely fails and we become tormented by the past. Our minds have a great potential to hurt us."

His students recognize the change in tone and sit staring up at him, pens still. Something comes across Bennie. He makes a connection.

"Our minds can work for us or against us. We are made of equal parts light and dark. Kind and cruel. This is the great battle of life. Every day we must struggle against the dark."

Bennie looks around at his class. Almost all the students have put down their pens and are staring blankly at him. They have been well trained through a lifetime in the American educational system to recognize what will not be on the test.

THAT AFTERNOON, BENNIE calls Sophie's teacher and asks what happened in school the day before. The teacher feels terrible, terrible. Some talk about parents and Career Day. Trying to get women in. Mothers. Sophie stayed quiet. A boy shouted something. Another laughed. Sophie blushed. The teacher wanted to bring her out. Such a quiet girl.

Yes, Sophie, what does your mother do? Would she like to come in to speak? The teacher hadn't known. She feels awful, awful. You know how kids are. The boys laughed again. One— always a troublemaker—said, "Sophie doesn't have a mom. She lives alone . . . with her father." He nudged his friend, the university president's son, who hissed, "I bet they sleep in the same bed." Apparently there was another incident in gym class. She wasn't sure. But you know how kids are. They pick anything, anything. But the boys had been dealt with. They were quickly sent to the vice principal and would most certainly be given a failing grade in comportment.

SUSANNAH'S HEAD HAS been hurting for three days straight. This brain tumor might be serious. Susannah is not as a rule given to panic, but she does not have that much else to occupy her. Precision flies away on wings like something or other. Her temples squeeze in.

Work is almost unbearable. She thought she had left this kind of thing behind her. She cannot handle being with the people so she tends to the pets instead. Before her eyes, the four basset hounds in Building A line up, one by one, behind their owner, an old religion prof. The first lifts its leg on his ankle, then walks away. The second takes its place, lifts its leg, and walks away. Then the third. Then the fourth. The religion prof stands there, ankle soaked, eyes closed, head shaking. Susannah said, "I'll take care of it," and cleaned up.

Every animal in Clarence has lost its mind. Baying. Meowing. Peeing. Running in circles. Singing to furry gods. The Sunny Shadows grounds are filled with clumps of dirt and holes. Things fall apart. The vet is overrun. One old mutt has been sniffing excessively. A normally eloquent parakeet is talking gibberish. A rabbit has not slept for a week. A golden retriever has done nothing but sleep for a week. Three ferrets have been piddling excessively. A neutered tabby male cat has rediscovered his sexual side with some stuffed animals. And a white cat named Eleanor Roosevelt has been grooming herself raw. Wherever Susannah goes in Clarence, dogs are barking and howling, jumping against fences, burrowing under gates. Todd rubs his hands together and postulates the cause; finally, we are seeing the effects of this airborne thing.

"Soon, Susannah, maybe we will all be digging holes in the

ground and howling at the moon and burrowing under fences."

Susannah is burrowing already. Dirt flies everywhere. She digs deeper and deeper.

There is something she is trying to get to.

Todd is beginning to catch on. At night, in bed, he runs his hands through her hair. He pulls a curl. "Susannah? What is it? You're not happy. What can I do? I love you so much, Zana. You are the only one for me. You know that, right? You know that. I can't make it without you. I do not care what happens. I want to be with you until we are ninety-nine. We will sit and rock next to each other. No matter what. Please, Zana. Zana Zana Zana Zana Zana . . ."

The touch of his hand is at that moment unbearable. The feel of fingers on her hair joins her with too many Susannahs past. Sex, adoration, anticipation, flirtation, forgiveness, anger, tenderness, quiet—all these moments echo in that touch and Susannah can hear nothing else.

She should tell him. Now they can relate. Susannah spends her nights how Todd spends his days in the lab. Each wrapped up in memory.

She has not been sleeping well—her mind hums and buzzes. She stays awake replaying crises of last week, last month, last year, last decade.

"I don't know, Susannah," her sister says. "Maybe that factory smell is affecting your brain."

"Oh, it doesn't smell anymore. Not since the factory closed."

But every other smell bothers her. The scent of peanut butter sends her tumbling back in time to junior high. Her best friend is telling her over peanut butter sandwiches that she is having an affair with a teacher. This could not have happened. She must have dreamed it. It might have happened. Could she have forgotten it all this time? How could that have happened? Did she dream it or did it happen? She remembers, but what does that mean? The images are thin and filmy and floaty. Do we remember in the same material we dream in? The textures are indistinct from each other and Susannah cannot tell the difference. It becomes the most important thing in the world for her to know whether or not this thing really happened and she cannot know it.

Everything is something. Susannah grabs a hair dryer and the cool plastic shrieks in her hand. Seven-year-old Susannah is staring at her mother. Her mother is standing before her, crying. "You be careful. You be careful with a hair dryer. Never use it in the tub. Look. Look at these poor girls."

She thrusts a bit of newspaper before Susannah's eyes. The image: two girls, sisters, smiling into the camera, in a picture just like the one of Susannah and Sara taken at that portrait studio where they got lollipops for being so pretty and well-behaved. The picture of the two girls is a Before shot. In the After shot, which is not shown, the girls are dead. Electrocuted. First naked and gleefully splashing in the bath, like Susannah and Sara do, and then life shorts out of them. Somewhere, a father walks into a room. A nice father, like hers, and finds his daughters dead. The parents had children and now they have none.

"Never use a hair dryer in the tub. Do you promise? Do you promise?" She shrieks these words, and then cries and cries.

Susannah whimpers, "Yes, yes, I promise."

Her mother crumples up in a little ball in front of her daughter. Susannah sits down next to her and strokes her hair the way her mom used to do for her. "It's okay, Momma. It's okay. I'm here. Shhh, Momma . . ."

Her father stands in the doorway. "Sharon? What is it? What's wrong? What happened?" He is not used to this kind of thing yet. His voice fills with alarm. "Sharon?" Susannah does not know what to say.

"What happened?"

"Look, Dad. Some girls died." Susannah thrusts the paper in front of him. "Isn't it awful? Isn't it just awful?" Susannah wants to cry, too.

Her father's eyebrows lock. He scans the article. He stares at his fallen wife. "It's okay, Susannah. I'll take care of her now. Don't worry," and then he picks up her sobbing mother—"Sharon, Sharon, what is it?"—and carries her away.

Seven-year-old Susannah crawls into the attic and sits in a corner and watches the shadow of the ceiling creep over her. She thinks it must be very, very sad for her mother to be so upset. She has never seen her mother like that, ever. It is just so sad. So sad. Poor girls, Susannah thinks. Poor poor girls. I'm so sorry.

The picture emerges again, a decade and a half old. Susannah sees the portrait studio Before photo with smiles and dimples and hair ribbons and she hears her mom's voice—quivering, then breaking down—and she wants to crawl back up into her attic at home and let the shadows cover her up. Susannah drops the hair dryer on the ground. The plastic case cracks.

seven.

Would you scare away his ghosts?

THE WEATHER CHANGES quickly in Clarence. Fall does not exist, at least as an entity unto itself. Fall is simply a direction, like west; fall is when things move winterward. One night the people of Clarence fall asleep to a lush green world; they wake the next morning to find themselves awash in oranges and reds. And then, the morning after that, the earth is brown and dead—leaves turn into powder with each step. Color has gone into hibernation and the white sky looms over everyone's moods. The dull brown branches of the trees reach out out out beyond the scope of the canvas, grasping something no one can see. The sky changes to a bright crisp blue, smelling of smoke and nostalgia.

And this year, isn't there another smell in the air? Stop in your tracks. Close your eyes. Breathe in. Separate out the whiffs of crumbling leaves and humbling regret, and there! Do you smell that? That lingering aroma, tinged with bitter almonds and burnt dinner. Yes, that one . . . Isn't it? Yes it is—close your eyes and breathe in the heady, unmistakable scent of foreshadowing.

Clarence blinks and suddenly October has almost gone. Life proceeds. Former factory workers accost the mailman to see if their first unemployment check has arrived. ("It will come," Harris Jones assures them. "It took some time. The paperwork. But it will be there. Any day now.")

At the high school, two fraternal twins, newcomers to the town, wander the hallways trying to fit in, a young nerd writes love letters to a sensitive jock, while his girlfriend sets her sights on the homecoming crown. The high school basketball coach lectures his young scholar athletes on their priorities. (Number one: God. Two: Family. Three: Education. Four: Basketball. Say it with me.)

At the elementary schools, yellow buses pull out of the tar-black parking lots. In the front, groups of small children dodge spitballs and swear words and plan their costumes for the Halloween parade.

At a Mansfield University dormitory, a sophomore wakes up as the sun sets, attempting to remember what he drank last night. Two virginal first-years try to figure out how sex works, while next door a sweating student tries to finish her Political Thought paper by the deadline.

In a large house in Mansfield Hills, the university president promises his son ten dollars if he'll pick up his socks.

At Davis and Dean Booksellers, a café worker with pale skin and dark hair spends her break burrowing inside the mythology section again. This woman has been reading myths since she was three years old. She will not stop until she finds it out. She does not know what "it" is, but it is something. "I am looking for explanations," she says to a curious supervisor. "I am looking for the Origins of Things. There is something I am trying to get to." And she pulls out another book from the shelf, flips through the pages, and raises a hand to scratch her neck. It itches and itches.

A few blocks away, at the house of the town's beloved pastor, the PTA president shrieks as pieces of silverware take flight and soar across her living room.

At Sunny Shadows Estates, two grandmotherly friends—one a writer you may have heard of—walk the garden wrapped in hand-knit shawls, analyzing the psyche of one of the handsomest residents. In a room in Building B, the subject of this conversation lies on the plush carpet of his room, ghost white, gray eyes frozen open, shreds of canvas in his hands.

THERE HAS BEEN a crisis in Innocence Falls. An accident. Death. Three students in a ten-year-old hatchback. Driving home from an evening at the beach. Mickey and her friends from the mansions up the hill break into Dr. Daddy's liquor cabinet. Cruising around in a sport utility vehicle. Back streets. Dimly lit. Interior of the Jeep. Pan frozen faces. Mickey screams and grabs the wheel. Two cars pass the point of no return.

There is a crisis on *Innocence Falls*. Past the point of no return two cars merge on a shadowy road. Metal slams into metal. The small hatchback, compressed. Mickey wakes up in a hospital bed. She calls a nurse. The people that were with me. Are they all right? Ray? Is he okay?

Yes. Yes. A concussion. Marsha and Robbie too.

And the people in the other car? Are they . . . ? Did they . . . ?

They didn't make it. They died instantly. I'm sorry.

Who were they? Did I know them?

Mickey does not go to the memorial service. The students plant trees. Mickey does not go to school. Marsha and Robbie's parents discuss boarding school, where their children can have a fresh start. There are fights. Students scream at students, adults ostracize other adults. The town is brokenhearted. A meeting is held in the auditorium. This has got to stop, a man in flannel screams. The people up there do not know how to raise their kids, and our kids die because of it. We need laws. We need enforcement. We need accountability. Let's sue the parents. Money is the only thing these people understand. Let's not wait until more children have to die.

Hubbub. Hubbub. Sounds of agreement. Shouts of anger. A few parents exchange glances and sink into their seats. Trevor stands up. He wears a suit and a tie. Twilight looks around nervously.

"I'd like to say something. I'm Trevor Barrett. My sister and I are new to Innocence Falls. Maybe there are things we just don't understand. A terrible thing has happened here. Death. Of youth, and of trust. We come from the city, and we have always heard that a small town is a community. This sort of suspicion and mistrust is the world we came from. We didn't expect to find it here."

Audience members begin to turn their heads toward Trevor. A few gaze down at the ground. The man in flannel looks around anxiously. Music swells.

"This is not the place or the time for neighbor against neighbor. This is the time to come together. To be a community. To help each other heal. Maybe if we weren't such strangers to each other this never would have happened in the first place."

A few heads begin to nod. Mrs. Barrett grabs her husband's hand and beams. Even Twilight seems to be proud.

"Right now, there are people who need our help. The families who have lost their children. And . . ." Trevor breathes in. "Mickey, Ray, Robbie, and Marsha need our help too." The hubbub starts again. "Now—" Trevor shushes everybody. "They made a terrible mistake, which they will carry with them for the rest of their lives. We've all made mistakes. Imagine having to pay for them the way these people, these children will pay."

Trevor sits back down. There is silence for a moment. Then, suddenly, the man in the flannel shirt gets up. People stare at him, holding their breath. The man begins to clap. Soon, the whole auditorium is standing and clapping and cheering. Trevor leans back in his chair while his teary-eyed dad thumps him on the back.

On her couch in Clarence, Susannah cries and cries.

BENNIE WOULD LIKE blood, it is true. He would like to march into the university president's office and say, Mr. President, your son must be dealt with. Mr. President, your son is a juvenile delinquent. Mr. President, your son is an ass. Of course the world does not work that way. The university president would stare at him oddly, smile accommodatingly, and then ask Bennie for a donation to the school. Little Robbie, fourth-grade terror, might be punished. Can't have the university president's son making a bad name for himself after all. But then the little punk would surely take out his revenge on Sophie.

Bennie's friend Phil assures him that the revenge may be long in coming, but it will be sweet. "Sophie will have her day. That boy will be a drug dealer and Sophie will be an astronaut. Don't worry, Bennie."

"Phil, I actually want to kill him. He's nine years old, and I want to murder him. I want him to die slowly and painfully."

Bennie and Phil have breakfast at Davis and Dean every few days. Strange Brew has better coffee certainly, but also more students. Bennie hates it—the nervous glances, the halfhearted hellos. Each semester he teaches either Intro to Psych (three hundred students) or Personality (a hundred and fifty students). He gets to teach his psychoanalytic seminars once every couple of years; the department is positive that this is all student interest will justify.

For Phil, it's different. They sit at Strange Brew and any student who has ever worked with him will approach him, frothing at the mouth, cracking jokes about the latest Hitchcock remake or bursting with a new trend in e-zines.

All that was Lizzie's forte, of course. Lovely Lizzie doing her dissertation on 1950s hygiene shorts. Lovely Lizzie, bouncing home from teaching her first seminar, eyes full of Sophie . . .

Phil has the job she was supposed to get.

Bennie rubs his temples. Where was he?

Yes, Bennie much prefers Davis and Dean. It is nice to have your bagel and fat-free cream cheese away from the life of the university, safely wrapped in the arms of corporate America. It is nice to live in a macrocosm every once in a while. To surround yourself in the assiduously familiar and yet at the same time to be so damn insignificant. A cog. You collect on the twenty-five-cent refill of your house blend, and at this same moment around the country the scene replays itself hundreds of times.

"That will be twenty-five cents, Professor Singer."

Bennie starts. The dark-haired girl—woman—at the counter blushes shyly. Probably because she has just destroyed his interior monologue. Has he seen her before? A student, of course. Sometimes it seems like everyone who works at this goddamn store is a former university student. Didn't Mansfield prepare anyone for a career?

Bennie smiles weakly and the young woman blushes again. "Oh, um, my name is Lilith. I was in your Jung seminar a couple of years back." She points to her name tag. "I liked it. Um, here's your refill. Have a nice day, Professor Singer." She smiles again and turns her attention to the next customer.

Bennie stands still and holds his coffee. He wants to lean over the counter and talk some more. Yes, Lilith. It's nice to meet you. You look tired, are you sleeping well?

He must walk away, of course. The line behind him will not wait for his ego needs. But still, he feels himself smile a little more. The interior monologue drifts off, and the conscious mind wonders, What was I saying?

Bennie walks to the table in the corner of the café. Phil has gotten ahold of the *Clarence Chronicle* and is reading the comics. He laughs uproariously, ignorant of the people around him, drawing air through his nose harshly on each inhale. Bennie adds four packets of artificial sweetener to his coffee. Phil looks up and shakes his head.

"I will never understand you and that stuff."

Bennie looks at the empty packets in his hand. Something stirs again. The encounter with the former student is gone, and he is elsewhere, stirring coffee, watching the door, waiting, face hot.

"So, what's Sophie going to be for Halloween?"

"Huh? Oh yeah. Do you know where I can get some homespun cloth? She needs it for her costume."

"Is she going to be a ghost?"

"Nope. Gandhi."

"Indira?"

"Mahatma."

"Oh." Phil sips his caramel latte. "Can she wear a white sheet?"

"No. Not authentic enough. It has to be homespun. She wanted to shave her head."

"Jesus."

"Yes, I suggested she reconsider. We're looking into what we can do with hair gel. She was going to go as deletrium, actually, but then she decided that would be passé."

"That's some little girl you have."

"Now I have to figure out how she will stay warm. I suppose long johns are not authentic either."

"I'm having my seminar students write down all the costumes they see. How many are TV and movie characters, how many are old standards, how many come out of a box. Around here, I swear, half the costumes are homemade by loving mothers with sewing machines."

Bennie's mind flashes back to Sophie's shaking shoulders and one tear-drenched cat. "She probably needs a mother."

Phil folds up his comics. "Ben . . ."

Bennie forces a smile. "It's okay. Hey, what time is it? I promised Mom I'd stop by before class."

"How's your mother's love life going?"

"I haven't heard about the big date, but, man, Phil. She said she's becoming 'smitten.' My mom is smitten. I don't know what's happened to her. She is a teenager in love, and she didn't even tell me about him until now."

Phil leans back in his chair and begins to say "Smitten" again and again. Bennie begins to gather his stuff and stops.

"Hey, what is that?"

"What's what?" Phil looks around.

"Don't you smell that?"

"Smell what?"

"I dunno." Bennie sniffs again.

SUSANNAH KNOCKS ON the door of Madeline Singer's room. She has been at work for just two hours today, but she has found herself rather irrelevant. There are four maintenance people scheduled on any given day and today two of them have called in sick. No one seems to care; everyone in charge is too busy calling doctors in, contacting families, tending to residents who have fallen ill. Susannah is trying to stay out of their hair. Everywhere she goes, someone on staff is telling her, "It's okay, Susannah, I'll take care of it."

Susannah always wondered if she would know what going insane feels like—can you feel your perceptions alter, your mind move ever so slowly out of center? Or do you have to wait until somebody finally tells you? This is a mother-daughter chat they have never had. If whatever's happening here does affect her, how will they tell whether it is caused by chemicals or by heredity? Will one lead to another? If it's caused by the chemicals, will they be able to cure it? If it's not, will they be able to cure it?

"Mrs. Singer?" She knocks again. "It's Susannah . . ."

There is a pause.

"Come in."

Madeline's voice sounds slightly tired perhaps, but still human. Something twinges within Susannah and for a moment she feels a sensation she had not been expecting—could it actually be fear? She pushes the door open and is surprised to find herself nearly praying to forces she does not believe in: *Please let her be well. Please let me find her all right, sitting at her desk typing away with her good posture and thick brown-gray hair.*

"Hi, Mrs. Singer. I just wanted to check in. I hope I'm not interrupting. . . ."

Susannah finds Madeline where she always is, sitting at her desk next to that funny old typewriter. She is dressed, like always, in loose pants and a bulky sweater. The only change Susannah can see is a proliferation of crumpled-up sheets of paper, scattered under her chair, her desk, next to her books, even over by the window—everywhere but in the dark blue trash can.

"No." Madeline smiles tightly at her. "I'm not getting anything done today."

"I could come back—"

"Don't be silly. Take a seat. I could use the company."

Susannah sits down. Madeline gazes at her vacantly. They sit a moment, not speaking, and that thing inside Susannah twinges again, and suddenly she expects Madeline to burst out crying, or yelling—or to ossify, there, in front of her eyes, not move for hours on end. And if that happens, Susannah does not think she will be able to take it, she might crumble into little pieces right there.

Susannah clears her throat. "Mrs. Singer, are you feeling all right? There seems to be something going around here."

Madeline pauses. "Really? I hadn't noticed."

Susannah blushes. "You haven't? Oh, well, people are just, I don't know, a little funny lately."

"Funny how?" Madeline looks stern—or so Susannah thinks. Susannah realizes she is being imprecise, and one should never be imprecise, with Madeline Singer most of all.

"Um, I took some animals in yesterday. They've all gone a little weird."

"Really."

"Yeah, um, the vet doesn't know what's wrong, though. The, uh, the basset hounds in Building A, they've all been peeing all over the place. It's quite a clean-up job." She breathes out a little laugh. There is a pause. Susannah shifts in her seat. Madeline is not here, with her. Susannah gets an urge to ask Madeline where she is right now, where her mind is taking her, and perhaps, might she come along, too?

Susannah coughs a little.

Madeline looks at Susannah for the first time since she came in. "I'm sorry, Susannah, I'm afraid I'm not very good company." Her words are languid, as if she is speaking through a hundred humid skies. Susannah bites her lip.

"Oh, it's okay, I can leave you alone if you'd like."

Madeline sits up and seems as if she is deliberately trying to focus. "No. I'm sorry. I'm just a little . . . preoccupied, I guess."

"Um, Todd—my fiancé—seems to think the deletrium is beginning to affect people somehow. He's in Memory Studies, so he's done neuro stuff. He knows all about this kind of thing."

Madeline purses her lips, and leans forward, staring into Susannah's eyes. "Ms. Susannah? Can I ask you a question?"

"Of course."

"Is that why you moved to Clarence? For your fiancé?"

Susannah blushes. "Yeah. Well, he got into Mansfield. I wasn't, really, doing anything. Um. I wasn't in school or anything."

"Where were you?" That is the other thing about Madeline Singer versus the rest of the world; Madeline Singer asks questions like she actually wants to know the answers.

"Oh, ah, I was home. There were some, ah, family things."

"And then you came here."

"Well, yes."

Madeline pauses again. She tilts her head. "You know, it's funny, I thought for a while you didn't remind me of anyone, but you do, very much so. It all feels so familiar. . . ."

"Ohh . . ."

There is more silence. Susannah wonders if the conversation is over. She wonders if she should make tea. She wonders if she should crawl under Madeline's bed and stay there. Then, finally, Madeline sits up and smiles faintly.

"So, what have you got for me today?"

"Huh? Oh, gossip!" Susannah suddenly finds herself talking very fast. "Well, this is an odd one. I was listening to Bertie Lundberg— you know, the church organist?—this was last week actually, while I was working in the garden, and she was telling some people that the pastor's wife has seen a real live poltergeist in the house! Silverware flying through the air and all sorts of things! Anyway, the gossip is that Pastor Hansen is having an affair, but his wife doesn't know it, even if the whole congregation does, so Bertie thinks that maybe the pastor's wife is kind of sublimating, if you know what I mean?"

Susannah pauses. Madeline doesn't say anything. She seems to be focusing on something above Susannah's left shoulder.

"Well, anyway, apparently the pastor doesn't really believe his wife, not that he's around enough to notice anything, and Bertie is up in arms. Bertie says that if your beloved tells you there is a ghost in the house, you hold her and vow to scare it away."

Susannah stares up at Madeline, with a sense of desperation. She waits.

Madeline breathes in, and says flatly, "How awful."

"Yes. Yes. Well, I thought that would be good information for you, all those church dynamics."

"Susannah?"

"Yes?"

"What is your fiancé's name again?"

"Todd."

"Well, then, what about you and this Todd? Would you scare away his ghosts?"

Susannah works that out in her head for a few moments and then looks at the ground. She bites her lip again. Her hand flies to her hair.

"Well . . . I don't know."

Madeline eyes her. "Do you mean that?"

"I don't know. I don't know if he has any ghosts."

And then, something happens, something comes over Madeline, her shoulders sink, and her eyes lose their color. She takes a deep breath in, and shakes her head. "Susannah. Susannah, that is so sad. That is the saddest thing I have ever heard."

Susannah opens her mouth and then wonders what exactly it is she intended to say. She does not think "What are you talking about?" would be an appropriate response. And then, before Susannah can answer, the telephone rings. Madeline reaches over to answer it.

Hello? . . .

. . . Mildred? . . .

What is it? . . .

And then Madeline turns the color of the crumpled sheets of paper around her desk and drops the phone down and without a word to Susannah, she runs out the door.

NO ONE IS on the grounds of Sunny Shadows when Bennie arrives. Bennie finds it odd—this bunch is usually out in all weather—reading, painting, taking walks, observing some animal or another. Bennie walks over to the library. No one is at the front desk to greet him. He walks into the reading room. The big maple tables are empty. The sunlight casts stained-glass-colored spots on the carpet. Bennie walks through the library peeking behind shelves. He reaches the Staff Only door and knocks. Once. Twice. He takes a deep breath and shouts, "Hello?" (How funny it feels to shout in this temple!) His voice travels up, bouncing against the ceiling. "Is anybody here? Hello?" The only response is the echo of his own call.

Bennie turns and walks out of the library. It seems to have grown colder just in the last few minutes. "Hello? Is anybody here?" He walks right over to Building E, his mother's building—maybe the cold has just kept them all inside. The smell in the air grows stronger and stronger. He can almost place it. Maybe everything is fine. Maybe there is a meeting. Maybe the library is closed today. The front hallway of his mother's building is empty. It is then that he notices the sound of the approaching sirens.

Bennie goes to the elevator. He is almost running, but not quite, because to run would be to admit he is panicking. Bennie does not panic, because panic is irrational. Panic is a vestigial stressor that causes the release of adrenaline, allowing the creature to run away from predators. But this is not appropriate right now. Panic does not help. Panic impedes judgment. He presses the button. He jumps up and down. The elevator won't come. He runs over to the staircase and runs up four flights of stairs to Madeline's floor. The hallway is still—he expects this now. A few doors ajar. His mother's door ajar. A sheet of paper sits suspended in her old typewriter, her desk chair stands askew in the center of the room. Bennie stands, stares. "Mom?" A weak attempt. He leans against the wall. (Robin's egg blue. Because then it will always be spring in here. Bennie had rolled his eyes.) Outside the window, there is noise. There, a crowd at the building on the edge of the property. Building B? Yes, B. His mother had looked at an apartment there. She wanted to be closer to the library. Bennie runs out of his mother's apartment, through the hallway, down the steps, and out the front door.

"What is it? What's going on?" Fifty Sunny Shadows residents stand outside the door of the building looking ashen. "Is my mother here? Have you seen Madeline?" The librarian grabs Bennie's elbow and points inside. Bennie pushes through knots of people—residents, staff, visitors—and finds himself standing in front of a small apartment on the first floor. Paramedics move in a flurried swarm in the doorway. He sees his mother, standing in a corner of the room, shaking and crying. The paramedics move away from the doorway and bend down. Bennie strains to see. Someone shouts, "Clear the doorway," and they lift a stretcher up toward the door. "Put a blanket on him," someone shouts, and Bennie sees the body of his mother's suitor. Calvin is naked, open-eyed, and frozen in fetal position. A strand of saliva runs down his chin.

eight.

Gandhi and the Glo-bot

EVERY HALLOWEEN, ALL learning at Jesse Ventura Elementary ceases at noon. After lunch, masses of children jazzed up on orange drink swarm into the bathrooms to don capes, leotards, and various types of plastic and vinyl to prepare for the Ventura Elementary Annual Halloween Party in the gym. Parental volunteers poise near mirrors with tubes of hypoallergenic greasepaint at the ready. A delegation from the Clarence Sewing Club stands in the corner fitting the fruits of members' labors on children who (for whatever reason— nobody is passing judgment here) don't have costumes.

Of course, the CSC members take their needlecrafts very, very seriously. The official club charter legislates that each member will put everything (he or) she has into (his or) her sewing and will try to better (his or) her technique with each piece. The unofficial charter legislates that each member will try to outdo every other member on each project. The club costumes, then, have become

more and more intricate each year—and have invariably won all
of the prizes at the Ventura Elementary Annual Costume Contest.
A few PTA members complained—after all, these kids are wearing
charity costumes, for God's sake, they aren't supposed to be winning. Some of these same PTA parents would occasionally find
the fruits of their own labors mysteriously stuck behind the bushes
near the bus stop, others simply would not find the time to make
a costume for their own kids, as what was the point, really?—and,
curiously, the lines by the CSC table would grow and grow each
year. The PTA met with the CSC to resolve the issue; a few PTA
members suggested that the sewing club simplify its efforts a little,
"to be more fair to all of the children," and the club members
bristled that, "it is not in our charter to simplify."

They had clearly reached an impasse.

This year, the CSC has been coordinating with local aid orga-
nizations to identify the needy families (of which there are many
more than usual due to certain circumstances) and provide just the
right number of costumes for those children. (Any non-needy par-
ent who thinks she will let the club do her work for her this year
will have another think coming.) Quietly, PTA parents, who are
so often called upon to serve as judges at the Halloween party—
agree amongst themselves that they, too, know who the needy
children are, and if these youngsters happen to be wearing some
intricate hand-sewn costumes well above the families' means, well,
they will just take that into account in their judging.

But the PTA president (and pastor's wife) has other fish to fry
this year. She has called an emergency meeting two days before
Halloween to discuss "a constitutional crisis in the school." Members stick hot dishes in microwavable containers for their families,
then scurry off to the junior high auditorium. On the stage they
find Lorna Hansen standing at the podium in a pool of soft light,

freshly styled blond hair pinned back in a twist on her small head, pressed pink pantsuit matching a thick coat of Xtralast lipstick. You can often find Lorna studying the fashion ensembles to be found in the career woman's section of the magazine racks at Davis and Dean. It makes sense; she is the pastor's wife and must set a standard for the community. I Know What I Am Doing. I Am an Authority Figure. There Is Nothing at All Amiss in My Household. Inanimate Objects Cannot Fly.

The clock strikes 7:00 and Lorna begins to talk. No time for pleasantries. This is serious. "What would happen," she begins, "if we staged a nativity play every Christmas?" A murmur passes through the auditorium. "What would happen if we put up crosses at Easter? Our children do not even have Good Friday off. And why is that?" She raises an eyebrow and surveys her audience. "Because some people would have it that our Constitution forbids it. Yet, every year, this school sanctions and celebrates a pagan holiday. That's right—pagan. All Hallow's Eve." Lorna Hansen pauses again and looks around the room, taking care to gaze at each audience member personally. "Teachers"—she glares at the few offenders who have deigned to come to this meeting—"decorate their classrooms with occult symbols of witches, vampires, and"—here she pauses—"ghosts.

"Halloween is a religious festival. And the religion we are condoning in our public schools rejects the Christian God as a matter of doctrine. And we must in turn reject this holiday. If you have any doubts, let me refer you to the First Commandment." Lorna, you are on fire. You have learned a thing or two from being a pastor's wife, that is for sure.

"This holiday celebrates mischief, trickery, the occult, and, yes, even the devil himself. Shall we continue to perpetuate this constitutional and Christian crisis? Shall we invite ghosts and goblins and witches into our homes? Shall we invite the devil himself? I think if we cannot bring the Lord into our schools we certainly should not invite the devil. Thank you."

Some of Lorna's friends in the audience stand up and applaud. Some teachers sneak out. The superintendent is called in immediately. The argument is made. An alternative is laid out. (Pioneer Days. A harvest festival. With corn and hay. Celebrating our forefathers. Celebrating our great heritage. Celebrating history. Celebrating virtue. And sharing.)

The superintendent sighs. He clears his throat. "Well. I do appreciate your concerns, and I think the matter requires further study." Lorna Hansen opens her pink mouth. "But Halloween is two days away and I do not see that we can make any changes this year. So, let's take the matter under advisement and discuss it more at a later date when we can put the issue to . . ." he sighs heavily ". . . a vote."

So this year, at least, Halloween will remain the same. All learning at Jesse Ventura Elementary ceases at noon. Swarms of children jazzed up on chocolate milk scurry into the locker rooms to don capes, leotards, and masks. Parental volunteers are poised near the mirrors. ("I am sorry. I cannot possibly. Far too much work to do," says Bennie, as he does every year.) The CSC costumes, you should know, are better than ever. At 12:30, students meet in the gym, lining up two by two behind their teachers. Picking buddies is always fraught with peril—Sophie Singer, for example, has two best friends, Leslie and Christine. Or rather Christine has two best friends, Leslie and Sophie. Or rather, Christine has two best friends, Leslie and/or Sophie. This week, it has been Leslie, and this Halloween the two have dressed up like characters from the chapter book series Girls of America. Curly-haired Christine is wearing the familiar plaits and gingham of pioneer girl Charity, while fat freckled Leslie wears the sailor dress and cap of Gilded

Age Emily. It is obvious to all concerned just who will partner up with whom. ("Whoever heard of Gandhi, anyway," states Christine. "And I bet he's not even American.")

Sophie wears a tan leotard and tights (Bennie's victory) under a white cloth wrapped around her like a toga. Her thin blond hair is plastered against her head, and she wears little round glasses from The Thrift Shop. Gramma helped her make a little mustache this morning. Gramma is staying with them for a little while. Sophie doesn't plan to accept any candy. ("It just wouldn't be right," she solemnly proclaimed to her father.) She has already explained to four children who Gandhi is in the past twenty minutes. Her teacher looks vaguely uncertain. Bully Brad (dressed as kickass afternoon TV superhero Captain Slaughterhouse) and partner Robbie Preston (dressed as wrestler M. T. Moose) overhear Sophie's repeated explanations ("He's Indian!") and make war whooping sounds.

In the immediate vicinity of the fourth grade, one can see three firefighters and four billowy yellow kids. Uberman, Piranhasaurus, and Dementia buzz around with parents running after them, while two girls lovingly admire their newly acquired hand-embroidered Gypsy costumes. Amongst the second and third graders three girls dress as their family cats and there are more than a few fuzzy bunnies. Several versions of Nilknarf and Zalfutz from the new animated musical *Alienz* jockey for position in line, and Sophie is nearly overrun by carbon copies of crime-fighting sixties girls Rosi, Daisi, and Lili from the show *FlowerKids*.

Rappers Cali Killas and D. J. Homey Cide begin bustin' moves while Sophie watches her schoolmates pair up two by two. She stands chewing on her lip while the lines form around her. She squeezes her eyes closed and counts to ten and when she opens them, she finds herself face-to-face with Jimmy—factory kid, class clown, vaguely tolerated by Brad and Robbie and co.—wearing black with an official-looking slip of paper pinned to his chest. Sophie leans in to examine the paper more closely, and the boy explains, "I'm an unemployment check."

They pair up and get in line.

IN CLARENCE, CHILDREN begin trick-or-treating around five o'clock, just as dusk begins to settle. The first round is always parents with young kids—by far the cutest—toddlers in indiscernible makeup and six layers of clothes, brash kindergartners sweetly impish in devil ears. These are the children that always say thank you. Kids begin to come alone at five-thirty, dressed in trademarked goods and shivering in the night air. By seven or eight, though, all the cute kids are gone, and the only children ringing Clarence's doorbells will be the Bad Kids, far too old to be trick-or-treating. Some are not even wearing costumes!

As the Sunny Shadows Annual Halloween Fair has been canceled, there are more children than ever on the streets this year. And more darkened houses. (Mrs. Lorna Hansen, for example, has shut off all the lights, locked the doors, and is presently hiding under the covers.) There are more doors answered warily, more strange gazes affixed to the packs of kids at the door. A few children report seeing adults hiding behind their curtains, peering at them from the safety of their homes. Other bewildered trick-or-treaters will have doors slammed in their faces. Actual grown-ups look at bogeymen costumes and shriek. Nobody seems to be very interested in ghosts this year.

Bennie is letting Sophie go out without him for the first time (after sticking a pair of mittens on her, explaining that Gandhi would have wanted it that way). He gives her glow sticks and some last-minute safety tips. Never eat unwrapped candy. Stick with your group. Stay out of the street. Stay in your neighborhood.

Don't take any apples. Don't go into anyone's house. Don't get into a stranger's car.

Of course, he would rather be with Sophie. He would rather be holding her hand, inspecting each bit of candy, staring down anyone who passes her. But that's just not possible this year. Bennie has enough on his hands. His mother has been in the guest room with the door shut since he brought her over yesterday afternoon.

Sophie arrives at Leslie's house at the appointed time. She rings the bell, and Mrs. Miller, a swollen mirror of her daughter, both fat freckled Mona Lisas, tries to give Sophie some candy.

"No, Mrs. Miller. It's Sophie. Is Leslie ready?"

"Oh . . . Sophie, I didn't recognize you. What a great ghost costume! Leslie's gone already. She and Chrissy left about a half hour ago." Sophie's face falls behind her little glasses. "Were they expecting you?"

Sophie shrugs. Her mustache is beginning to itch.

"I'm sure there was some sort of misunderstanding." Mrs. Miller smiles comfortingly. Sophie stands in the doorway. There is a pause. "Well, I will certainly tell Leslie you stopped by. Are you sure you don't want any candy?" Sophie shakes her head and Mrs. Miller leans in conspiratorially. "And tell that handsome father of yours I say hello!" She winks and closes the door, leaving Sophie alone, standing in between two grinning pumpkins.

Sophie sits on the stoop. She tries to decide if she should just go home. But her father would worry. He always worries. He would think she was giving up. He would be disappointed in her. He would insist on taking her out himself. The knots of children with glow sticks move closer to her. A doorstep is not a particularly good place to feel sorry for yourself on Halloween. When she is her own country, none of this will matter. When she is her own country, there will be a law about keeping appointments. When she is her own country—

"Hey, Gandhi!" Sophie looks up. Animate stripes of fluorescent tape approach her spot. "What are you doing on the Millers' step? Don't you have to save the Indians from the bad men?"

A form slowly emerges underneath the strips. It is Jimmy. "Like the tape?" He points. "My parents wouldn't let me go out in all black."

"Yeah. My dad made me wear mittens. Like they have mittens in India."

"Yeah. Like an unemployment check would wear glow tape!"

"Yeah!"

"What are you doing here?"

"Oh. Nothing. I guess I missed Leslie and Christine."

"Oh. Wanna come out with us?" Jimmy gestures toward a Globot and the Minister of Doom. "We just got started."

"Yeah, okay. Sure." Sophie bounces off the stoop and joins the group of boys. They move together into the night—the neon stripes and the superhero, Gandhi and the Glo-bot.

MADELINE REMEMBERS IN flashes. There was a phone call. Mildred's voice. Something wrong with Calvin. Collapsed. Not talking. Still alive. Heart beating. Had called 911. Come over. Waiting for paramedics. Word spreads quickly. Hear from me first. Don't know what to do. He looks like wax. I'm sorry. I'm so sorry.

Madeline does not recall much. She goes out the door and finds herself outside his building. People gathering, whispering. They part at the sight of her, fall silent. She thinks. Or else she imagined it. Or else none of it happened this way at all. But after some time, she was standing in his room, over him, Mildred in the chair crying. This body, this man, curled up, frozen—petrified. He looked like his skin was about to crack open. There had been so much promise there. She saw Calvin crack open in front of her eyes, his life oozing slowly out in front of her, as if his body could not contain what was in his heart anymore. She saw Calvin break to pieces and then she blinked and he was back together again, but the cracks were still visible, and then the men came wearing so much blue, and they pushed her aside—or else she moved, she cannot tell—and then there was Morris standing there, looking at her, talking to her, asking about dinner and coughing, ever so slightly, and she didn't know what to make for dinner at all.

Morris watches this new man that his wife loves. The new man looks twisted and pained and petrified and Morris can only mutter, "How lucky he is to have that uniform."

Now she is somewhere else, in some strange bed, and every time she falls asleep she wakes up and has to remember just where the somewhere is.

BENNIE CREEPS UP the stairs and knocks on the guest room door. "Ma? Ma, are you all right?" A moment of silence. He knocks again. The door opens—his mother is wearing the same mismatched sweatsuit he loaned her yesterday. "Ma, you should eat something."

She looks one century older. The pins in her smoky brown-gray hair have fallen out. Her wrinkles have sunken to the bone.

Bennie, too, has shut off all the lights on the first floor of the house and drawn the shades. A bowl of candy sits on the front steps with a sign, TAKE ONE PIECE, LEAVE THE REST. In the morning, he will find the bowl smashed.

"Here. I made some soup. Come downstairs, Mom." He holds out his hand.

Madeline nods. "All right." She puts her hand in his.

Eighteen-year-old Bennie leads his mother down to the

kitchen. A small victory. She has grown a century older since he left for school. No wonder. He shouldn't have gone. They should have told him. She has made it through the day she has allotted for sitting shiva. Family and neighbors marvel. How does she do it?—they whisper to each other. Every woman looks at her husband with the same thought—how will I manage without you? Poor Madeline. What will I do when this happens to me? But it won't, no, not for a good long time. A lifetime. Morrie brought it on himself. The smoking and all.

You are so strong, Madeline. They kiss her forehead. Remember we are here. If you need anything, we are here. God bless you. Eighteen-year-old Bennie sits in the corner munching rugalach and sending out bad vibes. Do you mean it? Will you really be there if Mom needs anything, anything at all? Or will you stop inviting her to dinner parties because you don't want an uneven number?

"You're the man of the family now, Benjamin," Fat Uncle Isaac says, a hand on his shoulder. Bennie excuses himself and goes to hide in the kitchen. His mother is making it through, strong and rosy. She laughs. She charms. The last person leaves. The door shuts. The sound sends his mother crumbling. Head, neck, arms, spine, waist, knees. His mother is in a heap on the floor.

Bennie does not hesitate. He carries her up to his parents' room. Now just her room. His mother's alone. His mother alone. He pauses a moment in front of the door. Does she want to wake up in this bed alone? He goes back down the hall and carries his mother to his old room, tucks her into his old bed, turns out the light, and goes to sleep on the sofa.

Bennie and Madeline sent God out the door that day. He will never be invited back.

The next afternoon. Bennie knocks on the door of his own

bedroom. "Ma? Momma, come on. The Schwartzes brought some soup. You should eat something."

Thirty-nine-year-old Bennie pulls his mother by the hand and leads her down into the kitchen. He sits her in a chair and wraps a blanket around her shoulders. She smiles weakly.

In her wrinkles linger Calvin's desiccated face, saliva dried on his cracked lips, chest heaving, eyes round and parched. The paramedics rushing out the door. His mother stumbling.

"Mom. Mother. Madeline." He grabs hold. "What happened?"

His mother trembles. "Mildred went to visit him. The door was open. She peeked in. She called me. I ran over. He was like this. He wouldn't respond."

Bennie doesn't know what to say. "A stroke?"

"He was fine last week. Wonderful. Exuberant. Talking and talking. Telling all these stories. I don't know. I came over and his face . . . He looked like . . . He looked like . . ."

Bennie thinks what his mother does not want to say. Catatonic Calvin looked like he had been quite literally petrified.

CALVIN'S DAUGHTER LAURA has come up from the city and stays with him while doctors put in tubes and take out samples. Laura is taking no calls. She will, she promises, call in to Sunny Shadows with updates. Thank you for your concern. Thank you for the flowers. He'll love them. When he wakes up. Bennie calls Madeline's friend Mildred to see if she knows anything. Her son (History Department, Bennie thinks. Civil War guy?) answers the phone. He is staying with his mother for a bit. Mildred is unwell. "They're really taking it hard. People aren't coming out of their rooms. Some have been crying all day. Calvin, well, the doctors are still doing tests. They haven't found anything yet. He hasn't come out of it." Bennie hears a distant shapeless voice through the phone wires. The Civil War Guy's voice becomes muffled, Bennie makes out a "Mom? Ma, are you okay?" Bennie blinks and the Civil War Guy's voice comes on strong and sharp. "Ben, I've got to go."

The phone goes dead.

Bennie hangs up and Madeline stares, stirring her soup.

"It was like this," she says. "I remember. When your father died. A blanket. Soup. The phone calls."

Bennie nods.

"At least that, we expected. We understood it. This—well—this—" She trails off. Her eyes close. "Yes. It was like this."

Bennie does not talk. He is remembering a different night.

Nighttime. The evening news is long over, the candy put away, lights turn off one after another in the houses down the street. Children lie safe tucked in their beds, visions of sugar dance in their heads. University students write papers under the blue-green glow of their computers, drink beer, watch cable, fornicate, sulk, study, sleep.

More than a few residents of Clarence find themselves awake. *Awake* awake. More than a few residents of Clarence turn on their bedside lamps and pick up a magazine, a mystery, a romance, a nice biography. More than a few residents of Clarence find they cannot focus on their reading from one sentence to the next. Others find themselves back on the couch, flipping through television channels, pondering a midnight snack. A young woman watches her husband twitch in his sleep. An old husband wakes with a jolt as his wife kicks him in the back while he's sleeping. Something is up tonight. Halloween. Full moon. Sugar highs. The change in seasons. Something in the water. That funny smell in the air.

Bennie lies in bed, twitching. Behind his eyes he is driving his

car. The same dream. Always. Over and over. He is driving his
car. He can turn right or left. Which way? The stop sign immo-
bilizes him. Right or left? He freezes. Lizzie teases. "You still
awake there, big guy?" Beautiful Lizzie, eyes full of Sophie. China
blue. She reclines back in her seat. She looks out the window.
Right or left? Right or left? Right or left? He's seen this movie
before. He knows how it ends. But he can change it, can't he? He
can change it if he just remembers: Right or left?

Sophie lies in bed, twitching. She hugs her bear close to her.
Eleanor Roosevelt sleeps on her legs. Eleanor Roosevelt is twitching, too. Sophie is on a little boat with a triangle for a sail in a
watercolor world. On the boat is a wolf. Sophie says, Get out of
my country. Leave us in peace. The wolf howls. There is a mas-
sacre in a mosque. The guards keep shooting. Her dad's voice.
Sophie, don't watch this part. Women scream. Sophie screams.
Leslie and Christine sit on the beach whispering and giggling. The
wolf spins wool. A man with a gun shouts, Death to Gandhi! Her
dad shouts, Who said that? Who? Who said that? Who? Her dad's
voice mingles with the man with the gun. Death to Sophie.
Where's her dad? She hears him shouting, again and again. Who
said that? The man with the gun gets closer and closer. She cannot
find her dad. Where's her dad?

Madeline lies in bed, twitching. The thin quilt slowly works its
way off her small body. Madeline is watching herself walking
through a garden. She knows this story. This is from a long time
ago. This is her own novel. She knows how it ends. This is when
Madeline was forty, except she is not Madeline. In this book her
name is Anna and the garden is filled with dandelions. It is a metaphor of some sort. She can remember how the words felt against
the typewriter. In the cottage at the end of the walk Anna will
find a dying man. She will fall in love. But first she must open the

door to the cottage once she crosses the dandelion garden. At the end of her dream she will find a comatose man lying on the floor drooling, with death mask eyes.

Todd dreams of molecules spinning. Flying through space. Hitting targets with a loud THWACK. Todd swims at the bottom of the ocean, sea creatures like dendrites reaching up. He touches one. It excites, erupts. He swims at the bottom of the ocean with Laurie Berg. Jane Porter. Catherine Nussbaum. Women he never got to touch. So beautiful, so smart, so kind, so sensuous, such nice brea—.

Susannah is on *Innocence Falls*. Susannah is in Innocence Falls. This is one of her favorite episodes. Trevor asks if she'd help with physics. Twilight passes her notes in study hall. She is so glad the twins moved here. Trevor asks if she'd like to walk the dog together. Trevor loves dogs. Trevor says, "I've never met a girl like you." Susannah blushes, he leans in to kiss her, and she says, "Come over for Thanksgiving dinner. I would love for you to meet my family. They are so nice, so very, very nice, and my mother makes such a lovely turkey," and Trevor smiles and says, "I'd love to," and leans in to kiss her again, and the credits roll.

nine.

Memory Studies

D EEP WITHIN THE bowels of the James J. Hill Building for the
Physical and Biological Sciences at Mansfield University (or the
Phy-Bye, as the students call it) a neurology professor cuts open a
rat's brain with a scalpel. On her laboratory wall hangs a poster with
a photograph of a brain, which sports the caption, GRAY MATTERS.
Another wall has a large placard decorated with an impressive bolt
of lightning reading, DOCTOR FRANKENSTEIN WAS FRAMED. Another poster shows a brain with scrawny arms lifting a dumbbell,
proclaiming, MIND OVER MATTER. Another shows a pen sketch of
a brain nearly covered in scattered mismatched Post-Its. The caption: THE ORGANIZED MIND. The neurology professor designed
that one herself in a fit of whimsy. It still cracks her up. They'd had
a contest among the senior faculty members in the department.
The adjunct lecturers did the judging. The department chair won,
of course, by a unanimous vote with the predictable brain-in-the-

garbage-can, A MIND IS A TERRIBLE THING TO WASTE. He col-
lected the free bed-and-breakfast stay and was very, very happy
with the discerning judgment of the adjunct faculty.

The neurology professor immerses the pieces of brain in electrolytic fluid in a petri dish and waits for sparks to fly. She measures
voltages, slices the pieces into cross-sections like fine ham, slides
the meat under the microscope, and hits a button on a remote
control. Beethoven. "Ode to Joy." She lets it play for a few
minutes, then stops, presses another button. Miles Davis. "Kind of
Blue." She waits a few minutes, then switches back to the Beethoven and peers under the microscope. Activity. There, there,
and there. Is it listening?

Or perhaps, is it remembering?

She checks the clock. Her research assistant is late. She turns the
music up a notch and leans back in her chair and begins to conduct
with her arms.

TODD IS RUNNING late. He is to be assisting his adviser as she en-
deavors to find the location of memory in the brain. This takes
more work than you might imagine. Todd is never late. But. Reg-
istration for next semester is coming up quickly, and Todd needs
a reading seminar. He wants Personality. Psychoanalysis. Freud,
Jung, and, um, those guys. He knows his adviser will understand.
("Ah yes. Benjamin Singer," she will say. "The Personality guy.
He's a little funny, I hear." She will wonder aloud why Todd
would even venture out of the ordered sphere of the cognitive
determinists and charge into the nebulous wishy-washy world of
the psychoanalytic/humanists, but, she will say, as a matter of policy she doesn't like to discourage her advisees from broadening
their horizons. To a certain extent.)

Todd would rather be at home, of course, but Susannah does

not seem to want him there. His class schedule, at least, is something he can control.

Todd had to beg to get Professor Singer to meet with him on a Friday. "I have a long-standing appointment at three," the professor had said. He will be out of the office. Far out. But Todd promised he would be brief. Todd's deep brown eyes danced, his grin flashed, his sincerity shined, and Bennie said, "All right. Two-fifteen. But I warn you, two-forty-five and you are on the street."

The two men sit in Bennie's office. Todd gazes at the shelves and shelves of books. (When I am a professor, he thinks, I will have this many books in my office. People need to know you are well-read. I will have elegant bookplates that proclaim, "From the library of Dr. Todd Lewis." I will loan out the books very judiciously, and anyone who does borrow this or that tome will always remember from whom it came.)

On Bennie's desk are scattered pictures of a little blond girl in various stages of evolution. Crayon drawings and watercolor paintings paper his walls.

Todd nods to the paintings. "What's your girl's name?"

"Sophia. Sophie. She's nine."

"She's really cute."

Bennie beams. This never fails to please him. "Yes. She's an angel." He catches a yawn. "Excuse me . . ."

Todd notices the thin silver wedding band and the lack of any concomitant photograph and is at least smart enough to put two and two together to equal a question he should not ask.

"So, Todd Lewis, what can I help you with?"

Todd is prepared. He brings a proposal out of his backpack and hands it to Bennie.

Bennie takes the letter and tries to skim the typewritten words. They blur before his eyes. His brain is so foggy today! He blinks and tries to put the sentences together, word by word.

Todd watches him expectantly. "So, I'm . . . I'd like to do an independent study with you. Next semester. In conjunction with my Memory Studies work. I saw your lecture in Advanced Personality. It was really interesting. Freud, and, uh, all that." He blushes. Bennie smiles. "Your theories are quite interesting. I haven't really looked at the, uh, your perspective. I thought it would help. I know neurons but I don't know people. Most of the psych I've been reading has been really, well, scientific."

Bennie gazes at Todd mischievously. "Well, actually, Mr. Lewis, we consider what we do here a science as well." A moment passes. Todd's brain goes slack. Bennie grins congenially. "Sorry, I couldn't resist."

"It's all right. I deserved it."

"You know"—Bennie leans in—"I can't help but be surprised. Usually the neuro people don't let people like you in here."

Todd grins. "Yes, well, I'm hoping we can keep this our little secret."

"Of course." Bennie smiles and eases back in his chair. It occurs to him that perhaps he could steal this boy over to his side. That would really piss them off. Who needs a sheep brain when you can have dream analysis, eh? It occurs to him as well that there is something in this boy. He remembers being this age. Eager. He remembers handing tweed-elbowed professors proposals much like this one. He was charming, too, then. Once he spent six hours writing and rewriting a one-page letter to the psychoanalysis professor, the one adviser in the department who wouldn't ask him to dissect a pigeon brain. He read and reread the letter he had composed and Lizzie laughed and laughed. "Just go in there and smile. That's all you'll need."

Lizzie giggles and brushes her hair out of her face, pen ink all over her fingers.

"Professor Singer?"

The boy is staring at him. Todd. Todd Lewis. "Yes, well. I tell you what. We'll do this. Just no pigeon brains, all right?"

The boy gives him an odd look. "Sorry, what?"

All of a sudden, Bennie isn't sure. "What time is it? I better run."

"Where's your meeting? I'll walk you."

"Oh . . . it's off-campus. Come back before finals; we'll go over your proposal for the department." Bennie checks the clock nervously. He hates the thought of Sophie waiting outside alone. It is part of the bargain, after all.

IT IS THE last thing Susannah wanted to do. It is the last place she wanted to go back to, but she is back—because as much as she doesn't want to be here, she cannot be there either, because there is home, and she cannot be at home right now. She does not belong there.

Madeline Singer got that phone call and turned all crumpled and white. Susannah had followed her out the door, down the stairs, through the garden, over to Building B. She saw the people gathered around the door, and more joined before her eyes, one after another. And then she stopped. She heard the sirens coming and she imagined she knew exactly what it was. Inside that door, there would be a person—Calvin Woodhouse, probably, given Madeline's reaction—who had taken all of this insanity to its natural conclusion, in some horrible way, leaving all the people here to deal with the consequences.

The voices around her quickly told her she was wrong, he was still alive, but the face she saw as the paramedics carried Calvin's body out, that awful shape his body made under the blanket—like a toppled statue—put any relief out of her mind. Susannah left, then, it was time for her to go, so she turned around and went home, without a word to anyone.

She spent Halloween, not under the bed as she would have preferred, but in it, which is second best. Todd stayed home from school that day—she didn't know he had it in him. She expected him to be twitching all day like a cigarette addict, but he did not. And somewhere inside her she found she wished he hadn't stayed home at all. She was not going to be well, not at all, and she didn't need him to see.

He'd come in to check on her, every hour or so, he'd kiss her forehead and shut the door behind him so she could sleep. "Do you want me to call a doctor, sweetheart? I know, sweetheart, you've had a bad shock. It's all right, sweetheart, anyone would be upset."

And she wants to say—but she doesn't say—even you, Todd? Would you be upset?

He comes and goes all day, and finally, late afternoon, as he closed the door behind him to let her sleep, she called after him—

"Todd?"

He turned around. "What?"

"Todd?"

"What is it?"

She breathed in. "What if this happens to me?"

"What do you mean?"

"You know what I mean. What if this happens to me?"

And Todd shifts his weight a little, and he says, "What are you talking about, Susannah? Calvin is an old man." And then there is this pause, this endless, teeming pause, and he says, "Now rest up, sweetheart, okay?"

And the next morning, Susannah said, "I have to take care of things. At work. They need all the people they can get. I have to take care of Calvin's cat. I have to go, Todd. I have to go."

So she is here, at Sunny Shadows. She went into the office and said, "Let me help, let me take care of things. I can stay here. In the guest rooms. Be here for a while. In case you need anything. I know how overworked you are. I know how stressful this all is."

"Are you sure?"

"Yes. Yes, I can help."

Reports are Calvin is in a coma. They do not know what caused it. Adult children pour onto the grounds from taxi cabs and rental cars, but all of the residents are in their rooms, doors shut.

Susannah is in Calvin's room. Kitty kitty kitty kitty kitty kitty good kitty. Come here kitty. Good kitty. Here you go, kitty.

Calvin's room is one of the smaller Sunny Shadows rooms, just a studio, really, overlooking the garden. There is one picture frame, on the dresser, facedown. Susannah picks it up and stares at the woman in it. She considers her for a moment, then takes a bit of her shirt and dusts off the frame. The bed is unmade; she strips the sheets and throws them in a heap. She will do laundry later. She loads and runs the dishwasher, she throws away several old cartons of milk and some bad fruit. The cat follows her as she works.

"What's your name, sweet kitty? Don't worry, I'll take care of you."

And finally, Susannah begins to pick up the pieces of green army canvas that litter the floor.

Susannah has done this before. She was seven, and she went up to her mother's room to see how her headache was. Her mother was sitting in the middle of the floor cutting her bright red cotton dress into shreds. She was surrounded by pieces of fabric and yarn and buttons—red, purple, white, and black, all kinds of greens and blues. Susannah watched and watched until her mother looked up. Her mother screamed.

"Oh, please, Susannah, you can't let your father see. Please, help me. Help me." Her mother started to try to put the pieces back together again. Susannah got a garbage bag and helped her collect the pieces. "No, no, Mom, that won't work. Here." Her mother started to cry and would not stop. "Please don't tell your father. We'll tell him we gave the clothes away. I needed new ones anyway. Please."

And in her memory, Susannah thinks, "What would Todd say?" This is, of course, impossible, because Susannah was only seven at the time.

Susannah did tell her father. She ran down to the kitchen and told him right then and there. And that's where he got the look on his face, the slowly shattering insides look, the one that still has not left him. Her father picked up her mother and took her to the hospital. That was the first time. "It's time, Sharon. Something is wrong." Her mother cried and cried all the way out the door, "I'm so sorry. I'm so sorry."

Later he would sit Susannah down—Sara was too young—and talk to her very slowly and softly, and then she would fall asleep on his lap, and he wouldn't move, not all night.

Here, in Calvin's room, Susannah suddenly has an urge to go see Madeline and leave all this dusty canvas behind, and she heads over to Madeline's building, holding her breath, and knocks on the door, and knocks again. One of the residents on the floor peeks her head out and tells her that Madeline is gone.

"Do you know where?"

"No, I'm sorry."

"But—"

Susannah stops herself. She can ask at the office. They will know. They will even know how she is doing, if everything's all right, or if this thing has gotten her, too.

She has plenty of time. She will be here for a good while.

Susannah has checked herself into the asylum, but—clever Susannah—she has disguised herself as a nurse.

Once upon a time.
Once upon a time there was.
Once upon a time there was a woman named Madeline.
And . . .

Madeline lies in the guest room of her son's house among the detritus of old magazines and garage sale furniture. She tries to tell herself stories. She cannot get past the first part.

Once upon a time there was a woman named Madeline and . . .

She approaches the phrase carefully, methodically—she considers each word, articulates it perfectly, pauses at the right places, but each time the same thing happens: She gets to the end of the phrase, she gets to the "and," and her mind fills with words (*and* she read a book, married a man, broke her wrist, stubbed her toe, made a dress, kissed a doll, lost a shoe, had a blue bonnet, had a blue bear, blue beard, had a hot paper rash singing for supper of milk and honey and toast crumbs in the doll forest with brother mother baby boy feeding husband and son), a life of possibility to end the sentence, and out of the cacophony of memory nothing can be heard. Madeline's head crackles with once upon a times and the matter cannot be resolved. Again and again she tries and again and again her mind electrifies, then short-circuits, then she breathes and tries, again and again, until she realizes that the sentence does not have any more ending, that this is all the truth there is:

Once upon a time, there was a woman named Madeline. And.

ALL OVER SUNNY Shadows well-groomed adults in travel clothes sit in the bedrooms of well-groomed apartments holding their parents' hands and talking in low voices. The parents lie in their beds—some trembling, some crying, some mute.

This goes beyond Calvin—the unspoken words are communicated between worried glances of the librarian, the janitor, the groundskeeper, the building managers. There is something wrong here. Are we killing them? Fifty formerly healthy elderly adults take to their beds, fifty sets of sons and daughters come flying in from fifty states turning to anyone on the grounds they can find. What has happened? What have you done? Not the librarian, the janitor, the groundskeepers, the building managers—none of them have any answers. Doctors come in from the university, from the cities, from the clinic. Water samples are sent in official test tubes to official sites in official parts of the country.

In Building A, Madeline's friend Mildred lies in bed sleeping fitfully. She dreams and dreams and dreams. She sighs and cries. Her eyes pop open and she leans over to her son, the history professor, sitting next to the bed in a folding chair, and she draws him close to her. She brings his ear to her lips and whispers, "This must be what it is to be dying. You close your eyes, the doors in your mind open up, and everything you have ever felt comes flooding into your head." She licks her cracked lips. "I don't recommend it."

• • •

DEEP WITHIN THE bowels of the James J. Hill Building for the Physical and Biological Sciences at Mansfield University, a neurology professor cuts open a rat's brain with a scalpel. She immerses the pieces into electrolytic fluid in a petri dish and waits for sparks to fly. She measures voltages, slices the pieces into cross-sections like fine ham, and slides the meat under a microscope. Her able—but distracted—assistant Todd records every detail. Their research keeps them in this lab well into the night this night like many others. This is their obsession. The neurology professor and her able assistant Todd are trying to discover the precise location in the brain where events record themselves into memory. They are trying to watch memory happen.

In a few days it should occur to this professor to add to her petri dishes and brain slices some samples of deletrium. It should occur to her to watch the sparks fly. She should be able to notice the condition of the town and justly hypothesize on the cause. This is, after all, her job. It should occur to her, but it will not, because by that point, she will be in no condition to hypothesize at all.

act two   spilling

ten.

Right or left?

URING THE FOURTH and fifth grade recess on the Ventura Elementary grounds, the girls usually keep to the swings and the monkey bars in little huddled clusters while the boys stake out territories on the basketball court, in the woods, or just run around and around in circles. A group of girls sits on the monkey bars beading necklaces while some boys trade Technosaur cards (which will soon be banned in all Clarence schools) on the stairs. On the court, Jeff and Freddie vie for alpha male status ("Did you see my moves?"/ "Did you see mine?"/ "Naw, I was going too fast!"/ "Yeah, fast like your mom's big butt!"/ "Screw you, your dad's on unemployment!"/ "Screw you, your mom's the biggest cow in the state.") while in the woods John and Mike and Matt play King of the Hill and stomp around waiting for the snow to fall. (A week later Mike will break his tooth during just such a game.) And behind the gym, members of the Fangs circle little Wally and taunt, "Wally collects stamps!" (This is the chant of the week. Last week it was, "Margie wears a bra," which showed somewhat of a lack of creativity because the preceding week it had been, "Wally wears a bra.")

Leslie and Christine perch on the sandbox as they do every day. It is their spot. They have recently begun to wear a lot of purple and to speak their own language. An icky person is a "neep," something cool is "trey" (Leslie's older sister having very recently begun French lessons), and something beneath their notice is a "fleck." Jimmy, the Glo-bot, and the Minister of Doom are all "koobies," (whatever that means) which means that Sophie, lately, has become a koobie, too. Jimmy has a word for Leslie and Christine, but his mother has told him it isn't very nice and he shouldn't use it.

"Sophie, they're so snotty," Jimmy says. "All they do is whisper to each other and think they're better. Christine thinks she's so cool because of her daddy."

"Yeah, but we're friends." Sophie hits a stick against the ground.

"Why would you want to be friends with people like that? They don't have a fort like ours, do they?"

It is true. They don't. Sophie has to agree. No one does. Jimmy, Sophie, the Glo-Bot, and the Minister of Doom have been building a fort (code name: Project Bombay) in the trees behind the school. Of course, that's where all the boys build their forts. Brad and Robbie have one four maples down, but the Glo-bot's father owns the town's lumberyard, and by extension, Project Bombay's fort is much, much, much cooler.

The Glo-bot stops by the lumberyard every day after school and is allowed to take whatever he wants out of the cull pile. The yard guys even let him ride around in the big trucks with them on deliveries and he picks up lots of scraps from the construction sites, because no contractor wants to deny Kenny McCusker's kid anything. So they have all the nails they could ever want. Their fort is insulated. It has twenty-year shingles. It has a plastic vapor barrier. On his ninth birthday, the Glo-bot's dad gave him a hammer. ("You are a man now, Son.") While the other boys are dealing in sticks and rotting chipboard, the team of Project Bombay is framing their fort with two-by-four studs and putting together a half-inch plywood roof.

And, their fort has windows.

The Minister is going to design a flag on his computer because his sister has a program that lets you print on fabric (he assiduously avoids mentioning that it is a Krissie Doll program) and then they are going to write their own anthem and have their own charter and Jimmy's mom even volunteered to make curtains but he demurred. (Now, of course, like everyone else in town, Jimmy's mom is not making anything—like his lunch for instance, and Jimmy is getting himself out of bed in the morning, which he wouldn't do at all except he knows if he doesn't and his mom finds out when she feels better, he is going to be in Serious Trouble.)

Of course, Leslie and Christine can't be bothered with forts. They spend recesses looking at Paul and Jason and whispering that the two boys are quite the delicious "bo-ums," while Paul whispers back to Jason that the two girls are les-bi-ans, which is a word Paul has recently learned from his father. (Jason's mother has recently vacated the house and his own father has just explained that word to him and Jason is very, very confused, but he snickers anyway, because Paul could beat him up at any moment.)

Forts are for boys, specifically for koobies, and now there is never any question over just who will partner up with whom in gym class or on field trips. Fortunately, Sophie has not found herself floundering for a partner because Jimmy always shows up at her side instantly. Classmates smirk because girls are not really supposed to be partnering up with boys unless they are "going" (which is a natural precursor to "doing it,") but only the popular fifth grade boys and girls really "go" anyway, nobody in fourth grade does except for Paul and Rachel, but they are really really popular so they can do that (and everybody knows that they aren't doing it, but Paul has stuck his hand up Rachel's shirt) and even then Paul still buddies up with Jason and Rachel still buddies with Mimi. Of course. So Jimmy and Sophie always partner up and Sophie really doesn't mind because Jimmy makes her laugh and everyone else in the class is a butthead anyway even though more than a few of the kids have asked her if they are "doing it." (Sophie knows exactly what "it" is, and cannot imagine doing that with Jimmy or anyone else really, and finds the concept frankly gross.)

Sophie has not been over to Leslie's or Christine's house since Halloween. She has not sat near them in class nor has she played with them at recess nor has she called them on the phone. Nor have they called her. Nor will they ever. Sophie is, in fact, an untouchable to them. They hold their noses high when she walks by. They snicker and pass brightly colored, intricately folded notes back and forth in class. They point and giggle and whisper. Sophie holds her head high and likens them to the British.

Plus they've been acting weird. They dress funny. They don't play foursquare anymore. They never know the answer anymore when they're called on in class. And Leslie, Leslie looks at Sophie and looks back at Christine and looks at Sophie again. She sits upright, eyes twinkling, slow grin creeping, fat little face doughy with joy. Christine is hers now. She has won.

Sophie doesn't know what happened. What did she say wrong? What did she do? The Minister of Doom tells her to stop thinking about it and Leslie and Christine are psycho-bots and that girls suck anyway. Except you, Sophie.

"Yeah, but I don't get to play with them anymore."

The boys don't know what to say and don't really understand so instead they plan Project Bombay and when Sophie isn't around they plan Operation Black Stab. Which is Top Secret.

You see, according to Jimmy, Leslie and Christine are [female dogs], for sure. The Minister and the Glo-bot agree totally, and besides, Sophie is the first girl that's spoken to them in years, and she is pretty cool for a girl, and Jimmy's mom told Jimmy all about what happened to Sophie's mom, and how Sophie's dad is a bit of a weirdo, even for a Mansfield type. Anyway, Jimmy and the Minister and the Glo-bot look after their own, and Sophie is now one of them, and Leslie and Christine are sure being boobies to Sophie and that really sucks big ones.

It is time for revenge.

ONCE UPON A time, there was a woman named Madeline, and she knew how to sleep through the night. She slept through the night straight for eighteen years. She slept best with one hard pillow and one soft pillow.

Once upon a time, twenty-one years ago, she did not sleep through the night for two whole weeks. She could not find the right place to sleep. She would go back and forth from her son's old bedroom to her room with its elegiac queen-size bed. She could not sleep in either place. Every time she woke up again, she would remember that she was alone. Better not to sleep at all, not to let oneself forget and then remember again.

Once upon a time, before that, she slept with someone next to her. A man. A husband. Rough skinned, itchy, whiskery, large. She slept through the night, and when she did wake up, she blinked at the lump next to her, trying to remember what world it came from.

Once upon a time, she slept alone for twenty-one years, in a dorm bed, in a twin bed, in a child's bed. She would stay up reading with a flashlight, and then fall asleep, book still in her hand, the flashlight fallen to the ground, and still she slept.

Now, once again, she does not sleep through the night. She falls into sleep, she dreams, she jolts awake—her whole body electrified, shaking. She looks around in the dark with an awareness like prey, breathes herself right, and falls asleep again, only to feel the electric current again minutes later. The dreams—what are they?—shades and shadows and flickers—shapes of bodies and tastes of experiences gone. Schoolyards, dinner tables, river walks, and bedrooms. She is Sophie-age, she is Sophie-size, with Sophie-eyes, in a fight with her girlfriend over playground teams. The girl—Penny—stomps and runs away, but not before shouting, "I hate you, Maddy, I hate you." Later the girl would be friends with Nina and never ever even look at Madeline again. She used to play in the street with Penny, not dumb girl games like the other ones, but real games with real plans and a very real neighborhood map that did not show all the hiding places. Once she hid and hid and Penny couldn't find her, and at first she was proud, then she was scared, then it got to be suppertime, and she knew Penny had forgotten.

Madeline jolts awake. The residue of all these images still lingers. She shuts her eyes and shapes flare up behind her lids. Madeline no longer wonders where the memories are coming from. At night, she is not aware enough of her present to know there is anything peculiar at all about all of this past.

THERE IS A first time for everything, Bennie knows. Yet he has always believed that that phrase implies that there is only a first time for everything that will happen in one's life, that if one is a caviar eater there must be a first time that one has eaten caviar. Bennie never, until today, took this expression to mean that there would indeed be a first time that everything in the whole world happens to a person, because if that were true, then impossible things would have to happen, like there would be a day when he would get a call from the principal about Sophie.

Yet it happened. He has gotten a call from the principal about Sophie.

There is a first time for everything.

A neuron fires and hits its target. ("It's very crowded in here!") A memory stirs: twelve-year old Bennie in the principal's office. Somebody had put dope in his locker. He hadn't known what it was—he pulled out the bag as a teacher was walking by. The principal (what was his name?) stands next to the wooden chair and stares down at Bennie. He smells like cheese.

I will NOT tolerate this lawlessness in my school. There are rules, you know, I can expel you, Singer, with a snap of my fingers. But I'm not going to do that. Do you know what I'm going to do instead? I'm going to call your father.

Dawson. His name was Mr. Dawson.

It has not been the best day for Bennie. In fact, it has not been the best week for Bennie. His mother has not been doing well. She lies in bed in the guest bedroom mostly watching TV and sometimes just staring at the ceiling. Just staring. As if she cannot quite comprehend it. He wants to call a doctor, he tells her, as he sits by her bed and strokes her hair, he is going to take her to the hospital.

"No. No, Benjamin," she says to him, "there is nothing wrong with my body."

Other times she does not speak at all.

He should know all about this. This should be his forte. He has volumes and volumes of books. He has written, published six articles. He is a Ph-goddamned-D and he cannot figure out what's wrong with his own mother. Depression. Stress. Shock it seems.

This is his mother, for Christ's sake. He calls the doctor. Dr. Jessop, Charles, Charlie—an internist at the hospital. Sophie and his daughter took figure skating together last year.

Dr. Jessop. Charles. Charlie. It's my mother. Please. "Could it be a stroke?" he asks. "Should I bring her in?"

The good doctor sighs. "Listen, Bennie, the beds are full. The emergency rooms are packed. Just about every person with a senior citizen's discount card has been in here. There's not a thing physically wrong with any of them, beyond symptoms of massive stress—sleeplessness, dehydration. We give them IVs and some sedatives. Bring her in if you want and I'll check her out, but I tell you there's not much we can do for her."

Bennie stammers, "There are more? I just thought—"

The doctor pauses for a minute. "Listen, Bennie, we're really not supposed to talk about it." His voice grows quieter. "But we think it's the deletrium. It's the only thing that really makes sense. Somehow over time it's been slowly stimulating people's memories."

"I don't understand."

"According to the psych guys, it's like every experience people have ever encoded in their brains have come back to them, as if their past has just come spilling out. The effects are similar to acute stress or PTSD, except of course in these cases, the trauma is just . . . living."

Behind his eyes Bennie sees Calvin, twisted and catatonic, eyes dried wide open. He realizes that the rumors must be true. Calvin had been there. He saw Dachau. And suddenly, inside Bennie, it is very cold.

"Listen." The doctor clears his throat. "I'm not supposed to say anything. Harris Jones, they're pretty powerful. They don't want this getting out. Fortunately the media around here aren't real, um, investigative."

"Well . . . isn't anybody doing anything? I mean . . ."

"Their people are working on it pretty obsessively. Their necks are on the line big-time here. Their guess is it will just sort of get out of our systems and go away pretty soon. At which point they plan to make reparations. Handsome reparations."

"Why isn't this affecting us?"

"It probably is. I think that's why nobody's noticed that everybody's experiencing the same thing, everyone's too involved with themselves."

"Then how come I'm not catatonic?"

"Well, how old are you?"

"Thirty-nine."

"Yes. Well, isn't it obvious? You don't have as much to remember."

(Charles is wrong. Bennie has plenty to remember. The town is overcome with the weight of their whole pasts, but his lifetime can be encapsulated by one moment, and that moment is what he relives again and again. Bennie shuts his eyes and he can only see one dark road.)

Later, Bennie lectures to his intro class about Jung. He has given this lecture so many times he can do it without notes. And without concentrating.

He does not concentrate. He thinks of his own dreams. He thinks of the images that have imprinted themselves in his head of late.

Torture. Psychological torture. But why?

He should be able to control this. It's the deletrium, yes. It's making him remember, yes. That is all. He should be able to breathe it away. He should be able to function. He will be able to function.

The classroom smells strangely today. It smells acutely. It smells.

Chalk and window cleaner, plastic desk and transparency residue, institutional bureaucracy and unwashed student.

This is how Bennie's life smells. Every classroom he has been in. Every department building. This is how his entire life will smell. The distinct aroma of apathetic class on top of industrial carpet.

(He knows every smell but Lizzie. He tries to call up Lizzie and instead all he can smell is burnt tire and bile. Lizzie Lizzie Lizzie Lizzie. He cannot call up her shape. Where is her shape? He gets in a car with her in every moment in time and he turns the wrong way and Lizzie is gone.)

"Of course"—he barely notices as he begins to deviate from his usual lecture—"the images that strike us are so often negative. We deal in pain and fears. We seek psychology because we want to examine the dark places. It's our modern obsession. If we look into the past and remember something that was joyful to us, we feel not happiness but nostalgia. If we lie in bed at night and let our minds wander, we will only worry about the future or mourn the past. Why? Is it the nature of our mind to play tricks on us? Is our collective desire for conflict and drama so great that we will sabotage our own mental wellness to get it?"

The more Bennie talks, the more he becomes convinced that what he is saying is true. He pushes his sleeves back on his blazer. It must be true. How else to explain . . .

". . . that after ten years with my wife every memory must be painful because she has died? That no matter how many times I try to think about our courtship or our wedding or the birth of our daughter all I can see is the car crash in which she died—in which I killed her?"

Bennie's now booming voice bounces against the back wall. The words fly back toward him and hit his face like ice.

What has he said? Seventy-five students stare at him. He drops his pen. It hits the floor with a clunk. It is the only movement in the room. Bennie looks down. The stage is made of long, tan planks. He looks back up, and seventy-five freshmen shift in their seats. He clears his throat.

"Um, we'll pick up next time. Class dismissed."

SOPHIE'S TEACHER, MS. Plum, stares up and down at the twenty children in their desks, all eyeing her with expressions ranging from suspicion to contempt. She hates this job. She had dreams too, you know. Once. She grew up in Lovelace, one of the smallest towns in the whole county, and she was going to get Out, as far out as possible, so she packed up and moved to Clarence, which was the biggest town in the whole county. Not to stay of course. Clarence was to be Step One. She would be a schoolteacher. For a while. Her three brothers and four sisters are all schoolteachers. She would interact with the community. She would be seen as feminine and caring, with good childbearing hips. She would latch on to some nice man on his way up and they would get married and she would see the world.

Twenty years later the only place she has moved is from the third to the fourth grade. Clarence smells bad. And all these germy children so very full of themselves. There are three worthwhile children in the class. The rest will grow up to be either all snotty like Lorna "Pantsuit" Hansen or lead meaningless, empty lives like she does.

So what, then, is the point?

The truth is, she never liked school. Her teacher in Lovelace was hairy and liked to use the ruler on Ms. Plum's hand. (Oh, there was one time . . . she can feel it now . . . one time! The stories she could tell you!) She doesn't really see the point of multiplying numbers of three digits together or all those phonics. Spelling is okay. She hates history the most, she always has. All of those facts to memorize. There are, of course, basic requirements, so she has the students read in their *Pioneer Dreams* or *Our Great State* or *Explorers!* manuals and answer the questions in their workbooks. Occasionally one of the kids will ask something about something and she doesn't have any idea of the answer, so she will answer in a clipped tone so that the class would know she strongly discourages questions.

Her sister Jane teaches up in Lake Labiner. She loves it. Ms. Plum complains about the stupidity of the course material and Jane just says, "Well, make it a teaching moment." Whatever that means. "Give them the context. Remember," she says, "your job is not to teach them facts. You're teaching them to think. And be good citizens."

So Ms. Plum got a filmstrip about citizenship from the library. Ms. Plum has been showing a lot of filmstrips lately. Her head is all cluttered with stuff and she doesn't feel like talking to the class. Nobody seems to mind. The dark lets the little terrors pass notes and poke each other. The notes are probably all about how much they hate her. Kids never liked her. Even when she was a kid.

NO ONE MOVED for a moment after Bennie dismissed class and he found himself having to repeat, "Class dismissed!" The students filed out silently, not even daring to look at him. But they would talk when they got out of the building—oh, how they would talk! What has he said? What's wrong here?

He stands in his empty classroom, the echoes of his own words still hanging in the air. So it is affecting him too. So he will be like his mother. He must already relive that past every night, now he will be thrown—

Something must be done. He finds himself in front of the Contemporary Studies building. He goes in. Phil's office door is closed. It is decorated with architectural phallic symbols. Normally, Bennie would find this amusing. He knocks. "Phil? Phil, it's Bennie. Are you there?"

There is a pause, then a small voice:

"Uhhh . . . come in . . ."

Bennie rushes in the door. He doesn't know quite what he expected, why he came—in his desperation, he went over to see his friend without any hesitation, but he wasn't expecting to find Phil like this.

Phil's office is filled with old magazine advertisements, action figures, tin toys, cartoon figurines, lunch boxes, old board games, propaganda, tourist collectibles. Phil is white and teary, holding a small toy car in his hands. He does not look up.

"Phil?"

His friend stares at the little red car and whispers, "I had this. One just like this."

"Phil!"

"Bennie?" Phil looks up, tears running down his face. His knuckles are white around the car.

Bennie stands in the doorway, stunned. Their friendship does not encompass moments like these. There are points of masculine empathy, but they linger softly under the bright talk of the day.

Bennie cannot take it—this much past. He could just break apart, here and now, dissolve, or petrify like Calvin Woodhouse. He needs normalcy and he gets tears over a toy car.

Bennie's eyes fill up too, and for a moment, he sees himself crying with Phil, hugging Phil, they sit here and sob over the weight of it all, they go through one hundred boxes of tissue, and they still fill the room with tears. Something must be done. Someone must stop this. And then, something alters, something rises up inside him, his mind goes somewhere quite else. He looks at Phil and in his head he screams, *This should be her office,* he screams, *so what are you crying about? Who cares about your goddamn toy when this should have been her office?*

This will not do. Bennie looks at his friend and whispers, "I'm sorry, I can't, I can't right now . . ." and closes the door. In his mind, he hears a screeching of brakes. His stomach plunges to the floor, his heart wrenches apart.

No, this cannot happen.

With his eyes firmly on the floor, Bennie walks out of the Contemporary Studies building and heads to the parking lot.

TODD IS JUST getting out of his car when he sees Professor Singer across the parking lot. Todd shouts a hello and walks over to him.

It isn't until Todd gets near him that he realizes Professor Singer hasn't even registered his presence at all, that he is just standing in the parking lot staring aimlessly. He looks sweaty, shaken.

"Professor Singer!?" Todd tries to smile with respectful concern. "Are you all right?"

"Umm . . ."

"Todd. Todd Lewis."

"Yes, Todd." Professor Singer nods abstractly and then, suddenly, snaps to attention. "You're in Memory Studies, right?"

"Um, yes. It was in my project proposal—"

And then the professor exhales loudly, and grabs Todd's shoulder. "It's the deletrium. It's stimulating memory. Find a cure."

And before Todd can respond, he walks away.

MS. PLUM HAS been showing a lot of filmstrips lately, Sophie has noticed. This one is on patriotism. It is very very old. The deep-voiced man explains to Sophie that it is her civic duty to vote. America is the greatest country on earth. We are now waged in an immortal battle between good and evil and it is America's job to make sure that good prevails. We are the custodians of democracy. We are the envy of the world. With freedom comes responsibility. The way to express oneself in a democracy is through orderly means. Write a letter to your congressman. There are those in this country that would let chaos be the rule. [Here, a picture of some messy people burning a flag. Another of someone smoking some kind of cigarette.] Rambunctiousness is not good citizenship. We must support our democracy as we try to make the world safe for the American Dream, because aren't you, after all, proud to be an American? [The music scratches off to a high note. A picture of the flag. And then the voice again.] And, above all, don't use drugs.

[Here a smiling picture of Richard Milhous Nixon (Sophie recognizes him right away. Thirty-seventh president of the United States, before Gerald R. Ford and after Lyndon Baines Johnson. His wife was Patricia (Pat) Nixon. His vice president was Spiro Agnew and then Gerald Ford for reasons Sophie doesn't quite understand. Nixon had a daughter named Tricia who was married in the White House. He had a famous dog. He was the only president ever to resign. He resigned because he stole some things from a hotel and then lied about it. Why he's on this stupid film strip Sophie cannot guess and she will ask her father when she gets home.)]

MS. PLUM CHECKS the date on the film strip. 1973. Oh, well. She sits on a stool in the back of the room, wondering how much of the day this will eat up. She kicks off her high heel shoes, and begins to leaf through a little book made out of purple construction paper she has found near Leslie Miller's desk. . . .

"MA?" BENNIE KNOCKS gently on the guest room door.

"Benjamin."

Bennie has put himself back together again. A little cold water on the face, a few deep breaths. The incident in class he has shoved to the back of his mind. He can deal with it later. Surely, he got more upset than he needed to. So the psychology professor is fallible too. He didn't need to get so defensive about it.

He stands outside his mother's door, and hears her call again, "Benjamin?" It appears he is having some trouble staying on task. He breathes. He opens the door and walks in. She is sitting up. It is an improvement, to be sure. "Mom, how are you feeling?"

"Oh, my head hurts a bit, but not too bad. I took some aspirin."

"Have you been sleeping?"

"No. I can't stay asleep. I've stopped even trying. . . . I've been trying to read, but . . ." She shows him a magazine. *Elle*. From 1993. Bennie winces. "I brought you some water."

Bennie sets the glass on the little green end table by the bed. He has forgotten how ugly it is. They weren't going to keep it for very long.

The guest bedroom is not decorated so much as thrown together. The walls still have the dark yellow wallpaper that was already tacky when they moved in. There's an old green bedroom set from grad school days that Bennie kept meaning to repaint. A quilt. A ratty brown throw rug. Pictures of Sophie. Books everywhere. They had wanted a three-bedroom house, because they were going to have two children, three years apart. That was part of the Master Plan. (They were making great progress on the first part of the plan when they bought the house—Bennie was on tenure track. Lizzie was taking a couple of years off because of the little project growing in her belly. The Contemporary Studies department was growing, they would need more professors eventually, things looked promising indeed.) For the time being, though, it would be a guest bedroom. For the grandparents (They giggle. Grandparents!) to stay in. They could keep the old bureaus there. They would redo it when they got pregnant again. For now, they would leave green bureaus with yellow walls with that old brown quilt. It may not be attractive, but, as Lizzie said, "Collage is the art form of the twentieth century."

His mother keeps the lights in the bedroom very dim so all of the colors look like different shades of mud. She keeps the shades down. Bennie sits down next to her.

"I talked to a doctor today."

Madeline opens her mouth.

"Just to talk, Mom. Listen. It's the deletrium from the factory fire. It's triggering activity in your brain. You're all right, Mom. Nothing's wrong. It's happening to everyone. It's going to pass."

She doesn't speak for a minute or so. She looks better, Bennie thinks. She is pale, but she is focusing.

"Where is Sophie?"

"Ohhh . . . she's in her room. There was some trouble at school today. The principal called me, if you can believe that. Something about her trying to get some girls in trouble. She says she didn't do it."

"Do you believe her?"

"Of course I do. It's Sophie."

"She's in her room?"

"Yeah."

"Maybe you should—"

"Oh yes. Yes I will, don't worry, Mom." Bennie closes his eyes and opens them again. "Do you know what I was thinking about today? When I was in junior high, and somebody put pot in my locker and they called Dad down at the warehouse."

Bennie's mother pauses a moment and then smiles kindly. "Bennie . . . that didn't happen to you."

"Yes it did." Bennie blinks.

She laughs slightly. "No. It was Stevie."

Bennie cocks his head and thinks a minute. "Stevie? No . . ."

"Yes it was, I promise. I remember his mother calling me about it. She was going to sue the school."

"No, Mom, you're wrong."

"Sweetie, it's okay. These things get confused in the mind."

"Mom, no!"

"Benjamin . . ."

There is a pause. Bennie closes his eyes.

"It's okay, sweetie. These things happen."

"No, Mom. This is horrible. Awful."

"Why?"

"How in the world do we ever know what really happened?"

TWO GIRLS SIT in the counselor's office with tears running down their cheeks. Wayne "The Weed" Weederson, the Jesse Ventura Elementary School counselor and vice principal, sits back in his leather chair. He wears a comforting wool sweater and khakis. The fluorescent light, as a rule, shines reassuringly off his bald head. He carefully stares at the girls seated across from him on the cold gray folding chairs. (He has a red plaid sofa, which is for kids to feel comfortable when he is discussing their issues with them. When kids are in trouble, he brings out the folding chairs. Children always know just what they've been called in for as soon as they discern the seating arrangement he has set out. He has occasionally forgotten to put the folding chairs away, and invariably the young charge whom he has hoped to help starts sniffling as soon as s/he sees these harbingers of doom empty and waiting. It was no mistake this time, and Leslie immediately began to cry.) Mr. Weederson is brandishing a little book made of purple construction paper tied together with purple yarn. He flips through the pages. Words are written in black marker in bright, bubbly handwriting.

"It's not ours," Leslie sniffs.

"You are Leslie Miller, are you not?"

"Yeah, but—"

"And you are Christine Sobleski?" Christine rolls her eyes. She is as cool as the proverbial fourth-grade cucumber under interrogation.

"It appears to be a little dictionary. A phrase book. How cosmopolitan of you children! Shall we learn some phrases? Hmmph?" His eyes dare the girls to speak. "Here's a nice page. Let's see. *Fruit* is your esteemed teacher, Ms. Plum. Well, that makes sense. Put that with the other word on the page, *Hooloo*— *Fruit e Hooloo*—and you say, 'Ms. Plum is a cunt.' "

Christine's eyes go very wide. Leslie looks at her, trying to decipher what that word means.

"Here's another, which I believe refers to certain parts of your principal's anatomy."

Leslie sinks down in her chair.

"And another. This is my favorite. *Weed nu bo neep*. Now, let's see what that means. Oh yes, Weed—I think we can all figure out who that is—licks . . . hairy . . . testicles. Well, isn't that lovely! I must say, you girls have picked out the key words for communication in contemporary society. You can really mix and match."

And then something very bizarre happens. The Weed is staring down the students, with that mix of indignation and disappointment that he has perfected over the years. And then he blinks. And then Wayne "The Weed" Weederson begins to cry. Before the girls' eyes, his hands fly up to his face, his shoulders sink, his head bows, and this sound begins to emerge, this hiccuping and choking sound, like so many dying geese, and Leslie and Christine sit very, very, very still.

For several long moments.

Then Leslie begins to cry, too.

And Christine, even Christine, bites her lip.

"Excuse me," Weed says through his hands. "Excuse me, girls. It's just— You kids. You kids can be so awful. You never ever ever change."

Leslie, between her sniffs, pipes up, "Weed, we didn't do it! We swear!"

"Then . . ." He peeks through his hands. "Who did?"

Leslie looks at Christine and sobs, "It must have been Sophie Singer. She hates us. She's crazy."

"You mean"—Weed's hands reach for a well-placed tissue— "Sophie Singer framed you kids?"

"Yes. Yes, we're sure!"

"Well"—he wipes his eyes—"that would be very cruel of her. I can see that, yes." He stops crying and purses his lips. "But how do I know you are not just shifting the blame? Maybe you could show me some handwriting. . . ." Leslie nods. "Yeah! It's her handwriting, I'm sure it is!" (Actually, it is very similar to Sophie's tentative strokes, but this is an accident. The Minister of Doom, in fact, is quite adept at mimicking a girl's handwriting, which would make him subject to considerable mockery if that skill weren't so damn useful.)

Weed takes the purple book and begins to crumple it in his hands. He begins to sniff again and pretty soon Christine's composure gives way and she withers and begins to cry. She cries for

The Weed, she cries for Leslie, and most of all, she cries for herself and all the sad things that have ever happened to her.

BENNIE HAS SPENT the evening hours murmuring, *It was Stevie, it was Stevie.* The words no longer have connection to reality. Not that they ever did. After his conversation with his mother Bennie went straight up to his room to try to put the past back together again. It would not fit, though.

Bennie now stands in the bathroom and fills a cup of water for his mother and then drinks it himself. He drinks another one. And another. It was Stevie. Bennie reaches into his olive green locker to get his math book and there is a plastic bag and there is something in it like spice and Bennie pulls it out and then he hears a voice. "Mr. Singer!" A teacher grabs him on the shoulder and then he is in the principal's office and the principal leans in and Bennie breathes in the smell of damp cheese. The principal will not tolerate lawlessness in his school. He could expel Bennie, but he won't.

They call his father, and his father says, "If my son says it's not his, then it is not his." Bennie can hear his voice grumbling through the phone wires. Bennie would be proud, but he suspects that his father is thinking more of work than of his son's integrity.

Bennie fills the glass again, and drinks it down. The principal unlocks his top drawer and sticks the bag in there. Bennie pulls open the drawer next to the sink and feels around for his toothpaste. The principal glares at Bennie while he brushes his teeth. If he drinks enough water maybe the principal will stop glaring. Stevie liked to wear cords to school, even on the hottest days. Stevie carried a briefcase through seventh grade. The principal never glared at Stevie, only Bennie, only Bennie's father got called at the warehouse, only Bennie's father said, "I believe my son," only Bennie saw the top drawer open and the pot go in and only Bennie glimpsed the other parcels locked away with his own private planted contraband. . . .

What else is suspect? What else is wrong? The past is a lie, Bennie's memories are Stevie's, and now nothing can be sure. What happened?

Where is Lizzie?

Bennie finds himself in his bedroom, where he unbuttons his light blue shirt. He shrugs it off. He unzips his khakis. He pulls off his pants. He lets them fall to the floor. He is still thirsty. He makes his way back to the bathroom. The soap dispenser is empty. He turns on the water and looks at his face in the mirror. He takes a glass of water. He takes another. He does not turn off the tap. He closes his eyes and opens them and looks in the mirror and is surprised to find he is still there.

(Where is Lizzie?)—

"Dad?"

"Huh?" Sophie is standing in the doorway. Bennie blinks. "Oh. Hi, sweetheart." What time is it? Why is she still awake?

". . . Are you okay?"

"Sure. I'm fine. How are you? What's up?" He is speaking through so much fog; he can barely understand himself.

"Dad, are you mad at me?"

"Soph, what do you mean?" Bennie has genuinely no idea. For a moment, when she appeared in the doorway like that, he thought she was a child-size Lizzie, back to help him clear his mind.

"About . . . school."

"What? Oh! Sophie, I know you would never do anything like that. I told the principal that. She said she certainly would not expect behavior like that from you. We talked about how mature you are. Don't worry about it, sweetie. Go to bed."

Sophie still stands there, looking at him. Bennie rubs his forehead. Everything is so muddled. It's very late, isn't it? Isn't it late?

"It's late, sweetie. It's time to sleep. Everything will be better in the morning." Won't it? Won't everything be better in the morning? He strokes her hair and kisses her forehead. "Good night."

How can she even understand him when he is talking through this much fog? But she must have, for she is gone now, and Bennie is alone.

Bennie crawls between the cream-colored covers and looks up. He does not see his reflection in the ceiling. But he sees something there, something like a shape of everything.

An hour later, Bennie is still staring at the ceiling. He is finding the day's events amongst the cracks in the plaster. There was a phone call from the principal. There was a doctor. There was the memory that did not happen to him. There was his class. And then, then Bennie remembers the thing he said in class and what happened when he said it. What happens when the psychology professor loses it in front of his class? He should show up tomorrow and provide an explanation, show up in class with the diagnosis and the cure and they would applaud and he will say, "For your next lesson I will demonstrate dissociative disorder," and they will applaud again and Bennie will prove to them all he has mastery of his own mind, like a good psychologist should.

But he does not want to go to class. He is having some mental dysfunction. That's it, his brain is not well. He is having disordered thoughts, delirium, dementia, which frequently happens to people when their brains are not well. He is a psychologist; he knows about such things. Bennie thinks maybe he will call in sick tomorrow. Maybe it is better that way. Maybe he will order a video for Personality. Maybe he can even get a grad student to do it. There's a psychopharmaceutical component in his brain and it is causing reactions with the natural chemicals in his brain, which are distorting his perception of objective reality. Like a drug. He can be in control. It is merely a biological reaction. It will go away, Dr. Jessop says. It will go away, Benjamin. You can control it. Mind over matter . . .

(Lizzie?)

Bennie's bladder is the size of somebody's head. He should get up. He should get up. He can't get up, because the ceiling is not finished with him yet. Order and disorder become one in his mind and he cannot get up until he figures out what that means.

And then, as it so often does, something lights up in the corner of his mind and a voice begins to whisper:

Right or left? Right or left?

eleven.
Singer . . . ?

As the denizens of Clarence lie tucked all snug in their beds, the temperature falls below zero for the first time this season, and a series of cirrus clouds blows into the upper atmosphere ready to plunk down for a nice long stay. While the dust of things past dances around in slumbering minds, water vapor latches on to the nuclei of mineral particles that live in the air. The vapor crystallizes, the crystals grow branches, then join with other crystals and begin to plummet toward the earth. Some evaporate into the air, some collect moisture and continue their descent to the ground.

(Snow can be induced artificially too, perhaps by seeding very cold water clouds with dry ice. It can also be manufactured. If this were a movie set, key grips and best boys would be setting up snow machines because you can never trust Mother Nature to provide you with a good natural metaphor when you most need one.)

In his house on Cedar Street, little Mike, now with a chipped tooth, jolts upright from sleep wearing his Technosaur pajamas. He senses something. Could it be? He flings open the flowery curtains (which he has begged his parents to change and until they do he will have to keep making excuses every time John and Matt want to come over and play with his new Basketron 3000, which pretty soon they won't even believe he has anymore. But he does. And it's sweet.) Mike looks out into the proverbial black abyss and stares off into the distance. And then, there, under the streetlight . . . snow.

It's about damn time.

Mike grabs his Junior Sergeant pager and crawls under his Junior Sergeant sleeping bag. (He has been sleeping on the floor for four months and will refuse to sleep in a real bed for another year.) He types in John's address and the message: *Redbird Four this is Redbird Three. We have powder at last. Notify Redbird Five.* Mike licks his lips and is about to press send when he remembers: *I gotta copy your math homework on the bus. Redbird Three out!*

By morning, the ground is gone. In its place is a world of white. Children all over Clarence leap to the radio and tune to the list of school closings. A number cross their fingers, the rest find Jesus. Then finally, ah the sweet sounds: *In Babbitt County: Clarence—all public and parochial schools closed.*

One by one in houses on every street curtains are pulled and shades lifted. Men and women stare at the white abyss—some filled with joy, others terror, others plain ennui—all for reasons they cannot quite place. One man eyes his snow-covered car out the window, then gazes longingly back at his bed. If he closes his eyes, he can picture himself shoveling his car out last year. The year before. The year before that. Suddenly it seems to this man that all he has ever done in his life is shovel snow. There was a time when he had dreams for himself. Big dreams. None of them involved middle management or shoveling his own snow. He looks at his buried car and crawls back under his electric blanket. His wife groans and rolls back to her side of the bed. House by house, the scene is repeated up and down Chestnut Street, Elm Street, Oak Street, and Maple Street. Rose Street, Lily Street, Daisy Street. Polk, Buchanan, Lincoln, Grant. House by house people crawl into their electric blankets and shut their eyes to the world. Clarence will not work today.

The town has changed in the last month. No less than six couples have filed for divorce since Halloween. Some people have moved back to the cities of their childhood, three people have hired private investigators to settle bets on conflicting memories, two women are independently checking on how stringent the requirements for joining a convent are these days, and of course the line at Madame Z's goes out the door every day. The five licensed psychologists in the area have gone on indefinite vacation.

Lorna Hansen has gone to stay with her sister down in the city— a development that has caused Pastor Hansen to develop a serious stress-related bowel disorder. Both of those developments have caused him to break off his affair and to pray a lot. He doesn't have time for extramarital dalliances anyway; the phone in his office sings with things members of his congregation just want to get off their chests. (My Lord, he thinks. Who do these people think they are, Catholics?)

In the Singer household, snow blankets every sound, every movement. The upstairs hallway is lined with closed doors. Little Sophie sits behind one of them, in her room, playing school with her stuffed animals, reading books, telling stories to her cat, giving her dolls new haircuts, and waiting for signs of life to flicker through the crack underneath the door.

Bennie sits behind the closed door of his room, surrounded by shoe boxes full of old photos. He takes out a stack and flips through them. Then he will stop and stare at one for several snow-covered minutes. He will touch it. He will smell it. He will turn it around and around. He will lock his eyebrows and purse his lips and stare more deeply into the faded flat colors as if the photo is a puzzle he is trying to solve. Something starts in his body and pain flashes on his face. He closes his eyes and takes a breath in, and whispers to himself, *No. I will not go down that road.*

Madeline sits behind the closed door of her adopted room. A life's worth of images flit through space. The writer's mind lures the flying creatures in, contains them, crystallizes them, and re-arranges them into a narrative. Cause and effect. Beginning, mid-dle, and end. Revelatory experience. History and significance. Once upon a time there was a girl named Madeline. A daughter named Madeline. A wife named Madeline. A mother. A widow. A woman. A writer.

Image: the mother has her young boy on her lap.

The boy has a shock of thick black hair, growing thicker all the time, her brother says. (Brother Isaac is growing thicker all the time, too.) The hair is Morris's—thick waves that Morris combs back every morning, each stroke carefully pushing the waves back from crown to nape. It takes him fifteen strokes to get across his entire head. Madeline has to fight back the urge to sneak up on him and comb right to left. Instead, she must comb her son's hair that way. Morris has not yet noticed.

The hair may be Morris's, but the boy seems to be mostly hers. She catches her husband staring at Benjamin occasionally with a look of bewilderment, as if the boy were a monkey that had one day manifested itself in their home. She wants to take her husband's hands and run them over his child and say, "It's just a boy. It's just your son. You do not have to be afraid."

So the mother spends her time sitting in the rocking chair that her own father had made for the occasion, and sings softly to her son:

You're the top!
You're Mahatma Gandhi.

She does not know any real lullabies, but the boy does not seem to mind. This is Benjamin's favorite. He used to coo to it. Now he is too old and he just shuts his eyes and kicks up his dimply little feet and listens.

You're the top!
You're Napoleon Brandy.

Madeline spends her nights here, with Benjamin. Someday soon he will be too old for this as well, so for now these moments must be grabbed. Later, she will have to find another reason not to be downstairs, where silence emanates from the immovable form of her husband on the easy chair, the only noise the endless murmur of newspaper pages.

You're the purple light of a summer night in Spain.
You're the National Gall'ry
You're Garbo's sal'ry,
You're cellophane.

Madeline holds her baby boy closer. She thinks she will ask Morris for a desk—perhaps her father will build one for her. She would like a desk, that way she could write letters to her friends. That would be a nice thing to do at night. She would like that.

Image: the new wife sits across the dinner table from her husband.

They are having meat loaf—Madeline's mother's recipe, and potatoes and canned green beans. Madeline is not used to this yet, this marriage, this way of being. She is not used to all the quiet.

We could go for a walk tonight, she says. *We could talk. Have a nice time. Get some ice cream. Look at the sky. Pick out constellations. Make up constellations. Tell each other stories about them. Our own myths. We could read poetry to each other under the starlight.*

No, he says. *I'm tired tonight. Work, you know.*

At night she rolls over and whispers, *Tell me a story. Tell me your story.*

There is nothing to tell, he says. He scratches his thigh.

They lie in silence for a minute.

Maybe I should go back to school. I could teach then.

Maybe it is time we had a son. That would be nice for you. And he takes his hand and places it on her hip.

Yes, all right, yes.

Image: the mother sits next to her son, tucked into his bed.

The comforter has blue stripes. Ben holds the comforter up to his chin, so only his head and hands can be seen. She would like to take a picture and have this image forever. She pulls up the rocking chair and picks a book out of his many shelves. He is too young for some of these, but he never complains. He never has to beg her to read more, she always reads until he falls asleep, and sometimes a little more, and every night she has to ask her son, "What's the last thing you remember?" And they would start from there.

The words from the books sing in her head for hours afterward, the characters linger, the plots twist and turn and she waters the stories and gives them the proper amount of sunlight and shade and soon they blossom and grow.

She worries that Ben needs some attention from his father. She cannot think of what to suggest. So one day when Ben is six, she says to her husband:

Why don't you read to him sometime? He would like that.

A pause. Then the words stumble out:

No, no, I can't. You do it. He wants his mother.

All right. All right. I don't mind one bit.

And secretly she is glad.

One day, when Ben is eight, he tells her he is a big boy now and too grown-up to be read to. She says she understands and puts the book back onto the shelf.

They talked about having another child, as much as they ever talked about anything. She wanted to have a girl. She would name her Mary. But by the time Ben was old enough for them to consider having another child, she and her husband only really talked about the weather and her family's health, and work, of course.

So she would have to read to herself.

The mother sits at her new desk.

In the letters she is writing, she jokes to her friends that she now has a room of her own—they read about such things in college. But it's true, she does have a room of her own, and in one corner sits a sturdy mahogany desk her father made for her. She and Morris do not need the extra bedroom and all her books had to go somewhere. Madeline spends her evenings here, with pens and fresh paper and endlessly reread books, hiding from her silent husband. Madeline's friends are all over the country and she writes one of them every night. One is a doctor and one is a bookstore manager and one is an artist and she, Maddy Singer, raises a boy. She never has any news, except about her son, of course.

There was one point in her life when she believed she would be something besides a mother and a wife. When she was young, she was going to be a fashion designer, and then a singer, and maybe at one time a gymnast. And then she got older and realized what she wanted most in the world was to be an English teacher. She was going to get her degree and move somewhere completely different with the friend who is now an artist, and she would teach high school students the wonders of Virginia Woolf and Jane Austen and all the Brontës. And then her mother got sick, and she did not get any degree, and now she has no news for her friends. But she writes them letters anyway. Her friends write her back and they have all kinds of news, it seems. Madeline keeps the letters, every one, inside her desk.

The wife sits next to the sister, Rachel Singer, on the couch during some holiday at the in-laws.

The air is thick with chicken broth, so the wife thinks. The wife and the sister are going through an old photo album. This fills the moments well. On the third page there is a shot of three boys and a girl. Two of the boys are older, taller. The wife says, "That is you and Morris, but who are the other two?" Rachel says, "You don't know?" and the wife shakes her head. Rachel says, "Those are Howard and Joe. Our brothers. Howard went to World War II and Joe went to Korea. Morrie never told you about them?"

On the way home the wife asks the husband, "Why didn't you tell me about your brothers?" and the husband does not have an answer. Something occurs to the wife, and the wife asks, "Why didn't you go to Korea?" and the husband is silent for a moment and then says, "Couldn't. Blood pressure."

And that was the end of the conversation.

The mother talks on the phone to her son at college.

She sits in the kitchen, twirling the cord around her fingers. "Things are well here." In the background, her husband coughs and coughs. Their evenings are coated with silence and she wants to grab him and shake him and say, "Is this really what you had in mind?"

And, would that he were a different person, would that he could express himself, he would say, *No. What I had in mind is that I would be a hero. What I had in mind is that I would honor my family. What I had in mind is that I would be strong. I did not have the warehouse in mind, I did not have this boy in mind, I did not have you in mind, but since I live my life in the shadow of what I am supposed to be, I will make do.*

And she plays her game with herself, she reduces Morrie to the smallest possible gesture. Morrie itches. He itches and itches.

And the wife catches her breath and finds that she wishes something, something either awful or loving, that she will never admit to anyone—except to her son a few chapters from now. And she imagines for herself what it would be like to have a husband free of regret. And then she imagines what it would be like to be free of regret herself.

The widow sits at her desk.

After two weeks of bedridden silence, of force-fed soup, whispery neighbors, and a worried son, Madeline Singer is back at the desk her father made for her ten years before. It is time to find a routine again. Her son says he will stay, he does not have to go back to college right now, and for a moment, just a moment, she wants to say, *Thank you, dear. I would love that. Stay with me, dear. I will tuck you in at night and read you stories. I will cook you dinner and you will fill my nights with talking.* But of course, she does not, and the son is sent packing. So she writes letters. They are short and sad, for now, filled with the echoes of days spent in silence. It will be some time before these letters she is writing become longer and longer and eventually evolve into something else. It will be some time before she realizes the letters are not addressed to anyone in particular. The characters in them will take shape and begin to breathe on their own, quite separate from her own experience. And, in a year, when she begins to put together the pieces, it will become an elegy for her husband, her rough-skinned, itchy, whiskery husband, for his dreams and for his fatal regret.

BENNIE HAS TURNED things at school over to a teaching assistant. They said it wouldn't be a problem, not for a few days anyway, if he really wasn't feeling well—some kind of bug, everyone out with it, it seems, if it got any worse they'd have to have a Mansfield holiday. School in the summer, the students would love that, eh Singer?

Singer . . . ? You still with me?

No. No. I was somewhere else for a moment.

Bennie has no plans to go back to school. Not right now. He can't stand the thought of smelling carpet and transparencies and all those indifferent postadolescent bodies right now.

Bennie lets himself out of his room every so often to check on his mother. Sophie he does not worry about. Sophie can take care of herself. She has not asked any questions, has not complained at all. She is fine. She is so fine. She understands, somehow she understands everything. Sophie is fiercely independent, supercompetent, so much like Lizzie—

He asked her to order groceries for all of them off the Internet. Quick and easy, as he doesn't feel much like cooking. Now, he rummages through the fridge to find something for his mom, who has not come down all day. She emerges, every once in a while, to get some water, to shower, to sit blankly in front of the television set, but since Bennie put her there ten days ago she has barely moved from the guest room. He comes in to bring her something—a nice apple, say—or those strange yogurt tubes that Sophie picked—and she barely talks to him. Sometimes, he sits down next to her and neither of them says anything at all. Time passes slowly in that room—if you sit there softly enough you can almost hear it run down. His mother doesn't care. She is somewhere else, with no intention of returning, it seems. She hugs the pillows close to her body as she sleeps, and Bennie does not realize he has been watching her until he sees her whole body shake and her eyes pop open—terrified seemingly—and then she closes them again and he stops noticing the way time moves.

And he would not admit this if you asked, but somewhere down deep Bennie wonders why his mother isn't coping with this all a little bit better. She knows what this is. A brain-chemical disruption—and he feels bad for her, really he does, but shouldn't she try to control it? Like he's doing.

He cannot find anything in the fridge that doesn't involve labor of some kind. She's probably fine. Not that she'd cook. She was never much of a cook. Dad didn't seem to mind, the less complicated dinner was, the less you had to talk about it. She said once that she used to try, when they first got married—

When he and Lizzie first got married she made him dinner every night for twenty-six days. She made him pastas and pies and meat and potatoes and casseroles and cookies. And then, one night, she served him leftover chicken, and then she never cooked again.

Madeline made lunch once, for Lizzie. The first time he

brought Lizzie home—it was three months into their relationship, and Bennie picked Lizzie up at the front door of her dorm and she was wearing a gray sweater and a long skirt with flowers on it. They drove the three hours to Bennie's house. He had called his mother the week before and said, "Mother. It is time. You have got to meet this woman. Mother I love her. Mother I am going to marry her. I love her from the very bottom of my toes. You will love her too."

And Madeline said, "I'm sure I will, Benjamin."

Lizzie was nervous. Bennie had never seen anything like it before. Her hands flew in the air as she talked, like two spastic birds. "Do I look all right? How's this skirt? Would you trust me with your son? I was going for Soft Stability. How'd I do? Is that right? Maybe I should have gone for more Gentle Competence?"

"Lizzie?"

"What?"

"What's the difference?"

Pause.

"I don't know."

"Listen." He reached over the gear shift to squeeze her knee. "This is my mom. She is not like that. She will love you, because I love you. I have told her all about you. She cannot wait to meet you."

"Has she liked all your other girlfriends?"

"Well, yes, she has, and none of them has been anywhere as dear as you."

"Well, great."

Bennie laughed. "Now listen, I met your parents, and that went just fine."

(Bennie remembers, just now, the way Mr. McCourt's—Tom's—hand felt in his. "You give my father a firm handshake and he will love you instantly," Lizzie had said. He gave Mrs. McCourt a kiss on her cheek and she giggled and said, "Oh, he's charming, Elizabeth!")

Lizzie raised her eyebrows. "We spent three hours picking your tie."

"Well, yes, but it went just fine."

Every time before, when Bennie had brought a girl home—and he had certainly done that, but never a girl like this—his mother had greeted her warmly, asked lots of questions, even given her a great big hug after the light lunch of limp lettuce was over. "It is so nice to finally meet you,————," she would say. "I've heard so much about you!" And did Bennie mention that none of the girls was anywhere near as perfect and wonderful and beautiful as Lizzie?

When they knocked on the door of his mother's house—his house—Madeline came to the door and opened it and she smiled her big smile that she had used on all his girlfriends. And then they all stood there, in the doorway, he holding Lizzie's hand, and he squeezed it, just a bit, and was filled with this desire suddenly to run his hands through her beautiful hair. She squeezed his hand back and said, "Mrs. Singer, it's so nice to meet you," and she dropped his hand and reached hers out to Madeline and he touched Lizzie's shoulder and then his mother just stood there. She did take Lizzie's hand, of course, and shook it, and said, "It's nice to meet you, too, Elizabeth," but something had altered. Her smile seemed fake and stiff instead of the fake-but-easy smile she had on when she opened the door. She led them into the dining room and fed them their wilted lettuce leaves—yes, this was his mother's cooking— but there was hesitation in everything she did. Lizzie could feel it—Bennie felt how stiff she was—and he kept reaching out to her, to her knees, her hand, her back, I'm here, sweetie, I'm here for you, I will never leave you, feel me here for you. . . .

Lizzie smiled at his mother. "That was a good salad, Mrs. Singer."

"Well, I got it from the store."

"Oh. Well, it was great!"

There was a pause. Bennie's mother was eyeing them with the oddest expression, like somehow some shadow had taken up residence inside her. Lizzie coughed and smiled and said, "So, what's for lunch? I'm sure it's wonderful—"

Bennie's heart sank. His mother raised an eyebrow. Bennie opened his mouth and his mother said, "Oh, Elizabeth, the salad is the meal. But if you are still hungry, I'm sure we can find something for you."

Lizzie turned the sickly pink of Mrs. Singer's preferred brand of French dressing. "No. No, I'm so sorry. It was wonderful, Mrs. Singer, really."

"Well then"—she smiled—"shall we go to the sitting room and all get to know each other?"

And Bennie found himself running the whole conversation, and when he couldn't stand it anymore, he got up and said, "Well, Mother, I want to show Lizzie around," and he took his beloved by the hand and they walked out the door and then Lizzie, whom he had never seen cry before, started to cry.

(No, he is not going to bring his mother anything. No, no, he is not going to knock on her door. He is not going to see how she is. She was mean to Lizzie. She does not deserve it. No, no, no, not one bit.)

Later he called his mother and nearly yelled, "What was that?"

"I am sorry, Benjamin. She's a lovely girl. I just . . . I had a headache. I'm so sorry. Please, bring her around again."

And Bennie would bring her around, bring her around in his car again and again and again—

And, then, as always, his mind begins to tire of this diversion and look for the road. . . .

Bennie barely hears Sophie open the kitchen door. He is too busy driving. He feels her presence next to him as she follows the path of his eyes into the refrigerator, but cannot quite bring himself to react.

Right or left?

"Dad?"

"Oh. Sophie. Hi."

"What are you looking for?"

"Oh, sweetie. Nothing."

"Then why are you standing there with the fridge door open?"

"Oh. I don't know."

"You know, you should figure out what you want before you open the door. It saves electricity."

"Thank you, Soap. I will."

Sophie stands and looks at him for a minute. Bennie obediently closes the refrigerator door. She is still there.

"Dad?"

"What?"

She opens her mouth and closes it again. Bennie smiles at her benignly. Isn't there something he's supposed to be doing? He is still in the world inside the refrigerator, he is not here at all. He is not in charge anymore. Bennie turns around and wanders back up to his bedroom, glancing at his mother's shut door as he walks by.

This isn't fair. His level of agitation is not his mother's fault. There is something he needs to do so he can be in charge again.

His mind, he is realizing, has its own will. It is trying to take him somewhere.

Perhaps if he goes with it, perhaps if he lets his mind do what it will, if he can get through it once, maybe he will be at peace. He can go back to normal, and live his life again and take care of his daughter and his mother and that night can relegate itself back to the pit of his stomach where it belongs.

He goes to his room, crawls into his bed, and closes his eyes.

twelve.

There is no warning.

THIS IS A partial list of things Bennie and Lizzie got into a car to do over their years together: Go to campus, go grocery shopping, go to the gym, go to the library, go out to dinner, go for milk, go to the movies, go to the video store, go to the bookstore on Fridays, go to the bakery, go for ice cream, go buy a Christmas tree, go buy a menorah, go visit Madeline, go visit the McCourts, go to coffee, go to the doctor, go to the dentist, go into the Cities, go to the North Woods, and sometimes, just go.

For years, they got into the car to go somewhere. Every single time, they both came back.

They had a brown hatchback from 1984. They would upgrade to a station wagon after Lizzie started working again, as part of the Ben and Liz Singer Master Plan.

One time they got into a car because Lizzie's water had broken. It broke two weeks before it was supposed to, which was not in the Master Plan. Bennie almost squealed when he saw the water stain. "Is that . . . ? Is that?" The late-night talk show audience roared behind him.

They called the doctor. She said, "Come in when the contractions are five minutes apart."

Then, they were five minutes apart.

Lizzie was the calm one. Lizzie got up (with some difficulty), got her night bag, and got into the car. The passenger seat. "Are you coming, Singer?" Bennie dashed to the car. "Did you turn off the TV?"

"I'm not sure . . ." Bennie was trembling.

"Are you going to be all right to drive?" She laughed.

"I think so." Bennie didn't see anything funny about the question at all. He started the car. He turned the wheel toward the hospital. He engaged the warp drive.

When they got to the hospital, Lizzie said, "You know, I'm not sure these are still five minutes apart."

"Oh. What does that mean?"

"I don't know. Maybe we're too early."

"What should we do?"

"I don't know. Let's drive around the block a few times."

"Okay." So Bennie turned around in the hospital parking lot and drove out into the street. He turned left at the stop sign, and left again, and left again. They drove around the block for fifteen more minutes before they decided to go in. Sophia Madeline emerged an hour later.

Like everyone else in the world, Bennie had always hoped that random, tragic accidents never really came out of the blue. That passengers on doomed planes always sensed they were doomed when they got on board. That their lives were somehow completed. That anyone who was about to die had some kind of precognition, at least from the swelling music or sudden, thundering bass.

Of course, like everyone else, he knew that this was ridiculous—that life, unlike movies, television, or novels, had a way of not giving any warnings. But, like everyone else, in his heart he had always hoped it happened that way anyway.

There is no warning, but Bennie stops at a stop sign and takes a left turn and Lizzie sings along with a radio commercial and the speeding car swerves and hits a tree while Bennie and Lizzie drive away singing with Sophie kicking her legs in her car seat in the back and the three Singers pick up some ice cream on the way home. Bennie takes a left turn and history rewrites itself and he smells Lizzie's hair every night as he goes to bed. They will drive together a million more times in their long lives, stop at a billion stop signs, and every single one of those times Bennie will always turn the correct way.

In the period of time known as After, Bennie never wanted to see the hatchback again. Selling it wouldn't have been any trouble, there was only minor damage, really. He never reclaimed it from the tow lot. After Madeline got in from the airport, she drove up to Clarence in a brand-new gray sedan. Bennie did not object.

But it didn't help. For a long time After, when he was driving in the car, he could see Lizzie in the passenger seat from the corner of his eye. But every time he looked toward her she had vanished. Soon, he trained himself to look straight ahead, so she would not go away.

One time they got into the car to go home from a day at the lake. They strapped sleeping Sophie into her safety seat in the back and set off on the two-hour drive home. There was no portent, no music, no bass. Just sand and picnic remnants and sleeping Sophie.

For a second, Bennie couldn't remember the way to the interstate and stalled at a stop sign. Right or left?

Lizzie looked at him. "You all right there, big guy?"

Bennie laughed. Lizzie reclines her seat back and turns her head to look at the moon. Bennie turned right.

Lizzie made a sound that Bennie did not process before he heard the sound of brakes and tires screaming in protest. Something collided into the passenger door. Bennie also did not process the sound that he would later realize was his wife's neck breaking as the force of the impact sent their car in the opposite direction and the little brown hatchback spun out of control.

In his mind Bennie said, We are having an accident. Not a very bad one. The door will need to be replaced. Insurance will take care of it. These things happen.

Bennie did not slam on the brakes. He let the car skid through, just as you are supposed to. In his mind, he said, Wow. I am turning with the skid. I am not a panicker. I am not a brake slammer. I am a turner with the skid.

And the car skidded and Bennie turned with it, and the car went into a tree at the side of the road and stopped.

Bennie unbuckled his seat belt. "Phew. Is everyone okay?" He turned around to the backseat. "Sophie? Baby? Are you okay?" Sophie was sitting in her seat, kicking her legs back and forth, looking slightly dazed but perfectly healthy. She wasn't crying. She never cried. At first, Bennie and Lizzie had thought they had been blessed, watching dirty crying babies in the supermarket, in movie theaters, in toy stores, while Sophie toddled serenely with them, her hands in theirs, studying the world around her with bemused quietude. After a while, though, Bennie and Lizzie started to think something was wrong with her. Babies cry. That is their essence. That is what they do. Whoever heard of a baby that didn't cry?

"You okay, Soap?"

The girl nodded, wide-eyed.

His hand reached for Lizzie's arm. "How about you, sweetie?" He stroked her arm a bit. She didn't answer. Bennie sat up and looked at her.

Her head was twisted around at an odd angle.

"Lizzie?"

No answer. Bennie squeezed her arm.

"Lizzie?"

"Lizzie? LIZZIE!"

They needn't have worried. At the sound of that yell, Sophie began to cry.

thirteen.

Wish you were here.

ONCE UPON A time there was a young man named Benjamin who loathed history. To him, math at least had built-in mechanisms for uncertainty. Science had a methodology for answering its questions about the origins of things. History was myth disguised as literature disguised as science and Benjamin didn't like it one bit. The human mind was complex enough—how can anyone put hundreds, thousands, millions of minds together to make a movement, a mind-set, a cultural consciousness? Impossible.

Jefferson and Hamilton College had certain requirements, though, certain philosophies about what it meant to be a truly educated person, something about a core foundation of knowledge and cultural literacy and broadening horizons, about dialogue and conflict being the essence of our great nation, about a belief that the true liberal arts education would entail both depth and breadth and some such bullshit so Benjamin Singer was forced to take not one but two courses in European and American histories to satisfy his humanities requirement so he could graduate. Needless to say, Bennie had put off the history classes until the last minute, and in his first semester senior year, in addition to his Psych Honors seminar and thesis class, he found himself in both American Foreign Policy 1945 to the Present and Medieval Europe. Bennie sat in the large lecture halls he should have left behind his second year and took notes alongside freshmen and sophomores who insisted on forgoing the complexities of individuality and instead were perfectly content to go about their daily business existing solely as types. In American Foreign Policy, eager beavers in the front row sporting a veritable rainbow of polo shirts jotted down the professor's every word, pausing only to lovingly finger their Reagan Revolution buttons pinned conspicuously on their woodsy chic backpacks. They fought for space with the men and women in dress shirts and briefcases that didn't need the buttons to express their allegiance. In the back sat pituitary cases still wearing their high-school letter jackets, women trying to grow out their perms, and a few stringy-haired socialists. Bennie sat in the middle. Meanwhile, in Medieval Europe, the seats were filled by pudgy women with frighteningly straight hair and tortoiselike faces wearing cloaks, young Society for Creative Anachronism hopefuls sporting (blunted) swords and T-shirts that read KNIGHTS DO IT GALLANTLY and SERF'S UP!, and of course a few stringy-haired socialists sitting in the middle. Bennie sat in the back.

Bennie does not remember a single thing he learned in either of these classes—academically at least. He does remember quite vividly learning that the average eighteen-to-nineteen-year-old is an idiot, and realizing that he wished he could apologize to everyone he ever interacted with during that period in his life. (Hindsight, as they say . . .) He also remembers the reading load—a book a week in each class, a requirement he did not have time for, given actual important things like grad school applications and his thesis, but then again he did have his GPA to think about (which was thus far excellent). So he would hole himself up in the back corner of Alter's Coffee Emporium for hours on Tuesdays and Thursdays, eating bagels, flirting with waitresses, drinking cup after cup of house blend (all the while developing a peculiar addiction to saccharin), and trying to get through whatever damned tome on William the Conqueror or Henry Kissinger so he could get on with his life.

And then one day, while skimming some book on the Black Death (and that, too, he will always remember. Plague and pestilence that killed one third of Europe, and he would forever associate it with . . .) he reached for the packets of saccharin and knocked his blue highlighter off the table. The marker rolled underneath the chair of the person next to him.

"Excuse me, dreadfully sorry, my highlighter seems to have—"

Stop action. Cue lights. Cue music. Cue cartoon effects. Eyes bug out. Heart jumps out of chest. Focus goes dim and Bennie is running through a field of sunshine and daffodils and he has a crown of daisies on his head and the birds are singing, singing, singing their birdie song of love just for him and this girl, this vision. She is a fairy queen, a knight-ess in shining armor, a princess so charming—and he in so much distress!—she is a paladin on her gallant steed who will take him and they will ride into the sunset happily, happily, happily ever after. She grabs his hand and she is wearing a crown of daisies too and they skip through the field and they kiss and they fall down and have splendor in the grass. There's a red brick house and a threshold and little Hasidic leprechauns who throw rice and he carries this aqua-eyed round-faced compact miracle with hair like the golden fleece into the doorway and they have more splendor, he and this girl, this vision, this—

"Here's your highlighter." The woman smiles politely. Her hand reaches to his, gives him the marker, and he opens his mouth to say:

Hello. I recognize you. I remember you. You are in my life every moment after now. You are the mother of my children. How could I not recognize you? You are my future. I remember. Our lives together will span decades and soon we will not even remember a time when we did not know each other. You are my wife, my soul mate, my dearest love, my every desire. My life has just begun. Our years together commence now.

But of course what he says is, "Thank you."

And she looks away.

Everything he has ever been, everything he has ever done is irrelevant now. Any other girl and he could have run his hands through his thick black hair and said, "And who do I have to thank for the rescue?" or "This highlighter has great sentimental value. It kept me alive during World War II," or something suitably goofy so the girl would be captivated by his insouciant charm and fine chocolate eyes, or whatever. But that was Before. The Old Bennie. B.C.E. Now, he is a new man, he wears a crown of daisies for all to see, and all he can do is burrow his head back into the Black Death and feel his ears turn red.

And pretty soon, just as the plague begins to spread up to England, the woman gets up and puts on her coat and tosses her backpack casually over her shoulders, leaves a few bills on the table, and walks slowly out the door. He stares into her back and thinks as loudly as he can: Turn around, turn around, turn around, turn around . . .

She turns her head back toward him. He smiles. She smiles back. And then she leaves.

Bennie spends the next week in the coffee shop. He reads every book for the rest of the semester for Medieval Europe. He brings highlighters of six different shades of blue to give him luck. He drinks ten cups of coffee per day. In that week he eats eight sesame bagels, seven lemon poppyseed muffins, six chocolate chip cookies, five cinnamon raisin bagels, four sticky buns, three French rolls, two turtle cakes, and one extra large piece of apple pie.

By Saturday he is in the waiting room of J&H Health Services (or Death Services, as it is frequently called) desperately seeking attention for a rather urgent stomach ailment. The kind that polite people do not discuss. He has no moisture left in his body. He cannot sit comfortably. His insides feel like they have been vacuumed. On the high setting. His hands are shaking. His skin feels so cold and clammy he thinks its hue might have passed from pale to clear. When he checked in the bored desk attendant asked him what was wrong as if he were having his car fixed and he leaned in to tell her and she squawked, "What? I can't hear you!" so he said very very loudly, "I have shat out all of my internal organs."

Now, he sits on a cold green vinyl couch and looks around at the other poor saps, most of whom are looking right back at him. He has been waiting an hour. Next time, he thinks, he should remember to be very nice to those who hold his fate in their hands.

He didn't bring a book. He has already read the "On Your Health" binder filled with articles the nurses have clipped, and the brochures on "How to Know When You've Had Too Much to Drink," and "Caring for Your Teeth," and "Your Growing Body," and "More than Just the Blues," and "The Great Smoke Out," and is now working his way through a brochure on living with an STD when the presence of a seatmate is announced by the telling squelch of vinyl.

A pause, then: "Hello."

He looks up. His mouth opens. Of course.

It is her.

If he had any blood in his body, his heart would pound. The

golden fleece is pulled back behind her head and she is wearing a fuzzy pink sweater that he would very much like to touch and maybe even stroke gently. She is small and sturdy, she looks like she would barely come up to his shoulders and still could probably beat him up if she needed to. She bounces slightly in her seat and in her grin linger the ghosts of one thousand mischievous thoughts. She looks like the secret of life resides as a ball of fire inside her. If he could touch her skin, he would live forever.

She looks down at the booklet he is reading and cocks her head sympathetically. "Are you all right?"

Bennie's eyes follow hers down and he drops the pamphlet in horror. "No, no, I was just reading this, uh . . . I've been here for about an hour. Next I was going to have to read the breast self-examination ones—"

She raises her eyebrows. He vows to kick himself in the head later. "Sorry, my brain isn't exactly functioning."

"I have to admit, you don't look like you're feeling so hot."

"Yeah, I have a, um, flu."

I'm Ben.

I'm Elizabeth.

I love you.

"Oh, I'm sorry to hear that. You came here so they could finish you off?"

"Exactly."

"Well, I'm sorry you had to resort to this. . . ." As her wry smile turns into a genuine one, some invisible and very, very malevolent and bad creature grabs Bennie's small intestine and begins to wring it back and forth in its tremendous, powerful, crushing hands. Bennie shifts in his seat. Please. No. No. There cannot, he thinks, be anything left to go anymore, except maybe his stomach itself. He feels his face grow clammy.

". . . Are you okay?"

"Um, yes." He grins. He blinks benignly. His stomach screams. "Uh. No. I'll be right back."

He sits on the toilet for a geological era. During the time he spends on the toilet, millions of insects the world over hatch, mature, lay eggs, age, and die. Governments of small countries collapse and the hole in the ozone opens a little wider while Bennie is in the bathroom and when he finally returns, the couch is empty. But there is a note on his coat:

Had to go for my appointment.
I hope you feel better and
they don't kill you.
—Elizabeth

351-4823

"Hey you!" The shrew behind the counter points to him. "Are you Benjamin Singer?"

"Yes . . ."

"Oops. You shouldn't have left. They called your name. You'll have to wait some more. Hope you don't mind."

Bennie smiles. "Not at all."

"Next time, don't leave the waiting area. We have a procedure."

And Bennie doesn't even blink.

HE CALLED HER later that day. He'd been rehearsing his message for an hour (please have an answering machine, please have an answering machine . . .), and he is now pretty sure he has just the right combination of charm and ingratiating awkward spontaneity. "Elizabeth, this is Ben Singer. The guy with the fleeing highlighters. I seem to have survived Health Services and wonder if you'd like to get some coffee with me to celebrate. Next week maybe. As soon as I recover from the Black Plague. Give me a call."

After he hung up, he thought of a thousand other things that he could have said. Should have said. Jokes to make. Flattery. Declarations of love.

Oh, and (Idiot!) he could have left his phone number.

It didn't matter. They would be engaged one year later.

"MOM," BENNIE SAYS into the phone. "Mom, I met this girl. She's magnifique! She'd be so nice to come home to! She does some-thing to me! I've got her under my skin! She is my life-to-be, my dream come true, she's the rose, she's Inferno's Dante, she's the nose on the great Durante!"

"Is she, now?" Madeline asks. There is a small silence.

AS IT IS with most Jewish–Irish Catholic weddings, the planning process for the Singer–McCourt union proved a little complicated. Bennie and Lizzie had planned a compromise. A celebration of heritage. Two religions, side by side. Honor both faiths. Honor both families. Come together, everyone!

Then, in the months before the wedding, a few individuals who by all reports had previously been entirely sane began to manifest bizarre behavior. Fat Uncle Isaac for one. When he heard about the engagement, he called up Madeline to find out what synagogue the girl belonged to. Wise Madeline broke the news to him gently. Bennie never had proof, but it was reported that in this conver-sation Fat Uncle Isaac said, among other things, "Oh, Madeline, what would Mother say if she were alive?!" and, "What is that son of yours going to do at the ceremony, chomp on a wafer?"

And no one can say for sure, but it was rumored that while

Lizzie was explaining the ceremony they had crafted to her parents, Mrs. McCourt fingered her crucifix and screeched, "What then, are we all going to sing 'Sunrise, Sunset'?"

Bennie and Lizzie had an emergency meeting behind closed doors. They came to a quick decision. They jettisoned the rabbi, the priest, and organized religion all together, and said their wedding vows to a judge in a vine-covered gazebo in the park.

In the gazebo, Bennie-in-Tux turned to Lizzie-in-White, slipped a ring on her finger, and said, "Beloved Elizabeth, since I met you I must look upon my life as blessed. I cannot regret a single thing I have ever done because every step in my life took me to the point where I first saw you. I promise you on this day to spend the rest of my life trying to give you what you have given me: a life without regret."

And then, Bennie was crying, Lizzie-in-White was crying, the McCourts were crying, Madeline was crying, Uncle Isaac was crying, rings slid down arched fingers, and Benjamin Singer and Elizabeth McCourt were pronounced husband and wife.

Fat Uncle Isaac even gave Mrs. McCourt a wet kiss on the cheek.

BY HER SEVENTH month, Lizzie was ready to pop. Despite Dr. Bende's assurances to the contrary, she and Bennie were positive that Lizzie must be pregnant with either nanotuplets or a baby rhinoceros. Despite the fact that she had to go to the bathroom roughly every three minutes, water never seemed to truly leave her body. Her hands had puffed out to twice their normal size. Her ankles swelled to the tops of her thighs. When she moved, Bennie thought he could distinctly hear the glub glub of water sloshing around. Or so he told Lizzie, who punched him.

There was an ocean inside Lizzie. If she sprung a leak, Lizzie would spout a second Niagara Falls. Or at least Old Faithful. "We'll charge admission. Honeymooners will flock," Bennie would say, kissing her earlobe. "You'll be a national treasure. People will send postcards from you. 'Wish you were here. The falls are amazing!' "

Lizzie's five-foot-two-and-a-half-inch frame found itself a little strained by the entire experience. Dr. Bende gave her orders and as a result Lizzie was to rest. So she spent most of her time sitting on the couch in the den, either studying the women's magazines that Bennie brought home faithfully from the college bookstore (for there would be no Davis and Dean store in Clarence for several more years) or just flipping the channels on the television. Three days of that and Bennie put the call in for cable service on Lizzie's behalf. Fortunately, this was all right in Lizzie's field of study.

"I'm doing research!" she grinned, raising the remote control triumphantly. "Think of all I am learning. Mansfield should give me a grant. They'll be sure to hire me now!" (Part of the Ben and Liz Singer Master Plan had it so Lizzie would teach at Mansfield's brand new Contemporary Studies department in a few years after the child, Sophia Madeline or Brian Joseph, had grown old enough for day care. Needless to say, Bennie was already starting to make the chair aware of the scholar in his midst. They had, in fact, planned to have a dinner one night during which Elizabeth McCourt Singer, Ph.D., would surely dazzle Professor Ian Zahansky with her wit, charm, and dedication, but Lizzie wanted to postpone any demands on her wit and charm at least until she had deflated.)

And then President George Herbert Walker Bush drew a line in the sand, and Lizzie turned all of her attention to CNN. Bennie came home one night and Lizzie waved the remote control in his general direction shouting, "This is bullshit. Bullshit! It's like a video game."

Bennie stood in the doorway and laughed. "Hi honey, I'm home!"

She turned to face him, her green eyes aflame. "The press is rolling over and playing dead. 'Press Censorship! Sure! We'll take it. Thank you sir, may I have another?' "

"Lizzie . . ."

"Do you know what it is? It's Vietnam. The press and the public want to alleviate their guilt. They're exorcising demons. They're trying to rewrite cultural memory."

"Lizzie . . ."

"Now, no one will ever accuse the media of losing another war, not in America, nosiree!"

"Lizzie!"

"What!?"

"I brought you a *Glamour*. The new ones came out today." Lizzie put the remote control down and leaned back on the over-stuffed couch and said humbly, "Thank you, sweetie."

Bennie smiled. Lizzie was wearing gray sweatpants and a massive flannel shirt. She hadn't bathed in two days and her hair was stringy and limp. Her stomach sat in front of her like a separate sentient being.

"This issue looks pretty good," he said. " 'Three Nights to Better Orgasm.' 'Ten Ways to Tell if Your Man Is Cheating.' I hope you don't mind, but I read that one in the car."

"Cheater. Did you take the quiz already too?"

"Yes, actually. Apparently I am too preoccupied with the shape of my thighs," Bennie said as he went to sit down next to his wife. He kissed her on the forehead and stroked her hair and they sat in silence for a while watching the explosions of light over the Iraqi night sky.

"Sweetie?"

"Yes?" Bennie said.

"Can you rub my feet?" Lizzie turned around and thrust a bare foot into his lap as she gave him her best plaintive look.

He appraised the foot for a moment or two, put it in his hands, and let the foot fall into his lap as he gasped, "Man, this thing is HUGE!"

Lizzie kicked him.

THEY GET IN the car and strap Sophie into her child's seat and Bennie turns left and they stop for ice cream on the way home and then go to bed, Lizzie in Bennie's arms. He whispers into her ear, night after night: *I'm a worthless check, a total wreck, a flop. But if baby, I'm the bottom, you're the top.* He buries his nose in her hair and breathes in.

TODD HAS BEEN working in the lab all day. He has made a discovery. Professor Singer still isn't in his office. He's been sick, the department secretary says. Todd cannot forget the urgency in Bennie's voice. Professor Singer will not mind. He will want to know. A couple of quick phone calls and a little bit of charm and Todd has the Singers' home address. He gets in the car and heads to Grant Street, leaving his scarf behind in the lab.

Neither the driveway nor the walkway of the Singers' red brick house has been shoveled—though, for that matter, Todd has noticed most of the houses in Clarence look like this right now. Todd's sneakers become soaked through as he makes his way up the sidewalk and chunks of snow stick to the cuffs of his pants and creep under the elastic of his socks. He gets to the porch, stomps his feet, rings the doorbell of the little house, and proceeds to wait. And wait. His breath seems to freeze in front of his face. His nostrils are congealing together. Finally, he hears footsteps. The door opens slightly and Todd looks down to see the form of a little girl who peers out of the half-opened door. Todd recognizes her from the photographs. How old is she? She looks like she's only seven or eight, but her blue eyes seem to contain memories of lost civilizations. And her name?

"Hi! You must be Sophie. . . ." He smiles and crouches down a little bit. The little girl frowns and closes the door a little more in front of her—she clearly was expecting someone else. Someone her height. Todd tries to lean in a little bit to get some of the warmth of the house on his face. "I'm sorry. My name is Todd. Todd Lewis. I'm a student of your father's. Or might be. Next semester—" Sophie pushes the door closed a little more. "Wait! Can I come in?"

Sophie opens the door just enough to stare directly into his eyes. "What, do you want to offer me candy, too? I am a nine-year-old girl. Do you think I am going to let a strange man in the house because he says he knows my daddy?"

"No, of course not!" Children are pure logicians, he forgets. Too bad they have to grow out of it. "Listen, is he home? I stopped by his office. Can you just tell him I'm here and I need to talk to him? It's really important."

"Dad isn't feeling well. He's in-dis-posed today." The door swings closed again.

"Please. Sophie. I might know how to make your dad feel better. Just tell him I'm here. Todd. Todd Lewis." If he stays out in the cold one more minute his nasal passages are going to freeze shut. His ankles are burning.

The girl chews on her lower lip and stares at Todd for a minute. "All right."

He motions to follow her and she whips her head around and purses her lips. "Wait there!"

"Right. Waiting here. Sorry." She turns her back and heads into the house and he calls after her, "Thank you!"

Todd crouches down on the front stoop and rubs his hands together. Mittens. He needs mittens. How long does frostbite take to set in? If his fingers fall off, can they be sewn back on? What if his mouth and his nose freeze shut? Crouching is a bad idea. He jumps up and bounces on his toes. Still there. For now. Todd is beginning to have empathy for ice. Boots. Soon he will buy boots. And a hat. A hat with a little pompom on the top. Hell, he'll buy snowpants if he has to—

The door creaks open. Sophie eyes him suspiciously. "Todd?"

"Hi!" He would sigh with relief if his lungs hadn't frozen solid.

"Dad says you can come in."

Todd bursts in the doorway. "Thank you. Thank you."

"Take off your shoes here."

"Of course."

"And maybe you should knock off all that snow."

"Sure thing." He does. She watches. When she is satisfied she nods and makes room for him to pass.

"May I take your coat?"

"Why yes, thank you."

Sophie grabs his jacket away from him and hangs it up carefully in a closet in the front hallway. She has to stand on a little stool to reach the hangers. (This gives him time to snoop a little; he has always loved to go to professors' homes. He imagines future students coming to his house, looking around, assessing the furniture, studying his book collection, evaluating the standard of living, appraising the value of everything—and making assumptions about salary and calculating that number against their own standards.) Bennie's house is charming. Quaint. The small front hallway, the low ceiling, and the delicate yellow wallpaper speak of the house's age. Victorian. A classic. This is exactly what he wants when he is a young professor. Though when he gets older and moves up in the department he'll need to have something a little fancier, with gaping fireplaces and lots of Oriental rugs and dark woodwork. Maybe red leather and a billiard table too. And a chandelier.

"Todd?" Sophie taps her foot impatiently. "This way. My dad's room is upstairs."

"Sorry. Coming." Sophie leads him through the hallway into a little dining room and to a small staircase. Sophie holds on to the rickety light blue railing and leads him up to the second floor. The hallway is painted the same light blue as the staircase, with a cream-colored rug spanning the space of the corridor. On the walls are countless pictures of Sophie and a few framed book jackets with author shots that span decades of fashion. Todd looks more closely.

"Hey, Madeline Singer. She's related to you?"

"She's my gramma. She's in the guest room. She's in-disposed, too. You can't talk to her."

"No . . . I just . . . She's supposed to be a really good writer."

"Have you read any of these?"

"Uh . . . no. But my fiancée has."

Sophie shakes her head and leads him down the hallway. Outside the last door, Sophie stops him and whispers loudly, "Now, don't keep him up. He has a headache."

Todd laughs. "Sure."

"I'm serious. Do you swear?"

"I swear."

"Okay. I'm going to come get you in five minutes." Sophie looks at him reproachfully then taps on the door. "Daddy! Todd's here. Are you sure you want to see him?"

"Let him in, Soph. It's all right."

Sophie pushes the door of the bedroom open. Professor Singer—Bennie—sits upright in bed wearing blue pajamas. (They must have been a present, Todd thinks. No man under the age of fifty wears pajamas unless they were a present. He, personally, sleeps in his boxers and maybe a T-shirt.) The room is a disaster. There are shoe boxes filled to the brim full of photographs, more photos on the bed, turned-over boxes of papers, letters everywhere, and, oddly enough, a huge stack of women's magazines seemingly from the '80s. Todd will not ask. Bennie grins congenially.

"I see you got through the front guard."

"Yes," Todd smiles. "She has a good career ahead of her in the Secret Service."

"Listen, Todd, I'm sorry about the state of things. I've just been . . . uh . . . reminiscing."

"Well, of course . . ." Todd nods and tries not to stare at the very unprofessorial mess. He does not know what to do with himself . . . should he sit in the chair? Should he stand by the bed? He finds himself standing near the doorway, which makes him look very much like he doesn't want to be there.

"And my outfit," Bennie says. "I wasn't expecting company."

"They're nice pajamas."

Bennie shrugs. "My mother got these for me. She's staying here, so—"

"No, they look comfortable."

Todd and Bennie smile brightly at each other while the dust on the old photographs settles. They both exhale at the same time.

"So. Todd. What can I do for you?"

"Well, um." Todd takes a step forward. "How are you feeling?"

"I'm all right. You?"

"I'm getting it a little bit. Not too bad. My fiancée, though . . . She's, uh, she's getting it hard."

"Oh. That's too bad. Are things going to be all right?"

"Well . . ." Todd shrugs. "We'll see."

"Let me know if I can do anything. . . ."

"Oh, no, that's very nice. This'll blow over." (I hope, he thinks, picturing the empty bed at home.) "Listen"—he steps forward again—"I've been doing some research at the lab. With the deletrium. I've been doing what you told me. I don't have a cure, but I think we don't need one."

Bennie looks at Todd carefully. "What do you mean?"

"Well, it is definitely activating the memory retrieval system, but I really think it will go away. The effects can't last. I mean, when it's in a drug the effects go out of your system in a day or two. Of course, the dosage is a lot greater here, but I think it will work its way out of everybody's systems pretty soon." Todd smiles comfortingly at Bennie and tries not to draw attention to the fact that he has noticed all the pictures on the bed are of one woman.

Something passes through Bennie's eyes that Todd cannot quite place. Bennie opens his mouth and inhales, then quickly shuts it again. He looks down at his lap and breathes in. He looks up at Todd, and Todd would swear the man's eyes were filling. Bennie smiles tightly and says, "Yes, yes, I've heard that, but—"

"What?" This is not what Todd has been expecting. Bennie's spine seems to collapse before his eyes and all attempt at dignity flies away. He is broken, his eyes spill over, his shoulders are hunched, and he lifts his head up and his eyes plead.

"Please." Bennie's voice is very soft. "It can't go away."

"Wha—?"

"You have to find a way to stop it. I don't want to lose it. Please."

Bennie's voice grows louder and more urgent. Todd finds himself beginning to back away.

"I'm sorry, I don't understand."

"The memories aren't tainted anymore. They're whole." Bennie catches himself. "No, they aren't even memories. I have her back. I got past . . . it, and found her again. Please. It can't go away. I have her back." Bennie shakes and shakes.

Todd is standing in the doorway now, stuttering. Bennie closes his eyes. He breathes in. He remembers now. He remembers. Lizzie's hair smells like cherry wood.

fourteen.

Let's go, Todd.

SOPHIE APPEARS IN the doorway where Todd is searching frantically for words, meanings, or convenient gaping holes in the floor.

"Come on, Todd. Let's let my dad rest." Sophie opens the door wide and steps behind it. Bennie looks down at the bed. "Dad, do you need anything?" Bennie bites his lip and smiles at Sophie. "No, sweetie. I'll be okay."

The little girl surveys him up and down. Todd can't tell whether or not she notices his red eyes. "All right, Daddy. You take a nap. Let's go, Todd." Todd is glad somebody is in control at least. He nods at Bennie and follows the girl out the door. She shuts it behind them very carefully, leads Todd down the stairs, and hands him his coat.

She shakes her head and clucks her tongue like a midget matriarch and lets out a heavy sigh. "He's been under the weather for a few days now," she confides.

Todd squats down to her level and says, "Listen, Sophie, your dad is going to be okay."

She nods slowly. "Well. We do the best we can."

"What about you? Are you feeling all right?"

"Me? I'm fine."

"And your friends. Is anyone feeling like your dad is? Is anyone sick?"

"Well . . ." She leans in and whispers conspiratorially. "Christine had a hissy fit recently, but I think she's okay now."

"A what?"

"A hissy fit. That's what Jimmy says anyway, and he would know because he saw it. I think she's better though because she looked fine in school yesterday. But she's not really my friend anymore anyway."

Todd smiles. "Who's Jimmy? Is he your boyfriend?"

Sophie gives him a supercilious eyebrow-raise and exhales. "You'd better go now, Todd." She opens the front door. Cold air bursts in and storms the front hallway. Todd straightens up, smiles awkwardly, and heads out the door.

He sits in his car and turns the heat on full force. The key is in the ignition but he can't seem to find the will to move out of park and put his foot to the gas. So he sits. And looks. White stretches across everything, as if someone has thrown a sheet over the world and abandoned it for an indefinite period of time.

Todd has been putting on a good show. He has always believed that knowing the cause of an ailment helps one suppress that ailment. That what makes any physical or mental illness unbearable is its nebulous nature; without clear cause and strict definition, one can only wonder where it will lead. The most weakening part of any illness is the sinking fear that it will never go away, that it will slowly consume you, and that it is simply the last road marker on the inevitable path toward death.

But knowing the cause means science has conquered the disease. Man is greater than his body. I have been feeling down. But no matter, you say. There is something wrong with the chemicals in my brain. Pretty soon it will go away and I will be a functioning member of society again, able to enjoy food, work long hours, and perform sexually.

Pain is like that, too. We don't cry from shots anymore because we can understand the pain, we know it will stop. (Of course, when we are little, we cry not so much from the pain as from disillusionment. How can such discomfort happen in a caring, nurturing world? This is before we realize that the world is not caring at all, a step Todd hopes to take his kids through early enough so they will not remember the shock.) What is painful is the interminable. Not knowing a cause and not knowing if it will stop.

So, too, Todd has felt his mind wander off yet can tell himself, No, that is the deletrium talking. There are chemicals running amok in my brain. Memories are being triggered. Understandably, the weight of life's experience would make anyone feel under the weather. But it is just chemicals. Concentrate. Mind over matter. Because I know what the matter is. So to speak.

And Professor Singer, well, he hadn't been in his office this week. Todd had thought perhaps that as a psychology professor he, too, could put mind over matter and the two of them together could work on the people of the town . . . and then maybe they would co-author a paper. (How would that look on his curriculum vitae, eh?)

It doesn't seem to have worked.

Instead, Todd saw primordial desperation grow in a man's eyes, an assured demeanor crumble and fall, and scattered pictures of an absent (dead, he must assume) wife stare pointedly at him from the distance of the past. Todd's mind whirls.

Matter takes charge.

Everything reminds Todd of something. The cold grabs hold of his mind and cycles back to every time in his life he has become aware of the hair in his nostrils. Snowballs smacking his friends on the playground. Waiting at the school bus stop without his scarf. That day in hockey. Trudging to the lab across campus.

And then something else fires. The image changes. Sitting in the car with the ignition running he is struck with a sudden and inescapable fear of death. Throat-closing terror. Ribs tightening against his heart. And he remembers: This used to happen when he was a kid. He had read about somebody dying of carbon monoxide poisoning in a book somewhere. He had had nightmares all night. For a year he always made his mother and father shut off the car the instant, the very instant, they parked somewhere. He made them promise they would do it when he wasn't there to watch them. He reminded them of their promise every week or so. He lived in fear that they would forget and one day die slowly, unconsciously, ignition running, no one there to crack open the windows and save them from helpless, meaningless death.

Todd, he tells himself. You are remembering. The memory has triggered an irrational fear. Not unlike someone with a fear of flying or an aversion to organized religion, you are reexperiencing a trauma of your youth that is causing a very real physical reaction. But you are in no danger.

Breathe. Breathe.

He inhales deeply and closes his eyes and feels his chest slowly return to normal.

There. You see?

(If he could only do this for Susannah . . .)

Everything has an association. Snow. Songs on the radio. Sensations against the skin. Association upon association activates the past, attaches to his consciousness, and grows like that much fungus. A word sends his brain spiraling back to an old spelling bee or a drunken late-night philosophy summit or an amorous whisper, and here in the present, ignition running and body perfectly still, he registers shock at what still lingers in the back closets of his mind.

Why is that still there? Why was that significant? What am I to learn from this? What does it mean?

It's déjà vu in reverse, and the mind tumbles and twists trying to understand why it has held on to that specific moment. Like a student trying to analyze a passage of literature, Todd scours each memory for clues. He remembers climbing a jungle gym with his friend Ernie. Todd remembers nothing else about the moment, how old they were, and in fact can barely remember Ernie himself who for all he knows could be dead right now, but he remembers the moment. Climbing.

His game, his award-winning interactive art project, he realizes now, is bullshit—no matter how nice it looks on his c.v. It is too clean. Too easy. A neuron hits its target or doesn't. We remember or we don't. We misremember or we don't. But what are the causes? What makes the damn thing fire in the first place? Why do we remember what we remember and, most important, why do we forget? And what is the effect? His game assumes the memory is good, you remember, you hit the target, you rack up points, you win. But now Susannah is remembering, Professor Singer is remembering, the whole town is remembering, and there is nothing but loss.

Susannah has left him. Temporarily, he hopes, but she is gone. She has been at that old folks' home for two weeks and he has not heard from her. If she were another girl, he would think she wanted him to come get her, wanted him to call, to send flowers, to write letters proclaiming his undying love. But she is not another girl, she is Susannah, and she probably left because she wants to be alone.

He wishes he knew what her mind is doing to her. Does she even understand? What must she be thinking?

Does she know he is thinking it, too?

He is on unfamiliar ground here, and the one thing that Todd hates is unfamiliar ground. But this is someone else's experiment, somebody else's controlled environment, and he is just an unwitting test subject. He knows suddenly how the characters in movies must feel. Like a volcano or earthquake or meteor or killer virus movie, someone has manufactured a very silly plot device just to make his Susannah leave him.

Why the hell is everyone calling it "The Spill" anyway? Nothing spilled. Vapor doesn't spill, it leaks.

The whole experience makes him want to empty out his savings account, use all of the money to buy clay, then work seven sleepless nights on some sculpture. When he is done he will take a gigantic sledgehammer to the work until all that is left is a flattened lump of clay, which he will then proceed to lie on, and will stay there for about thirty more years. He may in fact even die that way, his body sprawled in the eternal slumber across this flattened clay lump, with a placard on the wall reading, FORGIVE AND FORGET? He would end up in some progressively-minded art museum somewhere, where his corpse would gradually decay and the work would only grow more and more profound as more and more of his flesh rotted away.

Todd, you see, made a mistake, one that he is not entirely sure Susannah ever forgave him for. And surprisingly enough, it had nothing to do with girls. The mistake was not entirely his fault. It's just that, while he was getting to know Susannah, he thought one thing about her general way of being and orderliness, and was not quite prepared for an entirely different thing. The other thing took him a little bit back, and suddenly he was faced with his own shocking inability to cope with anything serious. Todd had rarely faced an inability to do something and was not quite prepared for the experience. Todd was not used to thinking long-term. You see, before he met Susannah, Todd wasn't always the present-hunting family man he is today. For a long time he considered himself an . . . aficionado . . . as it were, whose sensibilities were not attuned to committing to someone no matter what might happen to her when she is eighty. Or thirty-two. Or twenty-two.

Breasts. God's most wonderful creation. The only indisputable proof of a benevolent higher being in the world. Breasts. Like snowflakes. No two are alike. Each pair, so lovely. The adjectives used, so insufficient. Pert. Perky. Supple. Shapely. Satiny. Mountainous. Voluptuous. Luscious. Welcoming. Inviting. Calling his name. Todd, Todd. Breasts could be all these things, yes, but so much more; each one a carefully constructed intricate sonnet that must be studied assiduously to be fully appreciated.

Todd's mind explores avenues he didn't know existed and everywhere he turns he runs into the ghosts of past lovers. They are seated in cars stopped at traffic lights, they are riding double-seated bicycles wearing tight pants, they are waiting for buses, they are reading on benches, they are walking basset hounds across the street.

When Todd met Susannah, he was working as a physics tutor. He tutored a lot of girls at the time. His friends laughed and laughed. "You eat freshmen girls like candy." And in a way it was true. Juicy, sumptuous, voluptuous candy. Oh, but he savored each one. He was up front. *You, candy, and I, will have a short-term relationship. But it will be sweet, I promise. What do you think?* And none of the candy ever complained. In fact, they didn't seem to mind one bit.

It wouldn't be true to say that the first time he saw Susannah he felt . . . differently. That would do disservice to all those other lovely women. It wouldn't be true, exactly, though he has certainly told Susannah so. He adored her like he adored them all. He would explain a problem to her and she would play with her hair, like a child, twirling those complex curls around her fingers, it was so sweet the way she would do that. Those curls were physics problems in themselves. He wanted to dive in and solve them.

He didn't feel differently about her right away, by any means, but after they had drinks in the usual way and he explained to her his laissez-faire style of candy consumption she blushed again, cocked her head, tossed her mane, and said rather earnestly, "No. But thank you."

This had never happened to him before.

"I'm sorry, I hope I haven't offended you?"

"Not at all. It's just not my style." And she smiled brightly, paid for her gin and tonic, and left.

Style. He had never met a woman who had style before. The idea intrigued him. She intrigued him. She came back for extra help that week and he was very, very intrigued. They worked through equations together and he fantasized about diving into her hair and swimming around until he found scalp.

And then something happened. He doesn't know how, but he remembers being with her one day, and his sense of purpose somehow altering. It wasn't that the other girls weren't pretty, but he wanted Susannah. And it became very clear, very quickly, that both things were not an option, and he made his choice.

"Susannah? I love you."

Susannah had something no one else did. He had believed once upon a time that girls were acolytes of chaos. Susannah proved him wrong. She worshiped only order, she had things in glass cases that she carried with her. She had style, she had sweetness and light—he knew a lot of premeds, but none of the rest of them wanted to be a doctor because they actually wanted to care for the sick—and he realized that he wanted not only to throw her down on his bed and nuzzle her breasts for seven or eight hours on end, but he also wanted to pop popcorn and snuggle on the couch and watch an old Ingrid Bergman movie with her. And that, as sure as the world is round, is love.

The funny thing was, she would never introduce him to her family.

She had met his, of course. His mother loved her instantly—how could you not, all corkscrewy hair and blushing eyes? "Don't lose this one, Todd," she said. His dad beamed every time he saw her, bonked her on the head, and called her Sport.

They had been together a year and a half, and Todd was just beginning to think, I can do this. Love has changed me. I can do this and I can keep doing this, because doing this means being with Susannah and she is sweetness and light, and maybe we will get married, and we will be Dr. and Dr. Lewis. Or she can keep her name, I don't have a problem with that, the point is I can do this—

And then the order fell away.

Susannah got a phone call.

"Todd, Todd, I have to go home."

"Why, what is it?"

"It's my mother," she says so flatly. "She is sick."

"What's wrong? What happened? Let me come with you—"

"Um, I'm sorry, no, no."

He couldn't even be mad at her for keeping it from him. She was afraid he would act badly, and that he did.

"What's the number? Let me call you."

"I'll call you."

Susannah leaves and something happens to Todd. He is alone and he is afraid and he thinks, What is this strange thing that I am feeling?

A week later, he calls information and gets Susannah's home number. "What happened? Is everything okay? I've been worried sick. When are you coming back?"

And she says, "I have to tell you something."

And he says, "What? What is it?"

"I haven't told you something. But you need to know now." And there is some stammering and then Todd's heart plunges somewhere into his stomach and his intestines begin to wrap around it like snakes and squeeze. And Susannah stammers some more and says, *I have not told you, because, my family, well, we stick close, you see. I have not told you out of respect for my mother's wishes. I have not told you because we think it is no one else's business. I have not told you because I did not know how to bring it up. I have not told you because I was scared of what you would do. I have not told you, but you need to know now. My mother is very sick. Mentally. She has been very sick since I was seven. She used to be fine, and then she got sick.*

And he thinks, Why didn't you tell me? Susannah, you could have told me. You are so strong. You are so strong. He doesn't notice that something small and prickly has alighted on his shoulder. It begins to whisper in his ear, although he can't quite make out the words. He says, "Zana—"

"And the thing is, last week she tried to kill herself. She has never done that before. She says it has got to be too much for her. She says she had no other choice. She is still in the hospital. They are not going to release her for a while—"

The thing is getting very, very prickly. "Um, Zana—"

"And my father needs me. He cannot do this alone. My sister is too young. I am going to stay here and take care of things in the house. I am going to help him."

"Uh, Zana—"

"I am going to take a leave from school. Just until things settle. My father needs me."

"Zana—"

There is a pause.

"What?"

And then the whispering grows clearer, the prickling has meaning, and he does not say what he intended to say, which is, "I love you, let me come down and help, I will do whatever you want, whatever you need, I will see you through this." Instead, he asks something he had not even known he was thinking. He asks, "Susannah, is it hereditary?"

And there is another pause. It is very long.

Her voice grows very, very heavy. "They don't know. Sometimes."

And then there is this other pause, and Todd's intestines almost succeed in strangling his heart, and Susannah says, "I have to go now."

She hangs up.

And then, the worst part of the whole entire thing is, just when his Susannah hangs up the phone—getting exactly what she expected from him—the defiant click of the receiver startles the nasty prickly thing on his shoulder, and it flies away, leaving Todd very much alone with his own horrible mistake.

Is it hereditary?

Is it hereditary?

Todd hates it when he lives up to his own expectations of being a buffoon. Yes, okay, sure, he is a caricature of a commitment-a-phobe, yes, sure, he has a little, um, problem, yes, sure, Susannah is his first love, yes, sure he is supposed to put his tail between his legs and run in the other direction when things get too heavy, but is he really like that? No, no, no, he is not, and damn all the prickly things in the world, damn them, damn them.

Susannah. Susannah, I am sorry. Susannah, let me help.

Now, here, he is alone again. He wants to see Susannah. He has so much to tell her. I'm sorry, sweetie, you can tell me anything, I love you, I'm sorry, I've been so wrapped up in work, I'm sorry, I've been trying to find you a present for weeks, a Just Because kind of thing, I'm sorry, I make stupid games that are all wrong, I make everything so easy and it is not easy, everything is really, really hard. He spends the afternoon in the study with some clay, pounding and pounding and pounding and muttering to himself, "There is something I am trying to get to."

fifteen.

The broken remnants

SUSANNAH IS STAYING in one of the guest bedrooms in Building A at Sunny Shadows. She has Calvin's cat with her. The cat likes to sleep on Susannah's head.

She has been there over two weeks now. She has not gone home. She has not called Todd. Every time she leaves the grounds, if only to the grocery store, to the laundry service, to the pharmacy, she feels precisely as if someone is peeling off her skin, piece by piece.

Todd does not understand. Todd is made up of order. Todd's life works in theorems and constants and the shortest distance between two points. Susannah's thoughts travel through dimensions science cannot articulate.

She will not take to her bed. There are too many people here that need her—need somebody at least, and this is the only way she can keep her thoughts down. It is not as hard for her, perhaps because her memories are so much like her present.

She knocks on a door, softly.

"Mildred? It's Susannah. Can I come in?"

And Mildred—or whoever—will say faintly, "Yes." Susannah will open the door very slowly, so as not to startle the person inside. She will say, "How are you feeling today?" She will say, "Can I get you some water? I could bring you some food." She will say, "Is there anything I can get for you? I am going to the grocery store later." She will say, "But I have some time now. Do you need some company?"

And Mildred will say, "Thank you, sweetheart."

Susannah has done the same for her mother countless times. Every once in a while, when her mother has one of her breaks, she will take to her bed and will not move or talk for hours. Susannah will come in and grab her hand and sit by her. She never knows if there is any mother in there at those times, but if there is, she wants her to know her daughter is there.

Despite what Todd said on the phone that day, it had never really occurred to Susannah that she might get sick, too. She knew just about everything there was to know about her mother's illness—she had books, journal articles—and through most of her adolescence she wanted to be a psychiatrist and read everything she could. Onset, for most people, is in their early twenties to mid-thirties—later in women than men. This never struck Susannah as anything more than another red-flagged diagnostic criterion in her mother's medical history.

And now, for the first time in Susannah's life, her own mind is taking her down paths she never wanted to go, and Susannah is firmly inside the red flag zone.

If she never comes back from the edge, she could go back home.

Yes, that's right, it would be lovely, she could sit next to her mother and they could compare delusions, talk in word soup, lie catatonic for days, mother and daughter, together again after fifteen long years.

This is not really funny.

Susannah should have known better than to move to a town with a psychopharmaceutical factory. She knows what those things do to you. Her mother twitches, vomits, cries, shakes, faints, sleeps, and Susannah cannot even take aspirin anymore.

Her mother was on a drug for a while with the possible unfortunate side effect that she could lose her white blood cells, so Susannah and Susannah's father would take her to the hospital to get her blood checked every week. Susannah's mother would struggle and scream in the doctor's office because she thought they were trying to take away all of her blood, bit by bit.

Knock, knock. "Matthew? It's Susannah. Can I come in?"

Susannah didn't have a friend over to the house for fifteen years. Before her mother broke, before Susannah helped her pick up the shredded contents of her closet, just a little after her seventh birthday party, her mother stopped letting Susannah have people over. "I don't feel like it, today, Susannah. Another time."

After a time, her father would stand there and stroke his chin and say, "Sharon, I can watch the girls—"

And her mother would shake her head and begin looking off somewhere else.

"Can I get you something to drink? Some water maybe?"

A month after Susannah's seventh birthday, a girl in the city was kidnapped. Betsy. Betsy Benjamin. She had been out riding her bike one afternoon, and then they found the bike, but no Betsy. Her mother told her she could no longer play outside alone. She could no longer walk to school. She could no longer go over and play at her friends' houses because their mothers were not very, very careful with their children. She began coming home from work earlier and earlier. She wasn't sure she trusted Sara's nanny anymore. Because you never know with people. Her father would scratch his chin and say, "I'm sure it's fine, Sharon."

And then she quit her job. She wanted to be there for the girls, she said. She would be at home, certainly, but there was no *there* there.

"Do you need anything? Anything at all?"

Her dad would put Susannah to sleep earlier and earlier every night—stroke her hair and sing her songs and tell her stories—but sometimes she would wake up in the middle of the night with a bad dream or something, and hear her mother pacing back and forth downstairs, watching late-night television, talking to it. Packages started coming in the mail and her mother would smile and say, "Just something I ordered from the TV." Her father would stand there and tap his hand against his chin and send the things back.

And sometimes she would be fine. She took the girls to the zoo and Sara petted a llama and squealed, like she always did, but Susannah was much too old for the petting zoo and told her mom so. Her mom read books, big thick books, and laughed about them with Susannah's father. She liked to cook, until she started to worry about fires. She listened to baseball games and tried to teach Susannah how to play catch.

"Do you want some company? Can I sit here for a little bit?"

And then she would not be fine. They would sit at dinner together and her mother would start laughing all over the duck à l'orange and her father would hold his chin. She stopped leaving the house at all. She never called her friends back, she never spoke to her parents. "I don't feel like it," she would say, again and again, face as uninhabited as her eyes. Susannah would come home from school with an A on her spelling test (*twilight* and *mischief* and *exercise*) and her mother would cry and cry.

"Listen, I'm running some laundry down to the cleaners. What can I bring for you?"

Back when she and Todd were still skipping through the city together, she thought she might be able to get by with him never knowing. Here was a creature of pure normalcy, and Susannah could not believe her luck. He spoke in equations and laws and constants and he kissed Susannah on her forehead and ran his fingers through her hair and said, *Zana Zana Zana Zana Zana.*

She was well aware of his little, um, problem—that titanic struggle against imagining the possibilities of every pair of breasts he sees—and she tucked it away to worry about later. All it meant was she didn't have to tell him about her mother because sooner or later the allure of a lothario lifestyle would be too much, and he would answer the call of the wild, right? Because that is the nature of Todd, right?

How easy. How safe. Love in the present, but no future. It was what they both wanted, right?

A neuron fires and hits its target. The science building. A pencil in her hand. Todd the poet-physicist enveloping her in mahogany eyes. A blush forms, starting at her neck. *Is this how he tutors all the girls? It must be.* Uncomfortable pauses over gravitational constants. A pencil drops, eyes meet, a smile forms.

The answer to her question, of course, is yes. It is how he tutored all the girls. He smiled at all the girls just like that and they all blushed and he had this absolutely overwhelming urge to kiss all of their soft lips.

He assured her later that there was something different about her—something more . . . durable. That as much as he wanted to kiss her soft lips he also wanted to sit on the couch and pop some popcorn and watch an old Humphrey Bogart movie with her. Which, really, must be love.

"All right. I'll stop by again. You think of anything I can do for you, okay?"

"Mom, I don't have to go away to college. I can stay near here. Live at home. If you need. I'd be happy to."

"No. Go. Your father will call you if we need you. Lead a normal life, all right? I want you to go to college and be a perfectly normal girl with a perfectly normal family and I want you to tell all the boys and girls about how you have the most functional mother in the world." And she laughs, just a little.

"I will, Mom. I promise."

In her lucid moments, when the medication is working and the moon is in the second house, Susannah almost has a mother again. Other times, she and her father are trying to rob her mother of her blood, drop by drop, until she is a desiccated thing.

Knock, knock. "Mr. Czarnowski? Charles? It's Susannah Korbet. Can I come in?"

Todd would ask, of course, about her family. What her parents did, and the like. She never lied, per se. After years of putting off friends and inquiring minds, Susannah had become an expert evader. "It's nobody's business but our own," her dad would say. "They do not understand, and we must protect your mother from their ignorance."

In high school English, Susannah reads books and stories and plays about young lads or mysterious women in cloaks who have some psychological problem or other, and there is a noble doctor or psychiatrist or concerned citizen who tries to make them sane again. But soon, the psychiatrist or doctor or concerned citizen learns that the insane person is the only truly free one, and that it is he himself who must be healed.

Charles?

Susannah wrote a paper, once, about mental illness as literary shorthand for a truly free life. She said sanity did not actually equal constraint and insanity was by no means freedom.

Her teacher told her she didn't have an appreciation for metaphor and gave her a B minus.

Charles, are you all right?

She told Todd about this paper once. They were sitting in a Mexican restaurant talking about Todd's English course. The restaurant smelled so strongly of onions Susannah's eyes were watering, and she would not get the smell out of her hair for days, she thought. They never went there again. She told him about the paper and, even then, her voice caught, her stomach clenched a little. But Todd did not notice. Todd thought her paper made some good points, and maybe the teacher had no appreciation for good sense.

Charles. Answer me if you're okay.

Susannah went to a Mexican restaurant with her father and sister, once. She was thirteen and Sara was eight. Her mother was in the hospital for observation for a few days. Her father never explained why, but it was Sara's birthday, and she liked the Mexican restaurant because she liked the word *guacamole,* and the waiters always gave her extra, and it was her first choice for her birthday, but if you asked Susannah she would think that one smelled a lot like onions, too. The Mexican restaurant was right by the hospital, which smelled altogether different. Then, Susannah's aunt Charlie took them home and Susannah's father went back to the hospital to observe her mother, and Aunt Charlie would let them watch all kinds of TV, and then tuck them into bed and Susannah would just lie there, trying to wish the smells away.

Susannah takes her master key and unlocks Charles's door.

Then once, while Susannah was in her dorm room reading about the Black Death creeping into England, and her roommate was painting her toenails with the smelliest kind of toenail paint possible, the phone rang.

"Susannah."

"Dad?"

"I'm sorry. I'm so sorry."

"What is it?"

"We need you at home."

"Dad, what is it—"

She walks through the living room into his bedroom.

Susannah got in the car and drove away, barely glancing at Todd, who would not, could not understand. She drove right to the hospital. She ran in.

"She will be all right," her father says. "Physically I mean. But—"

And then he starts to shake his head, and she wraps her arms around him, and her father, for once, has no comforting words, and he crumples into her. Nurses scurry around them, while they stand there, father and daughter, a monument to all that has been lost.

The bedroom door is shut, and she can hear a rumbling sound.

There is a moment, then, where Todd is at her doorstep. Sara opens the door, and yells up the stairs, "Susannah? There's a boy here to see you."

Susannah runs down to see what she could possibly mean, and then there at her doorstep is Todd, looking very rumply. He says, with a small smile, "You haven't told them about me?"

"Uh . . . no. What are you doing here?"

Susannah is surprised he stayed after that. She is still surprised. She would not have stayed. But he comes in and introduces himself to her father and then later he folds her in his arms and says, "I am so sorry. So sorry." And then he says, "I would like to meet your mother, Susannah. Please."

He is snoring. Charles is snoring.

She expects her father to mind, but he doesn't, and Todd stands by her mother's hospital bedside amongst all kinds of tubes and beeping things. He shakes her hand and sits by her and he says, "I hear Susannah is going to stay at home for some time. I would like to come visit from time to time. Is that all right with you?"

And her mother smiles her old public relations smile and says, "Why, that would be lovely, young man."

And then her mother stopped trying to pull out her IVs and didn't scream at the doctors anymore, and came home.

Charles is snoring. Susannah sits down a moment, so she can put her heart back in place.

Todd went back to school, but he came back and back and back, and her mother would light up and they would get along famously, and Susannah's father would stroke his chin.

It is late. Susannah is tired. She goes to her room and sits down next to Calvin's cat. Kitty kitty kitty.

Within all these memories are countless others, some Mom-less and Todd-less, but most Mom-full. Susannah strokes the cat and neurons fire and fire.

There is a knock at her door. The cat jumps and scurries underneath the bed. Susannah peeks out of the peephole. Nobody is there. She opens the door and looks out into the hallways. She doesn't see anybody. There's a cardboard box on the floor. She bends down. On the top of the box, SUSANNAH is scrawled in heavy black marker. She runs her fingers over the lettering, then picks the box up (It is light. Pieces roll around when she moves it) and goes inside the apartment. She finds a letter opener and undoes the packing tape. She opens the flaps. She takes out tissue paper. At the bottom of the box she sees some marbles, some wooden pieces, broken rubber bands, and shreds of cardboard. She takes each of the pieces out and looks at them carefully. It takes her a few minutes to realize that she has in her hands the broken remnants of Todd's Memory Game.

LATER THAT NIGHT:

Susannah rolls out of bed, and looks inside the box again. Inside she thinks she sees reflections of the paths of her own mind. Susannah picks up the wooden pieces and caresses them. In their splintery shards lie a lifetime of Susannahs. Here she is a woman, here she is a teenager, and in these over here, she is a girl, seven years old again—and in some, some very broken pieces, she is even smaller. Some of the pieces even hold the secrets to Before. She wonders if she can put the pieces together, if maybe her mother— her real mother, her healthy mother, will reemerge.

sixteen.

Michigan, Minnesota, Mississippi

SOPHIE LIES. SHE knows she is not supposed to. But she also knows from her father's example that polite people don't talk about themselves, like when she and her dad are in a store and he runs into someone and they ask how he is, he says he's doing well, even if he told Sophie just moments before that he had a headache or it's too crowded in this blasted store or something. She tries to do things like her father wants her to because he says she is a good girl and he thinks she is the top, the Mona Lisa, the Tower of Pizza.

Sophie lies. Not habitually, but sometimes you have to, little white lies, Gramma calls them, like when that Todd man asked her some questions and she didn't know the answers but she does know that she isn't feeling exactly right on if you want to know the truth. Sophie likes to think about things, it's true, she thinks about things all the time, like during class when she is supposed to be thinking about math she is instead thinking about Christine or her dad or Gramma or something funny that the Glo-bot said or something.

But now Sophie is thinking of more things than she would like to be thinking of on a day-to-day basis. Like at school. Ms. Plum isn't there anymore. Sophie's teacher had been spending much of the school day telling stories about growing up and whining about the expectations of her mom and about how hard it is to be a single woman in a small town. And she'd been mixing up things about, like, explorers and the presidents and state history that even Sophie knows and she's not a teacher or an adult.

Now Sophie has a substitute teacher from another town named Mrs. Olsen and the teacher looks at the class and says, "Where are your heads, children?" And then someone will run out crying or something. Someone runs out crying just about every day, even some of the boys, and the boys aren't supposed to cry or Brad hits them. The Minister of Doom hasn't been at school for three whole days. Nobody wants to play anything at recess. Sophie doesn't want to play anything, especially, all she wants to do is hang out inside the fort and not say anything, except that's where Jimmy is, and he doesn't really seem to want to talk to anybody either.

The point is, Sophie is used to a certain amount of mind-wandering, which her father says is normal and healthy, but now it is like she is watching all these TV shows she has already seen, except the TV show is her life and she cannot turn it off. But she is not really excited about the idea of letting this on to the world, because usually in books when people start talking about their brain going all funny, people don't really understand and they end up sending a mob after you. Not that any kind of mob is going to be coming after Sophie, but you know what she means.

So Sophie is just sitting there, trying to learn the word of the week or taking a multiplication test or something, and then suddenly she looks at the word or the number, like *eight* or *elephant*, and she starts thinking about everything in her life about elephants, like whenever she's read about them or when she wanted to go to the circus with her dad or when she tried to teach her stuffed elephant Fluffy how to play "When the Saints Go Marching In" on the piano.

Your mind is a lot like your closet. You try to hang up your clothes well and line up your shoes like little soldiers and keep your toys from tipping over, but sometimes you just can't keep it all organized. Sophie, for instance, used to tell her father that she didn't know how to hang up her clothes when really she did, but really, it is so much easier to have your father show you than to do it yourself. She is nine now, and too much of a grown-up for that, but that doesn't mean everything always gets hung up just so. So sometimes the clothes end up on the floor of the closet, along with some toys and stuff, and after a time you don't know what's in there, and then you start putting the things you don't want to see anymore in that pile, like those shoes that Fat Great-Uncle Isaac gave you.

The point is, when you are taught something in school and you are supposed to memorize it, like the state capitals or something like that, it's like a really nice toy or dress or something that you put into your closet. If you don't keep peeking the toy or dress could fall down and end up in that really big pile on the floor that keeps growing and growing, and who only knows what's in there. So one day if you start cleaning it out you say, "Look, there are the multiplication tables!" and "Look, there's Charlotte's phone number!" and "Look, there is that day with Gramma!" But the more time you go without cleaning out your closet the more everything gets buried. Now, say there's a monster in your closet. (Sophie is well beyond the age of believing in monsters but if there were any, the bottom of the closet underneath all the clothes would be the place they would want to hide.) He lives underneath all the clothes and toys and Uncle Isaac shoes and multiplication tables, and the more stuff you pile on top of him, the more you can pretend he is not there. But the monster is there and sometimes he moves around and you have to smile brightly and say, "Look, my pile of clothes is moving," and pretend there is no monster even though you know perfectly well that there is. And then the monster jumps up and scares you and scatters all the toys and clothes you have outgrown or don't like or just want to forget ever existed all over your room.

This is a lot like what's happening in Sophie's head now, except that there are a thousand closets with one thousand monsters and they all keep jumping way up in the air and scattering things everywhere and all she can do is shake her head and say, "Oh I forgot all about those shoes that Fat Great-Uncle Isaac got me."

Sophie doesn't like it. Not one bit.

WHEN SUSANNAH KORBET was five, her mother began to get fat. Her tummy kept getting bigger and bigger and that was because there was a baby inside. This is because her mom and dad loved each other very much, and so they made a baby, just like they did with her. Susannah liked to go up to her mother's tummy and poke it, just slightly, and say, "Hi, baby, baby, baby, baby," just to make sure it was still there. Her mother would say, "Now Susannah, be careful, don't poke the baby." And then her mother got bigger and bigger and stopped going to her job where she did public re-lations, and Susannah would stick her mouth against her mother's belly button and say, "Hello, baby baby baby are you going to come out now?"

And Susannah's mother would laugh and stroke her daughter's red-brown hair and say, "You will help me take care of her, Susannah. You will bring up the baby with me. You will be the best older sister ever. She will be so lucky."

Susannah's father gave her the Very Important Job of keeping her mother company while she was in bed. So Susannah brought her dolls in and told her mother stories and read her books—well, her mother mostly read them, and sometimes she fell asleep next to her mom's big tummy, and her father and mother both agreed that she was performing her Very Important Job excellently.

And her mother said, "You are not worried, are you? That things will change? It will be different, but that will never change how much I love you. You know that I will always love you, no matter what? I will always take care of you. Nothing can change that, my Susannah, my precious, my little baby girl."

ONE DAY, WHEN Susannah was six, she left kindergarten crying. Her mother took her hand and led her to the car, and stroked her cheek and said, "Baby, what's wrong? What happened? My Susannah, my little girl." Susannah had been playing with the clay. Her teacher was named Mr. James and Mr. James was a bull-size man. He stared at her, nostrils flaring, eyes red, he pawed his foot against the ground one two three, he snorted and started to run at her, bellowing, *Susannah Korbet!* She hadn't done anything, anything, she was just playing with the clay, she didn't know. She hated him, he was scary, he made all the kids cry.

Susannah's mom took her home. She sat down on the big flowered chair and put Susannah on her lap. "He sounds awful, awful, baby. No one should yell at you like that. No one." And when Susannah stopped crying, finally, and had wiped her eyes and her nose sufficiently on her mom's shirt, her mom took her hand and said, "Come on. Let's play." They went into her parents' room.

She got to go through her mom's closet and play with all kinds of things. She put on her mom's perfume and her mom put lipstick on her. Susannah put lipstick on her mom. And then her mom took down a box and her voice got all whispery. "I am going to show you something. I am saving this for you, Susannah. These were mine, and they were my mother's too. You are not quite old enough, but when you are, I will give them to you. Now, shhhhh, shhhhh, Susannah my girl, Susannah my sweet, my baby, my little girl."

WHEN SUSANNAH KORBET was just seven, on her seventh birthday, in fact, as they were putting up pink streamers and blowing up silver balloons, her mother took her aside and whispered, "I have something special for you." Her father smiled and said, "You girls go ahead. I'll finish setting up."

It was a special occasion, because you don't turn seven just every day, so her mother was wearing Susannah's favorite shirt—that silvery, shimmery, shiny shirt. Someday, when Susannah has been very, very good for a very long time, she will ask her mother if she can wear it—of course she is much smaller than her mother, but she could wear it like a dress, roll up the sleeves, put a belt around it, and then she would have the prettiest, silveriest, shimmeriest, shiniest dress in all of school.

But Susannah knew she was not old enough for that yet, even though she was seven, and besides her mother was wearing the shirt now, and she looked like an angel and she smelled like lilies of the valley, which were Susannah's favorite flowers. She kissed Susannah on her seven-year-old forehead and twirled her seven-year-old hair around her own thirty-two-year-old fingers and said, "Come here, Suz, I've got a special present for you."

Susannah's eyes popped. "What? What is it?"

Secretly she thought she might know—she thought, she hoped, she wished. Her mom took her by the hand and they shimmered off together to Susannah's room and just outside the bedroom her mom whispered, "Close your eyes!"

And Susannah did, and she took a deep breath in and decided she would hold her breath until she saw her mother's surprise, and her mother laughed like bells. She felt her mom grab her shoulders and steer her toward the wall. Just as Susannah started to exhale, her mother said, "Here you go, sweetie. You are old enough now."

And it was just what Susannah thought, hoped, wished for! On the wall was a shelf filled with miniature things, dollhouse things, beautiful things—a silvery tea set, velvety cushions, a little piano, a mahogany chair, a brass bed, a couch with ball and claw feet, a crib with a little baby with red cheeks and a porcelain face, and even a small little basset hound with bead eyes and felt-y, floppy ears.

Her mom squeezed her shoulders and the lily of the valley smell moved closer. "Your father will put up a glass case for you to keep these nice. If you take good care of them, next year, on your eighth birthday, we'll go out and buy you a nice dollhouse, all right? You and I will go together, and that will be my present to you."

And her mom seemed to shine even more than her shirt and she wrapped her hands in Susannah's hair and said, "Happy birthday, my sweet Susannah, my baby, my little girl."

SOPHIE CAN'T STOP her brain. It keeps going and going and she is thinking of all kinds of things. Some of the things are bad and some of the things are silly and she can't make any of them go away, and everything inside her seems about to burst.

Sophie stands in the hallway. She looks at her father's door. It is closed. She doesn't want to cry in front of him too much. She doesn't want him to think she is a baby. Babies cry. He is not interested in her crying anymore. He must think she is too old. He would be embarrassed by her if she cried. He doesn't want her around right now anyway.

But Sophie cries. She can't help it. Her father's door is closed, now it is always closed—he used to never close it—but Gramma's door is open a crack. But. She steps toward her father's door and touches the knob. She keeps her hand on it and watches it for a while. Then she draws her hand back and goes to the guest room where her grandmother sleeps. Sophie doesn't know why they call it the guest room as they haven't ever had any guests, at least the sleepover kind. Sophie has, of course—Leslie and Christine slept over a couple of times, but they stayed in her room not in the guest room, but they weren't really guests anyway, just friends. Or at least they used to be.

Once when Leslie and Christine slept over they told Sophie, bouncing up and down on their sleeping bags, that Sophie hadn't gone to their school in first grade. They giggled and giggled and insisted that she hadn't been there, but Sophie knew she had been there, hadn't she? And what were they trying to pull anyway? And they laughed and laughed and she kept saying, "Yes I did! Yes I did!" but they wouldn't listen so finally she just stopped talking.

Sophie touches the doorknob of the guest room and it pushes open.

"Gramma?" Sophie can barely hear herself and Dad told her that when that happens she should probably talk a little louder.

"Gramma? Can I come in?"

Sophie stands in the guest room door. Her grandmother is lying down with her back to her. Sophie decides to wait. And to try not to keep thinking about things so much, maybe if she can think about other things—

George Washington, John Adams, Thomas Jefferson, James Monroe, James Madison, John Quincy Adams, Andrew Jackson, Martin Van Buren, William Henry Harrison, um, some guys in the middle, James Buchanan, Abraham Lincoln, Andrew Johnson, Ulysses S. Grant, Rutherford B. Hayes, Garfield, Chester A. Arthur, Grover Cleveland, Benjamin Harrison, Grover Cleveland again, McKinley, Theodore Roosevelt, Taft, Wilson, Coolidge—no—, Coolidge?, Herbert Hoover, Franklin Roosevelt, Truman, Eisenhower, Kennedy, Johnson, Nixon, Ford, Carter—

Martha Dandridge Custis Washington, Abigail Smith Adams, Martha Wayles Skelton Jefferson, Dolley Madison, Elizabeth Kortright Monroe, Louisa Catherine Johnson Adams, um, Mrs. Jackson, Mrs. Van Buren—ohhh . . .

Girls of America: Charity, Anastasia, Emily, Alice, Roberta. First series: Charity, a Girl of America; Charity Makes a Friend; Trouble for Charity; Charity Grows Up. Anastasia, a Girl of America; Anastasia Makes a Friend; Trouble for Anastasia; Anastasia Grows Up. Emily, a Girl of America; Emily Makes a Friend; Trouble for Emily; Emily Grows Up. Alice, a Girl of America; Alice Makes a Friend; Trouble for Alice. Roberta, a Girl of America; Roberta Makes a Friend; Roberta Grows Up.

Alabama, Alaska, Arkansas, no, Arizona, Arkansas, California, Colorado, Connecticut, Delaware, Florida, Georgia, Hawaii, Indiana, Iowa, Kansas, Louisiana, Maine, Massachusetts, Michigan,

*Minnesota, Mississippi, Missouri, Montana, Nebraska, Nevada,
New Hampshire, New Mexico, New York, North Carolina, North
Dakota, South Dakota, South Carolina, Texas, um, Tennessee,
Texas, Vermont, Virginia—wait—*

*One hundred, ninety-nine, ninety-eight, ninety-seven, ninety-six,
ninety-five, ninety-four, ninety-three, ninety-two, ninety-one,
ninety. Eighty-nine, eighty-eight, eighty-seven, eighty-six, eighty-
five, eighty-four, eighty-three, eighty-two, eighty-one, eighty.
Seventy-nine, seventy-eight, seventy-seven, seventy-six, seventy-five,
seventy-four, seventy-three, seventy-two, seventy-one, seventy. Sixty-
nine, sixty-eight, sixty-seven, sixty-six, sixty-five, sixty-four, sixty-
three, sixty-two, sixty-one, sixty. Fifty-nine, fifty-eight, fifty-seven,
fifty-six, fifty-five, fifty-four, fifty-three, fifty-two, fifty-one, fifty.
Forty-nine, forty-eight, forty-seven, forty-six, forty-five, forty-four,
forty-three, forty-two, forty-one, forty. Thirty-nine, thirty-eight,
thirty-seven, thirty-six, thirty-five, thirty-four, thirty-three, thirty-
two, thirty-one, thirty. Twenty-nine, twenty-eight, twenty-seven,
twenty-six, twenty-five, twenty-four, twenty-three, twenty-two,
twenty-one, twenty. Nineteen, eighteen, seventeen, sixteen, fifteen,
fourteen, thirteen, twelve, eleven, ten, nine, eight—*

Twelve, eleven, ten, nine, eight . . .

Eight—

Eight.
When Sophie was eight one night her father stopped reading to
her. He used to read to her every night as long as she could remember and tuck her in and kiss her good night and turn off the
light and then she'd count from one hundred back to one, very
slowly, and then turn on her bedside lamp and pick up another

book and read until she fell asleep. Her light was always off in the morning. (Sometimes she read her picture books under the covers, because she knew her dad wouldn't want her to read them, because those books are for babies and Sophie is big and advanced for her age. But she likes the books. She likes the pictures. They remind her of things.) One night, when she was eight, her dad just said, Well, good night, Sophie, and she had to tuck herself in.

Seven.

When Sophie was seven, she went out one day with Gramma and Dad and they went to the humane society and Sophie named all the dogs their different breeds because she could do that and she said *Can we have a dog?* And her father said *No, I'm sorry, sweetie, we can't take care of a dog,* and then she said *How about a cat? How about that cat over there?* And she pointed to the fluffiest whitest cat in the whole wide world. And her father said *No, sweetie, we can't, I'm sorry, but what kind of dog is that over there?* And then the next day her father came home and said, *Sophie, I have a surprise for you* and he had in his hands a little white puffball, and it was that kitten! the fluffiest whitest kitten in the whole wide world, and Sophie said I will love her forever and ever and ever and name her Eleanor Roosevelt.

Six.

When Sophie was six she started school. She had Mrs. Finn. Mrs. Finn always wore pants and she sang songs to the kids about numbers and Sophie already knew how to count and add and subtract, and Mrs. Finn said, *Sophie Singer, don't show off.*

Five.

When Sophie was five she broke her arm. She was playing in a tree and she couldn't quite reach a branch and she kicked her foot out and she fell very very slowly, like her life was in super slo-mo, and she put her arm out and she landed all funny and her arm was twisted back the way arms aren't supposed to go. Her father was watching her out of the window and came out of the house running and yelling. He kept saying, *I'm sorry, I'm sorry, I should have been more careful, I'm sorry.*

Four.

When Sophie was four she went to play in the playground and there was a girl named Charlotte there and Charlotte was the prettiest little girl Sophie had ever seen and Charlotte had a little brother to play with and Sophie didn't have a little brother so Charlotte said Sophie could have hers so they played all afternoon but then Charlotte and her brother went home and Sophie asked her dad whether or not she could have a little brother and he got very quiet and said, no, no, he didn't think so, and then Sophie started to cry and she screamed *I want a brother! I want a brother! I want a brother!* And her father didn't say anything, anything at all.

Three.

When Sophie was three—

And when she was three—

When Sophie Singer was three . . .

MADELINE HEARS THE voice distantly, a series of high notes behind the rumbling rabble of her thoughts. The notes come together indistinctly, and begin moving up and down in a melody of sniffing. Something within her grabs on to the melody and holds it. She has heard this crying before. That is Sophie. Sophia. Her granddaughter. Who didn't cry until her mother died and then didn't stop crying for a year it seemed while Madeline would hold her and stroke her hair and say, "Shhhhhhh, Sophie, Sophie, Sophie, Sophie, I am here. I'm here. Gramma's here. Shhhhhh." And the thing inside Madeline gives the melody meaning and context and Madeline sits up.

"Sophie?"

"Gramma?"

Madeline closes her eyes and opens them again. She takes a deep breath. She looks slowly over to the door where her granddaughter is standing, cloaked in shadow.

"Are you all right, dear?"

There is a silence. A few sniffs. Then, a small voice, "Can I come in?"

Be present. Be here, Madeline. Let it go. Let it all go. Talk to Sophie. Call to her. Say:

"Yes. Of course you can, sweetie."

Good. Now swing your legs over to the side of the bed. Good. Like that. Hold your arms out, toward your granddaughter. Tell her:

"Come sit on my lap, sweetie."

Ask her:

"What's wrong?"

Watch her as she comes over to you, crawls in your lap, puts her arms around your chest. She falls into you and the melody starts again. Stroke her hair and say:

"Shhhhhh. Sophie. It's okay. I'm here. Sophie, Sophie, Sophie, Sophie, Sophie. Shh, Soph, I am here. I'm not leaving."

And the girl seems to break and her chest can barely keep the rhythm and then something occurs to you. You know what is the matter. You have felt it yourself. And you stroke her hair and kiss her forehead and say, "Sophie. Sophie, it's okay, Sophie. You're remembering. Shhh, you're remembering. . . ."

AT THE VERY same time, Susannah is knocking on the door of her and Todd's apartment. She has not been there in two weeks, has not seen or talked to him in all that time. She barely realized she was going there, she was just heading for comfort, for familiarity, for a place she could do what she is about to do. Todd opens the door and stands and stares at her. Something comes in his eyes, something like tears, but that would be ridiculous, because Todd does not cry. Crying is not in the nature of Todd.

"Zana? What is it? Zana?"

And Susannah crumples on the doorstep—head, neck, shoulders, chest, stomach, waist, knees—she falls and falls. Todd kneels down next to her, "Baby. Sweetheart. What is it?"

Susannah whispers something, but it comes out like choking.

"Sweetie. Baby. Zana, Zana, Zana, Zana, I couldn't hear you. Tell me again. Please. Let me help. Tell me again."

Susannah lifts her head slightly. Her whole face has become a red bloating rashy thing. "Todd—" she says. "I miss my mom. I miss her."

act three   spilled

seventeen.

Norman Rockwell's American treasure

THE FACTORY WILL open again in fourteen days. After ten weeks and four different deadlines (and press statements that have numbered somewhere in the double digits), the construction workers and the engineers have slowly begun to move out of Clarence. In their place stands a wonder of modern engineering and architecture, a psychopharmaceutical factory to make all other psychopharmaceutical factories quake in their psychopharmaceutical boots.

At least this is what Harris Jones will tell the good people of Clarence, though in truth, the building looks pretty much the same. With a couple of added luxuries, of course—a beautiful new cafeteria and a sprawling workout facility to mollify any worker who may have found him or herself inconvenienced in any way by the wee little shutdown.

(Meanwhile, on the top floor of Harris Jones headquarters in

Minneapolis, a quivering epicene gentleman in a bow tie steps into the office of CEO Herman Nelson. He inhales deeply as the portly Nelson rubs his doughy hands together and harrumphs, "All right, Michaels, what did this little chemical spill cost us, all told?" Herman Nelson assumed leadership of Harris Jones after the untimely demise of his father, Stanton J. Nelson. And Herman, as long as he lives, will never forget the words of the Harris Jones patriarch as he lay dying: "Son. The company is yours. On one condition. Never ever let them litigate.")

The letters are in the mail. And, this time, they really are. In a day or two each former employee will receive a missive on bright, pleasing letterhead printed in a soothing font and signed personally by the associate vice president in charge of human resources, which contains the happy, happy news that the factory is reopening:

"Harris Jones deeply regrets . . . ," "doing our best to make things as easy as possible during this difficult time . . . ," "engineers have been working tirelessly . . . ," "prevent a disaster like this from ever reoccurring . . . ," "delighted to inform you that an opening date has been set . . . ," "we would like to offer you your job back . . . ," "we would like to offer you a pay raise and/or a dental plan . . . ," "please call a representative at your earliest convenience . . ."

And of course: "We at Harris Jones Pharmaceuticals would like to invite you and your family and friends to a holiday/grand reopening party to celebrate the good will and the indomitable spirit of the people of Clarence. . . ."

Harris Jones took out a full-page ad in the *Clarence Chronicle* (which is, in truth, not a very sizable investment) announcing the grand reopening party and inviting the entire town "to celebrate the indomitable spirit . . . ," etc., etc., etc. And in the fine print, careful readers would learn that representatives from the pharmaceutical division would be at the party to address any questions or concerns anyone in Clarence may have about the spill. Because Harris Jones scientists have been researching day and night over the past few months and after exhaustive testing have determined that the deletrium exposure causes absolutely no "permanent effects."

Clarence reads the paper over coffee and feels awake. More awake than ever before. All over Clarence, the scene is the same. Pancakes steaming, teapots screaming, children beaming, just like Norman Rockwell's American treasure "After the Spill."

All over Clarence, the scene is the same, at least in homes of the vast majority of townsfolk, ones who managed to pry themselves away from their beds and find their lives waiting patiently for them, and some who never fell victim to the deletrium's effects at all.

But in some homes, Norman Rockwell is conspicuously absent. A few people find themselves staring down the long cool barrel of a divorce proceeding, others wake up in a strange town (where they had planned to start over), others wake in their childhood bedroom (where they have tried to go back and confirm their version of the past), or wake up in the hospital (where they find their sense of reality has been altered once again), or, in the case of a few of the most senior of senior citizens, they wake up confused and missing time and in an unfamiliar room (where they find themselves attached to tubes). And two men and one woman who could not live with the weight of their own pasts now sleep forever.

Now that the pancakes are cooking and Clarence is awake, Pastor Hansen wakes up in his office at the church. He has been sleeping there since a week after Lorna left. He has not gone home in four days. He will admit this to no one, no one at all, but there seems to be something . . . unholy in his house. Supernatural. Pissed. Doors slam. Plates smash. Books fly through the air.

Pastor Hansen does not fear for his sanity. He knows the spirit is real. He knows what it wants. The weight of his sins has taken shape, breath, motion, and is now haunting his house. He broke one of the Commandments, and not number Three or Nine or Ten, which everyone breaks. He broke a biggie. Now he is being punished. And until he purges his soul of his sin (which will involve a good deal of embarrassment and some real-life plate throwing on his wife's part), the malevolent, knowing ghost will surely follow him until the day he dies.

So for now he will sleep at the church.

LIKE THE MINISTER of Doom and the Glo-bot, Jimmy Rose wakes up happy. He smells pancakes. He hears his dad downstairs. His dad has been in bed for a while. And he wasn't feeling so good himself. His brain felt all buzzy.

Jimmy wants to get back on track. He has a plan. He has taken it as his Solemn Duty to take good care of Sophie, because she is the only girl worth talking to in the entire world.

Before he got all busy-buzzy-brained, his reign of terror against Leslie and Christine had been going extremely well, and he is looking forward to getting back on track. The Glo-bot had been packing their boots full of snow and then dumping the snow out right before the end of the day. The Minister of Doom, resident wordsmith and forging aficionado, had been leaving little notes in Christine's cubby that read, "Someone likes you. But don't tell Leslie." And, in turn, he left notes in Leslie's cubby that read, "Someone has a crush on you. Don't tell Christine." (The next in the series will be, "Do you know who I am?" and then "Why don't you write any notes to me? I check my cubby all the time.") Jimmy is the idea man, and is also in charge of rumor spreading. Right now, with the smell of pancakes inspiring great things, he is dreaming up a particularly juicy one about a recent exposure to leprosy.

Sophie of course has no idea about the machinations of Operation Black Stab, or even its very existence; girls can be pretty funny about that sort of thing, and it's better not to involve her. (As a child born in the nineties, Jimmy has a good instinct for the principles of subterfuge, like plausible deniability.) He felt pretty bad about her getting in trouble about the phrase book (Code Name: Koobie This!), but she didn't stay in trouble for long. (Any girl that can build a fort can talk her way out of The Weed's office, that's for sure.) The search for a suspect in that matter is still on. Meaning that the three boys have had to proceed very, very carefully. Use code words. Leave no traces. Always have an alibi. Deny everything.

His mom acts very happy whenever he mentions his new friend. "Who is this Sophie? We should have her over for dinner." She leans in and smiles and winks. "Is she your girlfriend?"

Jimmy rolls his eyes and kicks the ground and says, "Jeez, Mom. Ick." It seems to Jimmy that grown-ups are always thinking about doing it and stuff.

It doesn't matter. Jimmy feels good today. He can just close his eyes and lick his lips and plan.

THE DAVIS AND DEAN manager wakes up in a foul mood. After several years of only profit, only praise, only progress, Davis and Dean Clarence's sales for November are at an all-time low. Important people are beginning to take notice. Friday again, time to prepare his weekly report to the district manager (who will pass it on to the regional director, who will then pass it on to the vice president in charge of development, who will hit his desk and cuss if this week is anything like the previous weeks.) He knows the other managers make fun of him. (Which is true. They all like their jobs, like the company, but not *that* much.) But before he had his store's success to assuage him. Now, though, they can just laugh. People have stopped coming to the bookstore.

Maybe it was the rather poor customer service evidenced by more than a few booksellers who have all seemed pretty darned touchy lately. Maybe it was the incredibly short staff. Maybe there was some kind of plague like the one that wiped out the café workers. (Though he is quite certain that attributing low sales to plague or pestilence generally does not fly well with the muckety-mucks. He has heard tales of other managers trying it and they did not get promoted to district manager.)

He is indeed worrying (as are the higher-ups at a time when sales in the rest of the country are skyrocketing) that the Clarence Experiment is failing. Maybe the store has been a novelty. Quickly digested and discarded like romance novels and paper coffee cups. Maybe now the people of Clarence have decided en masse to boycott this superstore for small-town down-home family-run businesses, buying into the propaganda that chain stores are evil when in fact Davis and Dean is just as much of a family organi-zation as Mom and Pop's Books. Just a more successful one. Right time, right place. Up by the bootstraps. Eyes on the prize. A little entrepreneurial instinct. A bit of capital and a little thing called ambition. A belief that good books, good coffee, and good cus-tomer service are the last things holding this country together. Franchising is the American Dream. Mom and Pop are welcome to throw their hats into the ol' ring. Like Vanguard Books did. The nasty little copycat weasels.

Well, whatever the cause, the store has been frighteningly empty. The muckety-mucks are not pleased. It's the Christmas season, the most important time for the store, calendars line the walls, gift books are scattered by registers, the children's section is teeming with overstock, and every bookseller has been trained to say, "Would you like a gift certificate today?" But there is nobody to impulse-buy those little extras, nobody who needs their carefully researched suggestions, nobody to appreciate the decorations, nobody who cares about staff recommendations, nobody to say, "Yes, in fact, I do need a gift certificate today. Thank you for asking. What wonderful service!" The manager's future at Davis and Dean is in serious jeopardy. He needs to turn things around. And fast.

LILITH, THE PERPETUAL café worker, wakes up feeling calm for the first time in weeks. Her mind had been playing all kinds of tricks on her, and she has been away from the Davis and Dean café for a week, due to some strange bout of something.

She gets dressed and drives down the snowy Main Street for her opening shift. People are on the streets today, even this early. For a while, it seemed the falling snow would be the only movement on Main Street this winter.

It is hard to go back to work. Lilith stands in the café kitchen wearing her official Davis and Dean red and tan apron, organizing the overstocks and trying to hide from the hoi polloi. Fortunately, business is slow today. When she went to punch in she could not find her official Davis and Dean name tag anywhere even though she could swear she left it in her mailbox before she went, so today she is labeled Brenda. Occasionally, a customer will call her Brenda and she feels her entire sense of reality shift.

At least she is appreciated. When she arrived at the store a little before noon the manager nearly skipped up to her and looked very much as if he wanted to hug her. "Lilith!" he squealed. "My café superstar! Thank god you're back."

Apparently the entire store had been short while she was gone. The bookshelves are in chaos, and the café kitchen looks like an ancient ruin. Not that she minds staying in back to clean up. So far in the day, her human interaction has not been exactly pleasing. Her third customer of the morning, a woman in a pink pantsuit, greeted her with a simple, "Get me the usual."

Lilith did her best to smile. "I'm sorry. What is the usual?"

"I come in here every day and you don't know what the usual is, Brenda?"

A few customers after Pink Pantsuit (the usual: regular cappuccino skim milk and just a splash of sugar-free vanilla flavoring. Just a splash, please!), a portly man cut through the line and slammed his empty cup on the table.

"This coffee stinks."

"I'm sorry, sir. Why don't I make you another one."

"No, Brenda. I just want my money back."

One of the supervisors, who had been standing in line when the gentleman cut through, shook her head and gave Lilith a look of such profound compassion and empathy that Lilith thought she just might start to cry right there in the man's empty cup.

She spends her break wandering indiscriminately through the career section. This something, this lapse of sanity, this vacation of her mind must be for a purpose. There is meaning glimmering behind the mystery, but what is it?

The career section seems as good a place as any to start.

SUSANNAH WAKES UP in her own bed, next to Todd. Bits of the past week come flashing back to her. Most of it involves lying here, in bed, with Todd—he pressed close to her whispering, *Susannah my lovely my dear my Susannah my sweet my lovely love love.*

Susannah's mind feels different. Better somehow. She wakes up and looks at Todd sleeping next to her, and for the first time in she does not know how long, she does not feel like she is moving underwater. She reaches her hand out to touch Todd's head. At this moment, she could sit here like this, watching him sleep, all morning long.

Todd wakes up to find Susannah looking at him. He sees how clear her eyes are, and then he registers that it is he who can now see.

"Hi."

"Hi."

"Whatcha doing?"

"Just looking."

Todd likes this answer, he likes it quite a bit. She runs her hands across his cheek. He rolls over and lets her caress his face. He closes his eyes and tries not to let the moment go.

"Todd?"

"Yeah?"

"I've been thinking. I might really like to be a nurse someday."

"Good. Good. You would be wonderful."

He dozes off again to the tingly feeling of Susannah's hands running through his hair.

"Todd?"

"Yeah?"

"Do you like dogs?"

"Yes I do."

"Good. It can be nice to have something around the house. You know."

She puts her head back down and rolls over. He puts his body against her curved back, his arms over her shoulder, and she grabs his hand. Moments tick lazily away.

"Zana?"

"What?"

"I didn't tell you something."

"What?"

"Well, the past weeks, the deletrium—"

"Yeah?"

"It's been pretty bad for me, too."

"Really?"

"Yeah."

They lay their heads back on the pillows, and sleep just a little more.

After some time passes, Todd feels Susannah sit up next to him. She leans over and he barely hears her as she whispers into his ear. *I have to tell you something. I have figured some things out. I love you very much. But I am not sure where I need to be right now. Something is pulling me away. There is something I am trying to get to. Please understand. I have been unhappy here. I owe you an apology. It was not because of you. I am sorry I have been acting so badly. Let me figure things out. Give me time.*

Todd tries to pretend he has not heard these words, and instead falls asleep dreaming of presents for his Susannah.

SOPHIE WAKES UP in her own bed for the first time in a few days. She has been falling asleep next to Gramma for a while. It is Monday now, and that is a school day, and that means she has to go to school. The thought of school makes her feel a little queasy. There is something still there in her stomach that is not quite right. School is a place where people do and say mean things, where there are people like Brad and Leslie there to look at her funny. Sophie's brain emptied out a lot of stuff, and a lot of that stuff was about how some of the other kids made her want to crawl under the desk, and how they didn't treat her as they would like to be treated, and how maybe she should talk to her dad about home schooling, which is what the girl in the book she is reading is doing and she likes it quite a bit.

MADELINE WAKES UP in the guest bed in her son's house. She has slept through the night for over a week now and has actually been able to concentrate enough to read, write a little bit, and most importantly to cook dinner. Which has been necessary because her son has been in no condition to be a father lately.

She would have moved back to Sunny Shadows days ago if it hadn't been for little Sophie. Sophie has slept next to her the last few nights, while Bennie has barely left his room in over a week. Meanwhile, she has arranged for a sick leave for him, delivered lesson plans to the Ph.D. candidate taking over his classes, done the grocery shopping, fielded his phone calls, helped Sophie with her multiplication problems, paid the bills, taken the cat in for her check-up, and functioned as all-around mother to her son and granddaughter, much like she did after Lizzie died, while Bennie lay nearly catatonic with grief and three-year-old Sophie kept looking in drawers and under beds trying to find her mother.

As she wakes up this morning, Madeline notices that her head is perfectly clear. She closes her eyes for a moment and revels in the beautiful stillness of it all.

CLARENCE IS WAKING up, going to work, reentering life. People wake up all over the little town and remember what it is to feel clearheaded. And, just at this very moment, in his room in the intensive care ward in the hospital, amidst a mess of tubes, charts, and beeps, Calvin, too, wakes up.

eighteen.

The workings of ghosts

BY TWO O'CLOCK, Madeline still has not heard anything from Bennie. This is not unusual these days. He emerges, eventually, always, wandering around the house with the fervor of a lion in a zoo habitat. He will find his way into the kitchen to stare into the refrigerator or will sit on the couch flipping through thirty-four television channels again and again. Madeline hears him more than she sees him; at night, she can make out the sounds of kitchen cabinets opening and shutting, stairs creaking again and again. She woke up yesterday morning to find the entire kitchen scrubbed perfectly clean, as if despair would dissipate in the presence of lemony fresh scent. And then, this morning, it was chaos again.

His movements have become more biological than psychological. He stalks, scavenges, forages, burrows, nests. In the mornings, she finds evidence of his behavior—like a zoologist she studies his activities and tries to discern their place in the natural order of things. Benjamin. My son. What can I do?

During the days, though, he stays shut in his room; sometimes he answers her knocks, sometimes he does not. She knows what his trouble is, she knows it will pass, she will just wait for the fog to leave her son. It has left the rest of them. It will leave him. It is just a biological reaction. Chemical. A malfunction of the brain. There is nothing really wrong. It will leave him, and when it finally does, when he is human again, when he is Benjamin again, the mother will go back home.

Madeline aches for her typewriter. Her fingers protest the misuse . . . buttering bread, turning door handles, combing through a nine-year-old's hair—this is the quotidian life that is the fate of other hands, Madeline Singer's past hands, not her present. Her present hands quiver with electric thoughts; the past has returned to its rightful place in Madeline's world but her mind still buzzes in harmony.

And there is Calvin.

Calvin with blue eyes and that embrace of a smile, Calvin now comatose at the horror of it all.

But first, she is a mother. Actual, and now surrogate.

At first, Madeline thought Sophie was taking her father's respite from the world rather well, considering. Sophie would only tiptoe quietly around the house, asking Madeline every so often if she could do anything to help. She never once asked what was wrong with her father, only went about her daily life with perpetually wide eyes that seemed to contain the Dead Sea Scrolls in their depths.

It took Madeline several days of this to remember that Sophie is, in fact, a child. Perhaps her subdued behavior reflected not understanding but something quite else.

After much deliberation, Madeline decided to sit the girl down on the couch and explain as much as she knew about the deletrium spill and its effects on the human mind, particularly on that of the Singer family. Sophie listened solemnly and scratched the cat's ears.

"So . . ." she whispered, ". . . this is why Dad's been in his room?"

"Yes."

"He's not mad at me?"

"Oh, Sophie, no. . . . No. No. Not at all. Oh, Sophie . . ." Madeline drew her granddaughter into her arms and held her there. She thought, for a moment, of how desperately awful her son is going to feel when all this passes.

"It's all been very scary. For us all. It's okay to be scared, Sophie. But I'm here for you. And everyone is getting better. You feel better, don't you?"

Sophie nodded slowly, then cocked her head and scrunched up her face and thought for a minute.

"So Dad should be getting better pretty soon, huh?"

"Yes. Yes, he should . . ."

Now, Madeline gets her granddaughter ready for school each day (despite Sophie's protestations that she has been able to dress herself and make her own lunch for a couple of years now), bundling her up in five or six different layers before she allows the girl out of the house, ("Do you have any idea how cold it is out there?") and usually watching her until the door on the yellow bus slides open. ("Honestly, you'd think they could just drive up to the house so the kids could wait inside!") Sophie protests at all the attention, but Madeline suspects she really does not mind too much.

Today, with Sophie safely on her way, Madeline has spent the day on the phone checking in on Mildred and her other friends at Sunny Shadows. ("Madeline, Calvin is awake. It happened this morning. But no visitors yet. He's going to be fine.") She does not want Mildred to hang up, she does not want to lose the soothing sound of normalcy. (Her heart jumps, her breath catches, her palms sweat. Calvin, Calvin, Calvin . . . What on earth will they say to each other now?) Indeed, everyone seems to be well now. Everyone is living again.

If only she could say the same for her son.

SOME OTHER KIND of clarity has come over Todd. It is certainly not a supply problem. There are still women everywhere. They still have the same soft skin and solicitous breasts. There are women everywhere, but lately Todd has not had the desire to nuzzle any one of them.

This has never happened before.

Before, of course, he knew he Could Not, Should Not.

Please Do Not Touch the Women. Stay Behind the Red Line. Display Copy Only.

And because of Susannah, he Did Not.

Now, though, there are women, women everywhere. In his classes. Working at the lab. Wandering around campus. Next to him at the grocery store. The laundromat. Passing him in economy cars. And where before there was appreciation, itching, twinging, urging, now there is nothing. No Thing. An Absence of Thing. Lacking the Thing.

There is Just Susannah.

And so, what is the point?

The thought of losing her has quickly become unbearable. No Susannah. An Absence of Susannah. Lacking Susannah. Nosusannah. Nothing. Left alone to face the world, to deal with these other, lesser women who are by no means Susannah. Who do not possess her patented blend of pragmatic rectitude touched with wide-eyed ameliorism, her unshaking compassion for all things fuzzy, her studied tolerance for all things Todd—and even Susannah with the secret of the sick mother (who simply adores him, by the way), and even, yes even, Susannah who has the potential for madness lurking underneath her skin.

Susannah. Maybe the most beautiful name in the whole history of the universe.

The thought of losing her is intolerable. It makes him want to smash some more things. Every Thing. If he could smash up enough things, maybe she would emerge through the rubble, arms out, lips open. Todd. I have figured it all out. I will spend my life with you.

In lieu of smashing, he can clean. He starts by cleaning the office. Turning it into an office again. Art is not for him. Art is not the essence of Todd. And his clay doesn't seem to hold the same lumpy allure anymore. It seems the problem is solved. The clay is shaped. The canvas painted. His project complete. What he has been trying to get to, he has gotten. And he cannot bear the thought of losing it.

Todd goes out to the living room and begins to look around. He dusts the table. He fluffs the pillow on the couch. He finds himself staring at Susannah's dollhouse things. Susannah has not dusted them since she has come back. He takes down the little piano and looks at it. The little keys are very sweet, fifty-two little white ones and the thirty-six teeny painted black ones. Todd dusts the piano. He dusts the little end table and the ball-and-claw sofa and straightens the doilies. He dusts the tiny mahogany rocking chair and sets it in motion. He straightens the little silver service. He tucks the baby into the little crib. Cute baby with its rosy porcelain cheeks. Cute fuzzy little teddy bear. Cute little blue cotton nubby baby blanket. Good night, baby. Sleep tight. No bedbugs.

The mom and dad are standing near the big brass bed with the embroidered flowery bedspread. The bedspread is fraying a little; "You should get that fixed," he tells them. They do not respond. They eye him with an infuriating expression of painted-eyed complacency. "Did she ever think about leaving you?" Todd asks. The man regards him thoughtfully. "What did you say? Were you able to stop her?"

He looks at the woman. Her hair is chipping off a little bit. Todd bobs her up and down and begins to squeak, "Oooh! Darling! I think I need some time to myself!"

The man in Todd's other hand gasps and turns toward her. His voice is pretty squeaky too. "Oooh! Darling! Whatever you need! But I love you, I need you, I can't live without you!"

"Ooooh! Darling! You're right. I will stay. Have you fed the basset hound?"

"Yes, I have, I love you, I love you, I love the basset hound, I love everybody!"

Todd clears his throat. The couple eyes him slightly warily. He picks up the man and gives him a more dignified voice this time.

"Susannah?"

The woman turns and squeaks back, "Yes, my darling?"

"I just wanted you to know that, if you want, we can move away from here. If you want, I will come back home with you to be by your family. Or we can go to a big city or something. I won't mind. I'll be glad to do it for you."

"Oooooh, Todd, you don't mean it!"

"We will go anywhere. I'm not going to be away so much either."

"Oooooh, Todd, really?"

"Yes, I want to be home with you and the, uh . . . basset hound. . . ."

"Oooh, Todd, you handsome devil!"

"Susannah, I will do anything to be with you."

And the basset hound barks and barks and bobs up and down too.

AT TWO-THIRTY, MADELINE gives up waiting for Bennie to emerge. She makes a tray of food and knocks softly on his door.

"It's Mom, Bennie. Can I come in?" There is no sound. She knocks again. "Benjamin?"

"It's all right, Mom. Come in."

She opens the door slowly. Her son sits up in bed as she does. The lights are off. All of the shades are down. The piles of pictures and papers around the room have seemed to grow bigger and bigger by the day, but Madeline has never seen him look at any of them. Artifacts of the past just accumulate, reproduce endlessly, real-life clutter made manifest by an acute remembering.

She smiles at him, trying to convey the right balance between maternal compassion and respect for his privacy and his status as an independent adult.

"Do you want me to clean up your space a bit?"

"No."

What can she do? Why is he the last one? What if she has lied to Sophie? What if he doesn't ever get any better? What if he lives the rest of his life like this, pacing and foraging, trapped in an artificial habitat? A town goes mad, a town finds itself again, and it is the psychology professor who cannot heal. The shrink needs to get shrunk.

"Can I turn on a light?"

"Uhh . . . sure . . ."

Madeline flips the light switch and Bennie blinks. Her son is pale and he looks shaky. His skin is tinged with blue. He smiles at her weakly, and it is as if his entire face has atrophied. No son should look older than his mother.

"Have you been sleeping at all?"

"Ummm . . . off and on . . ."

Madeline looks at him for another minute, then goes over to pull up the shades. He stutters in protest.

"Listen, it's not healthy for you. You need sunshine."

"But . . ."

"I insist."

"I've been an adult for several years now."

"Benjamin." She pauses from her rearranging to glare at him.

"Always the mother." Bennie shakes his head compliantly.

"Absolutely. It is my job. Here, I made some toast for you. And some tea." She goes over to the door and gets a tray.

"Mom, I'm not hungry."

"Ben . . ." She perfected this voice in the early years of her son's life. She still has it down cold, and it still works on the thirty-nine-year-old man.

"Sure, Ma. I'll have some. Thanks." He is almost saucy, like a teenager. Do the dynamics ever change? She puts down the tray on his lap and pulls up a chair next to him. Bennie looks at her and nods at their staging. "We've switched places," he says with half of a laugh. "Are you still feeling better?"

"Oh yes. I'm just fine now. Things at Sunny Shadows are back to normal too. I spoke to Mildred today. Calvin woke up. People seem to be putting themselves back together."

"That's great," Bennie says dully. Both of their voices have the false levity of most sickbed conversations. The air in the room, though, weighs their words down, so they sound muffled and bloated. Silence coats everything. Madeline tries to articulate as best she can.

"And you, how are you feeling?"

"I don't know." He does not look at her. He occupies himself with his toast, tearing the crust into little bits. He used to do that as a child. He never wanted to eat. He could not be bothered. He had far better things to do. Madeline would have to bribe him with sweets because at least sweets were food. Fruit juice will at least have some fruit in it. Anything else he would much rather play with than eat. The great game of toast shredding. Is this regression or is it just what it is? She watches him in silence and has to actively resist the temptation to order him to eat.

"Do you want to go out? We could go for a drive."

"I'm not quite ready for the world yet, Ma."

Silence again. More shredding. More bloated air.

"You know, Ben, it will get better. Things will fall away. Your mind will clear. The clutter will lift."

"Hmmm . . ."

"Do you want to talk about it?"

"Not really."

The sun ducks behind the clouds (you're leaving me alone in this, Madeline thinks) and now the room is cast with sickly yellow artificial light against a gray day.

Madeline leans in and speaks to her son in a soft, low voice, deliberately redolent of a distaff lullaby. "You know, Ben, I do know what you are going through. It's very strange, to relive your life like that. But the distance does come back. Slowly. The veil will lower again. I promise you. It gets better."

Bennie pushes air through his nose, which Madeline gathers is to be some kind of reply. She sighs with him.

"You know, I've been thinking about your father a lot lately. Well, naturally, I have been. But even now, now that the effects are gone, I have been thinking about him and about the week after he died." Bennie still will not look at her. He pours spoonful after spoonful of sugar in his tea, staring at it as it dissolves.

"I might write about it. I never have, you know. We never write about the things closest to us, do we? That week, I didn't think I could actually live. I thought grief might actually swallow me up whole. Drown me. I thought it might in fact be possible for all of the figurative representations of sorrow to come to life, to take body, and I would die by the manifestations of thousands of metaphors."

"Mom . . ." Bennie holds up his hand to stop her.

"I'm not talking about you and Elizabeth. I'm talking about me. The situations were very different." She stares him down, and when he relaxes, she continues. "I didn't realize it at the time. But I think that week I was not just grieving for your father. I was grieving for what I thought would be the death of my life. I was a widow at forty-four. I didn't think I could possibly make it alone."

He tears the last whole piece of toast in two and tries to look her in the eyes but only makes it to her chin before he has to stop.

"Mother . . ." He bites his lip. "Are you saying I am just feeling sorry for myself? You know, I am fairly well versed in the workings of the human psyche."

"Just listen, Benjamin . . ." She tries to modify the impatience in her voice into affection. (Sometimes, still, so like his father . . .) He exhales and leans back on his pillow. "That's better." She pauses a minute and searches for a place to begin. "Marriage was so different in those days. For many of us, anyway, us in the neigh-borhood. Getting married was something you were supposed to do. Love wasn't as much of an issue, marriage was just the natural order of things. A decade before, men came back from the war wanting to marry and forget everything that had happened to them, and the women wanted to marry whoever was still alive. Somehow, that never stopped. We all wanted companionship."

"Well, Dad sure didn't give you too much of that."

"No. No, he did not. . . ." Her voice trails off for a minute. "But he had his reasons. Do you know what the central tragedy of your father's life was?"

"Not getting district manager?"

Madeline chooses to ignore his tone. "No. No. His brothers were both killed in the wars. One in World War II, the other in Korea. He never got to go."

Bennie snorts. "That's a bad thing?"

"To him, yes. He never said as much, but I think he always felt like he was somehow less of a person because of that." She swallows. Somehow, she still feels as if she is supposed to protect her husband's secrets. And, of course, her own. "I've never admitted this to anyone, barely even to myself until this all happened, but I used to wish he had been able to go to Korea, and then maybe he would have been . . . different. I don't know. It's an awful thing to wish for someone, and I know he could have died, would have seen horrible things, could never have recovered, but at least he wouldn't have been so subsumed by regret."

Bennie stops playing with his toast. "I didn't know that."

"He never mentioned his brothers. His sister told me." Madeline shakes her head. "Benjamin, you must understand, your father and I were never as close as you and Elizabeth were. It was an entirely different kind of marriage. Of course I loved him, but our love was more habit. It never even occurred to me that there was any other way for a marriage to work. Even my friends who had marriages like you did . . . I didn't realize . . . until after I saw you two."

Now, it is his mother's turn to look at the ground. "You know, when you met Elizabeth, the first time I saw you two together, part of me was a little . . . jealous. Morris had never touched me as much in his life as you touched her in those first five minutes on my doorstep. I'm sure you remember the way I acted toward her?"

Bennie nods slowly.

"The two of you were magic to each other. You both swelled over with life. You were radiant together. I will never forget it. I have tried to write about it and I cannot find the words. Your love was ancient, literary. It was the way it was supposed to work. You never believe such a thing is possible until you see it in real life."

She looks up now and finds Bennie's eyes have filled. Madeline reaches over to grab his hand.

"And I see it, that love, every time I look at Sophie. She is a remarkable child. And she would have to be, coming from such a blessed union."

Madeline smiles at her son. He sits, gazing at nothing, red eyes spilling over. She holds his hand and they sit silently for a while, occupied with the workings of ghosts.

After an eternity, Bennie speaks. His voice is husky, his words are slow.

"Mom . . . do you still remember Dad?"

"Remember? Of course I do."

"No, I mean, do you remember what it was like to be near him? Do you remember what he was *like*?"

"Ben, I don't know quite what you mean. Of course things fall away. It was such a different lifetime then. I was a completely different person."

"But I don't want it to be a different lifetime." His voice grows loud and whiny. The tone shocks him. He breathes in and almost whispers, "Mom. I'd forgotten things about her." He stutters so Madeline can barely understand him. "Before this week. In my head she didn't have a body anymore. She was a ghost. A cipher.

I could not remember what her skin felt like or how her hair smelled or just how she lay in my arms. I kept losing her, more and more." Bennie is crying now. Madeline holds his hand firmly and lets him.

After a minute or two, he looks up at her humbly. "Uh . . . Mom. Can you get some tissue?"

"Of course . . ." She goes into his bathroom (a mess) and searches the cupboards. Toilet paper will have to do. She takes a deep breath and goes back to her son's bedside.

"Ben, sweetie." She hands him a sheet of toilet paper. "Bodies are temporary. They are not important. Memories are temporary. But Elizabeth is indelible. Her impression will always be with you. You don't need to worry. This is the way our minds work. The details go—and it is good that they go, otherwise we'd go completely crazy—but the important things linger. Don't worry about that."

He sniffs and nods. "What do you remember?"

"Oh . . . I remember your father as a sensation, a phrase, a smell, a presence. I remember instances. But I can never conjure up his entire self at one time. They're just feelings." She watches her son for a moment. "But the thing is, Bennie, all of those feelings are not necessarily pleasant ones for me. I've gotten to know myself a lot better since your father died. I've written. I've left these books behind. And I have you. And the dearest granddaughter in the world." She smiles. Now her eyes are shining.

"I can't even remember the person I was twenty years ago. But it was different with your father and me. We all make our choices, Bennie. Eventually I had to get up and start a new life for myself. Since Elizabeth died, you have led the same life, just without her. You live in the same house, same job, same routine." Madeline holds her breath for a minute and tries to decide whether or not she should say what is on her tongue. "But, you know, that's not necessary." She leans in and grabs his hand again. "You don't need to live as a monument to the departed. If you moved out of this house, moved out of Clarence, packed Sophie up and went to New York or London or Calcutta, Lizzie would still be with you. Nothing can ever change that."

Bennie sits quietly. "Are you saying I should pack up and leave?"

Madeline leans forward and squeezes his hand quickly. "No. No. I am saying that there are some things that are permanent, and you do not have to be afraid. . . ." He closes his eyes and she wraps her other hand around his and they sit together, mother and son.

AFTER SCHOOL SOPHIE stands at the appointed entrance and waits for her father. On their Fridays, whenever it rains, or every time in the winter, she waits in the west doorway. If it is nice, she waits in front of the school. Now, she watches the students pile on the school bus, Leslie and Christine walking by her with their noses pointed directly at the sky. She loves being picked up by her father. She loves it best when he gets there as the school bus is still loading, so all her classmates see that she has somebody to pick her up. Today, though, the bus loads up and drives away and she still is waiting. Teachers file out next to her in twos gossiping about students and complaining about the cold.

"Hey, Sophie!"

She turns around. Jimmy walks toward her wrapped in several layers. He had some after-school subterfuge to do, but Sophie does not know that. She is just glad to see him. "Are you still here?"

"Yeah."

"Don't you take the bus?"

"It's Friday. My dad picks me up every Friday. We go to the bookstore."

"Oh yeah. Isn't he sick?"

"Yeah, we haven't gone in a couple weeks. But he said today we would."

"My dad was sick too. He's feeling better, though."

"Oh."

Jimmy smiles at her, his big front teeth protruding out like vestigial tusks.

"Yeah, he thinks the factory is going to give him a big ol' Christmas bonus. I'm going to ask for a computer."

"Cool!"

"Yeah!"

"We can e-mail each other!" Sophie chirps.

"Oh. I dunno. Mom says she doesn't want me to use the Internet, because there are . . ." He pauses and forms the word slowly with his mouth, "pred-a-tors out there waiting for little boys. Hey, do you want me to wait with you?"

"Oh. No, that's okay."

"Are you sure? I think your dad's late."

"Yeah. I'm fine."

"Okay. Wanna go sledding tomorrow?"

"Yeah!" Sophie grins and waves good-bye to her friend.

Jimmy waves back and begins to walk over to the Glo-bot's house where the three boys are meeting to plan Operation Black Stab Phase II: The Secret Santa. Sophie leans against the wall and continues to watch for her father's gray sedan.

nineteen.

Will you do that for me?

AT FOUR O'CLOCK every Friday, Ventura Elementary Principal Dolores Small locks up her office (because you can never be too careful) and heads out of the school. She will schedule no meetings, allow no exceptions. Because at five o'clock on Friday nights, she goes to the Clarence Municipal Building for pottery class. Because her recent bout of acute self-reflection has led her to believe that in the quiet yearnings of a shapeless lump of clay lie her True Calling. (She will, in fact, achieve modest success a few years down the line. Among some circles in the Cities it will be quite something to have a Dolores Small bowl.)

But for now, Dolores Small is a principal, which has been her True Calling for a good ten years (long enough for any calling to get its due). And now, as she walks down the hallways this principal sees one of her charges standing in the doorway of the west entrance well after hours. She approaches cautiously, so as not to startle the child, so she can assess the situation before she makes contact.

It's a girl, blond. As she creeps up she can almost make out the face. Ah, yes. Um . . . (P . . . Q . . . R . . . S . . . , yes. S. Singer. Sophie Singer. Ms. Plum's fourth grade. Father, a Mansfield professor—something in the social sciences. Mother, Out of the Picture. Interests include gymnastics and figure skating. In the Junior Great Books Club. Celebrates Christmas *and* Hanukkah. Recent flap over forging issue. Cleared of all involvement. Suspects still at large.)

Dolores Small engages the subject. "Why, Sophie Singer!"

The girl turns and smiles tiredly.

"Hello, Principal Small."

"What are you still doing here?"

"I'm waiting for my dad."

As she talks, Sophie Singer rubs her left foot against the ground. A sign of shyness. Common in children when confronted by a principal. The principal, in such situations, should try to talk to the subject like an equal.

Dolores Small looks Sophie Singer directly in the eye. "Oh," she replies with a studied casualness. "Is he supposed to pick you up this late after school?"

"No. But he might have gotten held up in traffic or something. He wouldn't forget. He never forgets." The girl speaks seriously, frankly, as if she were all too familiar with the ways of the world. Here, too, Dolores thinks, is a girl with a True Calling.

"Well." Dolores Small stands straight up. "Why don't we call, just to make sure."

Sophie Singer sucks on her lip in thought. "Um. Okay." She looks at up at principal (gratefully, it seems) and follows her into the school.

. . .

SOPHIE READS HERSELF to sleep. (An old book. She and her father will go to Davis and Dean on Sunday and she can pick out three books. That's right, three.)

Sophie has had a most peculiar day. Principal Small was leaving a message for her dad on the machine using that answering machine voice when she stopped. "Oh, Mr. Singer?" She smiled at Sophie and mouthed, "Your dad is home." Principal Small listened and then said into the phone, "Are you sure? You must be very very ill indeed. I can certainly drive her home." Then she nodded encouragingly at Sophie and hung up and told Sophie, "He'll be right here."

And he was. Right away. The gray sedan pulled up by the school and Principal Small walked her to her dad's car and then her dad thanked the principal again and again and Principal Small said that it was no problem and then she looked at him the way she looks at kids sometimes when they are Acting Out. Her dad gave just the same look back that most of these kids do, except more so.

Sophie got in the car. Her dad apologized a million times. Then he talked to her very seriously. He wouldn't even drive until he finished talking to her. He looked very, very tired. He was shivering slightly. He wasn't wearing enough layers. He said he hadn't been feeling well. He said that there was something making his head sick.

She told him that she knew all about it. She told him what her grandmother had said. She said she understood. She wanted to tell him she didn't mind, but really she kind of did, and this was not an occasion for a little white lie. Her father said that he would spend the whole day on Saturday just with her. She said she had sledding plans, but how about Sunday. He said that would be very nice and they would go to the bookstore and she could buy three books. Three. Three books. He promised he would be better. He promised that everything would be better. Now. Better now. "You are such a good girl," he says. "You are so grown up. You are taking all this very well, Sophia. You are such a good girl." He said this again and again, and Sophie didn't know what to say.

Sophie lies on her bed and puts her book down and closes her eyes.

Something doesn't sit right.

When Sophie was waiting for her dad to come pick her up, Leslie and Christine walked up to her with their heads in the silent treatment position. This was very, very different from the way she saw Leslie earlier in the day, which was on the floor of a bathroom stall crying.

Sophie didn't know it was Leslie who belonged to the crying body on the floor until she knocked tentatively and asked if she could help at all. The sniff that followed, though, was definitely Leslie-brand sniffing, as was the retort that followed it—"Sophie Singer, this is your fault. Your fault."

"Leslie?"

"Go away!"

"Leslie, what's wrong?"

Leslie's round head appeared underneath the bathroom stall. Her face was red and bloated, giving her the appearance of a drowned Christmas ornament.

"Why do you care? You're the one that's saying all those things about me."

"What things?"

Leslie looked up at her supposed maligner with hating eyes. "I think you know, Sophie. You and your koobie friends."

Then the head disappeared under the stall and Sophie was left to bite her lip and wonder what exactly it was that Leslie thought she did.

Now as she lies in bed and thinks about her weird day she is slowly beginning to get some idea.

SOPHIE PLANS HER confrontation very carefully. Boys can be a little jumpy. She thinks a long time about what to say and how to say it. She thinks all morning. She thinks as her still sorry father drives her to Jimmy's house for sledding. She thinks as the boys skip toward her. She thinks as her still sorry father gives them a ride to the park. She has been thinking so much lately; everything is so hard. She thinks as they sled down Suicide Hill. In order to think clearly, she has to try to forget two things. Thing One: How hurt Leslie looked and Thing Two: How much hurt Leslie had given her (wrapped up with a bow).

To forget these things is hard.

She has to handle this by herself because she is a Big Girl and a Good Girl and her father is so sorry and he has those things in his head. She thinks and thinks and thinks. It is all so hard.

After their bodies have hurtled down a hill as many times as can be contained in one afternoon (all this time she is thinking), Sophie and the boys begin to walk back to Jimmy's house, where Mrs. Rose had promised cocoa with marshmallows. It is at this point where Sophie decides to make her move.

"You know, I saw Leslie crying yesterday."

"Really?" Jimmy blinks girlishly. The Minister of Doom tries to repress a snicker. Their chests swell up. They have kept it all a secret. Has Sophie figured it out? This is their present to her, the token of their esteem (wrapped up in a bow). They hadn't planned to give it to her yet, maybe for Christmas ("Hanukkah, stupid-heads," Jimmy hissed). The secret puffs up inside of them. It could leak out at any moment.

"She was really sad. She accused me of saying bad things about her."

The boys look at each other. (Should we tell her?)

Jimmy comes up with the logical response. "Oh, Sophie, she can't really think you'd do that. You're too nice." At that the Glo-bot starts to laugh. He can't help it. The puff is just too much. It tickles inside him. Such is the way of the Glo-bot.

At the sound of the snicker, Sophie turns around and glares at all of them, trying now to focus on Thing One to the exclusion of Thing Two.

"Are you guys spreading those rumors? Like that Leslie's mom is a space alien?"

Sophie is actually a little behind the times. They are well past the sphere of space aliens, into the high-risk, high-gain world of genitalia, nocturnal habits, and boogers.

It does not appear to the boys, though, that Sophie needs to know any of this right now. Or that she'd want to. The four children are stopped in the middle of the sidewalk, halfway be-tween Suicide Hill and a finish line made of cocoa and marsh-mallows. This is not going exactly as the boys had planned. Their chests sink in inconspicuously and they look at one another, slightly bewildered. Sophie stands tall and firm. Even the pink-and-blue pompom on her cap stands tall.

Jimmy, again, takes the lead. "Sophie, are you pissed off at us?"

"Yes, I am. I am pissed off. Why would you do something like that? You can't do that to people." Despite all of her best efforts, she cannot keep the tears away. They run hot down her face, as conspicuous as blood. Before, it was easy to be rational. Because there was still a possibility that her friends had not done this thing.

"Why not?"

"Because it isn't nice." Sophie stomps on the ground.

"But Sophie. They were mean to you!" Jimmy says. He is still standing firm. Perhaps she does not understand. Perhaps she thinks they were trying to frame her. Perhaps she does not get that this was all for the love of Sophie.

"We just wanted to help." The Minister of Doom is having some trouble articulating, either because his entire conception of the world has shifted or because his woolly scarf has frozen to his face.

"I don't care!" Sophie yells. "I don't care. It isn't nice. You shouldn't hurt people."

A girl had never yelled at them, much less a Girl Who Could Build a Fort. The Minister of Doom and the Glo-bot stare at each other while Jimmy scrunches up his face and kicks the snow.

SUSANNAH SITS WITH Madeline in Strange Brew. Madeline does not like to go into Davis and Dean; she says whenever she goes into a bookstore she still feels compelled to sneak her books onto the front tables, and she does not consider this decorous conduct.

Susannah is back to her normal shift at Sunny Shadows. She came into work yesterday to find a message for her from Madeline in the office, "Ms. Susannah, I am back. I've missed you. Let's have tea."

Susannah folded up the note carefully and stuck it in her pocket, to keep.

Now, Susannah is spending her lunch break with Madeline. She has not heard anything from her in weeks. She cannot imagine what it was like for her. Susannah has not yet dared ask Madeline too much—at least she seems much better than the last time Susannah saw her; her voice has lost that exhausted tremor.

"I have heard you were rather indispensable around the place, Ms. Susannah," says Madeline, stirring lemon into her tea.

Susannah blushes and cannot think of a thing to say.

"I have been taking care of my son. I cannot imagine what it must be like to take care of that whole place."

"Your son. Is he all right?"

Madeline considers her tea. "I think so. He will be. It is passing."

"Yes."

Madeline smiles gently. "I do not want to get too personal, Ms. Susannah. But how are you doing? This has been very rough on everyone, it seems."

Susannah blushes again. "I—it was hard . . ." She looks down. Her hair falls in front of her face.

Madeline looks closely at her, then casually wipes her mouth. "I heard you moved into one of the guest apartments."

"You heard that?" Now Susannah smiles a little.

"Forgive me. Sometimes Mildred and I have nothing better to do. May I ask, what did your fiancé think of this?"

And then something strange happens. Madeline looks at Susannah gently, probingly, and something releases inside Susannah and she finds herself talking. She does not stop. She tells Madeline about her mother. She tells Madeline about how she left school and never went back. She tells Madeline about leaving home and coming to Clarence and this feeling that someone is carving her in two and all the best parts about her are escaping in the process. She tells her how her father wouldn't even hear of her staying home, how he told her that she must live her life, that he could take care of it. She tells her how strange she has felt around Todd, and how strange she feels about going home. She tells her how lumpish and aimless she has felt since coming to Clarence, and how she doesn't know how to get away from that. She tells her how Todd offered to take a leave of absence. How Todd offered to move anywhere with her. She tells her how frightened she is that she will become like her mother, and that Todd will leave her, and how strange it has been to see things out of place in Todd's life for once, not so assiduously normal, and how somehow that made her feel better.

And the funny thing is—funny to Susannah anyway—while she does all this weird talking, Madeline listens. She does not say a thing, she does not cluck or shake her head, she just leans in and listens. Susannah talks straight, she barely takes a breath, her hands fly in the air, her eyes tear up, and Madeline does not say a thing. She listens and she waits. And then when Susannah is done talking, Madeline leans backward, and says, without blinking:

"Susannah. I have three questions for you. Think about them before you answer. The first is obvious: Do you love Todd? Don't answer yet. The second is: If you could do one thing right now with your life, what would you like to do? That's harder. And the third one is the hardest of all: Whatever that thing is, Susannah, what is stopping you from doing it?"

And Susannah drops back in her chair, and takes a long drink of her tea. And she thinks for a while. Her right hand twirls a curl around and around. Madeline drinks her tea, too, and waits, never taking her eyes off Susannah. And then, Susannah breathes in, and says:

"Yes. I do love him. I do. I have just felt so out of my own skin lately. So displaced. But I do love him. I love him because—he is Todd. I love him for his Toddness. For the second question, I don't know. I've been thinking about it. I've thought of this before, and then after these last few weeks, well . . . I think I want to be a nurse." Susannah takes a breath. "And for the third, well, I just don't know. These choices, they are permanent. I could start school and Mom could get bad again. My dad doesn't have much more money for tuition. I just . . . things just happen. I don't know what it is like to have choices. Things happen and I react. I don't know how to do it any other way. . . ."

And then Susannah takes a deep breath and she is done talking and she puts her head down and regards Madeline through her hair. Madeline is not speaking. And then Susannah brushes the hair out of her eyes, and something changes in the way Susannah looks at Madeline. She sits up and regards her more plainly and realizes that it is not approval she wants from Madeline, it is something else entirely. Susannah has never noticed before the small streaks of red in Madeline's hair, nor the way Madeline rubs her collarbone when she is thinking. And for a moment, just a moment—at the very same time that Madeline has stopped noticing the way Susannah's hands fly to her hair—Susannah sees the ghost of a girl behind Madeline's kind eyes and good posture. And Susannah is suddenly filled with something beyond respect, deference, admiration, and at that moment realizes what she feels for this woman is love.

She sees Madeline is looking at her, too, and so is the ghost of the young girl behind her eyes. There are two women before Susannah; one looks maternal and wise and the other looks empathetic and sad, and Susannah wants to gather both in her arms.

Madeline finally speaks. Her voice is low and husky. "I want you to know, Susannah . . ." She pauses. "I want you to know that no matter what happens, no matter how helpless you feel, no matter where the tide of life takes you, you always have a choice. You can always take action. Will you remember that? Will you do that for me?"

And Susannah nods slowly and says, "Yes, yes, I promise."

twenty.

It's nice to see you.

Bennie Singer sat on a wall.
Bennie Singer had a great fall.
All the king's horses and all the king's men
Couldn't put Bennie back together again.

As MUCH AS Bennie hates to admit it, his mother makes a certain amount of sense. He has been processing their conversation for days, when he is not lavishing attention on little Sophie. Bennie has never felt guiltier in his whole life, and now Sophie tiptoes around him in a manner that reminds him far too much of the way he acted around his own father.

He will talk to her, again. He will talk to his mother. He will rejoin the world. But there is one more thing Bennie has to do, first.

He sits on his bed and writes out his wedding vows, word for word, on a sheet of white paper. He had forgotten it, before—how is that possible? He should have told her, night after night, whispered it into her ear as she fell asleep. He should have written it out then, posted it up above their bed. And most of all, he should have blessed every single day he could live under its words.

He wrote the vow two weeks before the wedding and spent every day after that muttering it to himself. His friends told him he was an idiot, he should bring it up there on a sheet of paper, that he could forget the entire thing, and he would be standing up there with nothing to say, and then he would be the biggest idiot in the entire world. And for a moment, of course, standing up there, he did forget. For just a moment. But then, the words came back to him, because they were true, they were how he felt. Bennie looked in his wife-to-be's eyes and told her:

I cannot regret a single thing I have ever done because every step in my life took me to the point where I first saw you. I promise you on this day to spend the rest of my life trying to give you what you have given me: a life without regret.

He hopes, now, that he lived up to his promise. She died so quickly, she wouldn't have had time to consider it, which perhaps is a blessing. As for the eight years in between his vow and her death, he can only hope he succeeded.

Bennie stares at his vow and chews on his lip. Bennie has regret. It will never go away. It is not a matter of forgiving himself, it is not a matter of coming to peace with anything, it is not a matter of moving on. Those who do not understand have never lost their wives. Bennie had someone who filled him with such love and joy, and he lost her, and he can never have her back. This regret he will always carry with him. His life is burdened, and this burden cannot be eased.

The question is, what will he do with himself while he carries this thing around with him?

He runs his fingers over the wedding vow. He folds up the paper and kisses it. Later, he will bury it under the tree where they scattered her ashes.

And now, he must speak to his daughter.

He gets up, brushes off his khakis, and goes to her room.

Sophie sits on the red carpeted floor, chewing her lip, paging through a big white book. Her stuffed animals sit in a precise semicircle around her, gazing at her respectfully. Bennie knocks on the door frame. She looks up.

"Hi, Dad. Uh, are you okay?"

Bennie smiles. "Yes, Sophie. I'm fine. Can I come in?"

"Sure, okay." She puts the book down. He gets on his knees next to her. Fifteen stuffed animals sit in front of him, appraising.

"What are you playing?"

"Oh." She motions to the group. "We're learning multiplication."

"Oh. Good."

Sophie sucks on her cheeks. "What's up?"

Bennie looks her in the eye. "Listen, Sophie, I want to say something to you. It's very important." Her eyes seem to grow fearful. "No, it's not scary. I want to apologize. For the past month."

She pats his knee. "It's okay. Gramma explained it all to me."

"She did, huh? I have to apologize to Gramma too, actually. Anyway, it's not okay. There's no excuse for the way I behaved. You know you are the most important thing in my life, right? You know that."

Sophie nods, still not looking at him. "Yeah . . ."

"And whatever happens, that will always be the case. I don't want you to ever forget that."

"Okay."

"You handled it all so well. I imagine this was all hard on you. Gramma, um, told me that you had some . . . effects as well."

She shrugs. Bennie sits for a while. She plays with her stuffed elephant's ear. Bennie takes a deep breath.

"Soap? I want to ask you something."

"Yeah?"

"Were you able to . . . Can you remember your mother?"

Sophie grabs on tight to Fluffy and shakes her head.

"I'm sorry. You would have liked her."

Sophie nods.

"She had so much energy. I had almost—well, almost forgotten what it was like to be around her. She had this magnetism. You look like her, you know. Your eyes are full of your mother."

Sophie does not speak, does not look at him.

"She would be very proud of you, you know. You are so big, so smart, such a grown-up girl."

And then, before his eyes, Sophie disintegrates. She is a shaking mass on the floor.

Bennie sits up, reaches to her, brings her close. The words rush out. "What is it? Soph, what is it?"

Sophie whispers, "But Dad. I'm not."

"What do you mean?"

Sophie squeezes her elephant to her face and sniffs into him. Bennie can barely hear her words, and when he does make them out, he is not sure he has gotten them right.

"Dad? You know I'm just a kid. You know that, right? I'm just little."

TODAY, SUSANNAH KORBET will get two surprises.

Right now, she is just waking up, and she has no idea that today will be the kind of day where she gets one surprise, let alone two. Of course, her mind is other places. She has not stopped thinking about her conversation with Madeline, and she has realized what she needs to do.

After breakfast, she sits Todd down.

"Okay. Sweetie, I need to go home for a while. I need to talk to my dad. I need to be with my mom. I need to sort things out there. For a little while. I'll stay through Christmas, and then I'll come back."

Todd bites his lip. "You will?"

"Yes."

"You should come back. The factory doesn't smell anymore. Do you notice that? They must have cleaned, um, something."

Susannah smiles. "So you understand?"

"Well, no. Can I ask something?"

"Of course."

"What does this mean?" From the look in his eyes and the sound of his voice, Susannah would think that Todd is insecure, but that is not possible, insecurity is not in the nature of Todd. Right?

Nonetheless . . .

She grabs his hand. "Nothing. All it means is, I need to spend some time with my family right now. I have to be there to . . . make the transition. I have to see them like they are now. Does that make any sense?"

Todd sucks his lip further in. "Do you want me to come with you? I would like to. I can work things out with school, no problem. Whatever you want . . ."

"No." She rubs his hand. "No, I need to do this by myself. But I appreciate it. And I will call you. I promise, you won't need to call information this time."

"Good, because, you know, I still have your home number. And I'm not afraid to use it."

"I promise."

Todd does not speak for a minute. In that time, Susannah can see all kinds of ghosts flicker behind his eyes, and she wonders how to scare them away.

"Well, when are you leaving?"

"In a week, I think. If I can get the tickets."

"Wait. What about your Christmas present?"

Susannah laughs. "We can have Christmas when we get back."

"No, no, I have to get this for you now. You can leave it here. Since you're coming back, right? You did say you are coming back."

"Yes, yes!"

"Okay. It's at the lab. I'll go get it. I'll be right back."

And he rushes out the door. Susannah, who still has no idea she will be getting two surprises, laughs as the door closes in front of her eyes. And then she runs to open it.

"Todd! Your coat! It's freezing!"

But he is already pulling out of the driveway.

Susannah starts to close the door, then sees an envelope sticking out of the mailbox. She picks it up and goes back inside. Her name is written across the front of the envelope, in the elegant writing of Madeline Singer. Susannah opens it up and unfolds the letter inside.

Dear Ms. Susannah,

I have been thinking a good deal about our conversation yesterday. I did not tell you this, but I went through a period of my life where I did not make any choices. As a result, I lost twenty years of my life. I was a wife and a mother, but I was not a person. You remind me of myself, and I feel a need to help you. I have an opportunity to help you as I did not help myself for a long time. I do not want you to float aimlessly as I did.

My wish for you is that when you are my age, and you look back on your life, you are able to say you conducted yourself with bravery, that you made choices, that you took action for yourself, and that you have no regrets.

I have contacted the director of the nursing program at MSU, which is one hour from Clarence. I have arranged to pay your tuition for the program. You may apply for the upcoming semester; there are still spaces available. Should you like to pursue this or another degree in another state, we can make some kind of arrangement.

Ms. Susannah, I have a good deal of money saved, and I do not have anything to do with it. My son and my granddaughter will already be exceedingly well provided for. And if you decide not to go to nursing school, it must be because you truly do not want to go, not because you don't want to accept this gift from an old lady.

All I ask in return is that you continue to visit—or, if you move away, that you write me, that you listen for gossip for me, and perhaps if I need a nurse someday you will consider the job.

Yours truly,

Madeline Singer

Susannah stands rooted to the floor, mouth open. She reads the letter again. And again.

The doorbell rings. She peeks out.

Todd is standing there with a huge blanket-covered thing. "I can't get the door, Zana!"

She opens it, holding the letter in one shaking hand. He rushes in with the cold air.

"I went all around," he said. "I went to antique stores everywhere until I found just the right one." He pulls off the blanket to reveal an intricately crafted turreted Victorian-style dollhouse. "I thought you could put your furniture in this, instead, and we could move the people around—"

He stops and stares at her.

"—Zana? What is it? What's that in your hand?"

AFTER HE WOKE from his coma, Calvin was instructed to stay in bed for another few days. Nurses came in hourly to check his vital signs and to exercise his legs. Daughter Laura had rushed up from the Cities as soon as she got the call Friday morning, and soon visitors from Sunny Shadows Estates began to swarm in during visiting hours like shoppers the morning after Thanksgiving. Eventually, Dr. Kartopolis had to restrict visitors to just family for the sake of the patient ("You will see him when he is released. Let's let him rest."), but Laura has snuck Madeline in on Calvin's request. He has something to ask her.

Madeline has not spoken to him since his collapse. He has been better for over a week now, but she did not know how to come, what to say. There had been such promise, but things have changed now, haven't they? Have they? Calvin cannot now put on his hat and ask her to a double bill; there can be no formality now. Her feelings for him have not changed, really—well, they have altered, but they still lead toward him. Something inside her has been stripped away, something else has been added, and what remains begins to look like love. And need. All this past has made her want a future.

(A half-remembered image from late-night flickers of nightmares: Morris comes out of the ether and sits down on her bed and mutters, "You love him because he is not me."

And she shakes her head. No. I love him because he is him.)

But Calvin, Calvin, who cracked open before her eyes; she knows now the rumors are true, she knows what he must have remembered, why he collapsed. Photographs from television documentaries flash in front of her eyes, and part of her would like

to turn around and walk away from him, so she does not collapse, too.

"Calvin. How are you?" Madeline blows into the room effortlessly, trying to convey just the right blend of concern and casualness. Calvin lies pale against the bed, with tubes and wires sticking
out of him at every possible space. As soon as Madeline walks in,
he presses the button to push his bed up so he is nearly seated and
rubs his cheeks to add a little color.

"I'm sorry I'm not better dressed for your visit." He nods at the
checkered hospital-issue gown and tight circulation socks.

"No, it's very dapper." Madeline smiles gently. "Is that your
dinner?" She nods at the IV.

"No, that's just extra. I'm allowed to eat now, in a manner of
speaking." He laughs slightly. "I went from water to clear liquids
to juice just like that." He snaps. "Yesterday I moved up to chunky
broth. Apparently that's quite a big step. You know, I've always
been precocious."

It is a pleasure to see him joking. (It is a pleasure to see him.)
Madeline hopes he is not just laughing for her.

"Calvin. Are you really feeling all right?"

He nods slowly. "They say I can go home in a couple of days.
They just want to give me some more fluid, walk me around a
bit. Teach me to sit, bark, and shake. You know."

(Is he flirting?)

They pause and stare at each other for a moment. Madeline has
grown so used to awkward silences lately. She thinks that maybe
she will write an entire novel one day that takes place in one of
these pauses.

Calvin looks searchingly at Madeline. "Madeline . . . Sit down."
He motions to the little yellow chair that daughter Laura has called
home on and off for the last month. "I'm afraid that's the best I
can do. What a lovely host I am."

"Calvin, don't worry." She pulls the chair up to his bedside. (Is this too close?) Calvin purses his lips and inhales. She smiles and waits for him to speak.

"Madeline"—he clears his throat and speaks very, very slowly— "have you ever heard anything about my experiences during the war?" His face is down but his eyes look up at her deeply, searchingly.

Of course Madeline has heard. Everybody has. No one has ever asked him about it, though—who could ask?—and no one has ever confirmed that the rumors were true. Who would dare bring something like that up? Who would dare make him relive that?

Madeline speaks very very quietly. "Do you mean, about the . . . ah . . . camp?"

"Yes." Calvin nods cautiously, does not look at her.

"Yes." She takes a deep breath. "Yes, I guess I have."

"Well. I was wondering. I've never really, well, talked about it. Nobody really knows . . . Um, I think it's important to, uhhh . . ." He stops and starts again. "I'd like there to be some record. I know you have a lot of projects, but I was hoping . . ."

He trails off.

Madeline leans in. "What, Calvin?"

"Madeline, I'd like you to write about it. The war. What we saw. I would tell you and you would write about it. Could you . . . ?"

The air grows very still.

Madeline cannot speak for a moment. Calvin stares at her, stares through her. She feels her chest burn. Something in her cries, "No," and she pushes the sound back. She opens her mouth but nothing will come out. His eyes do not leave her and she is transparent, naked, cold.

"Of course." She breathes in. "Of course I will."

"Good." He straightens up. All business. "We'll start when I get home."

"Of course." She gets up and grabs her coat. "I will see you then." She starts to leave, pushed by the current of a hundred nameless emotions.

"And Madeline?" Calvin stops her.

"Yes?"

He smiles, red-rimmed eyes dancing in the old way. "It's nice to see you."

twenty-one.

It will take time.

Oh, CAPITALISM! OH, consumerism!

Oh, boom economy!

Oh, Visa, MasterCard, American Express!

Oh, Christmas—uh—the holiday season!

Oh, gift books, holiday sampler albums, cards, bookplates, tie-in merchandise, journals, calligraphy sets, address books, page-a-days, weeklies, twelve-month, sixteen-month!

Oh, eggnog lattes!

Oh, consumerism, you many-bosomed demoness, you fickle faerie, you bestial virgin, you bitch/goddess, you Madonna/whore. How you toy with us. How we try to break free. We pack up your belongings, throw you out of the house, laugh as you land right on your plush twin buttocks of supply and demand. We change the locks. We swallow the key. But your sweet venom stays in our mouth, our nostrils. We twitch. We burn. We cry out. Please. We're sorry. We take it all back. We need you, we can't live without you. We've grown accustomed to your face. How we beg to have you back. We fling open our doors again, bray into the night, fall on our knees, slither on our bellies, and plead with you to bestow your sweet supple moist wisdom on us again.

Thank you, Clarence. Atta boy, Clarence. Hello, movie house!

(Thus thinks the manager, going over the sales figures for the last week.)

Tu ra lu ra lu!

Oh, holy night!

Pat a pat a pan!

Oh, consumerism! We stand on guard for thee!

Did you find everything you needed today? Oh, this is an excellent selection. Would you like a gift certificate today? May I gift-wrap that for you? Can I interest you in a cup of our special holiday blend? Would you like an Xtra-big Xmas bag for all your shopping needs? Have a nice day. Thank you for shopping with us. Do come again.

There are contests among the various Davis and Deans. District-wide, region-wide, and even country-wide. Bonuses for the winning managers. Who improves their sales the most? Who sells the most small-ticket items? Bargain books? Gift certificates?

Davis and Dean Clarence is going to win them all (the manager says, at the weekly supervisors' meeting). Every single one. Let's make this the best year ever! Huzzah!

Yes (thinks the manager), something has been wrong in Clarence. Something dreadful. Something that kept these good hard-working small-town folk from engaging in their God given right to participate in commerce. Something was out there. ("But what?" asks the lady with heaving bosom. "In a word," says the manager, steely eyed, iron jawed, "Evil.")

But, the plague has ended. None too soon. Commerce and man are in accord. The bookstore and even the café are at full strength again. Better than full. Applications keep coming in. (We all want a little extra money at the holidays, a little pocket change to buy that extra-special something for extra-special somebodies. The holiday spirit spurts up into the air and falls on everyone like little flakes of Christmas snow.)

The café workers wear special red-and-green aprons and all have a sprig of holly pinned to their name tags (the manager's idea). They sell eggnog lattes, mint cocoa, and hot apple cider with a smile. And cinnamon scones by the truckload. The smell of baking scones wafts over the entire store. Customers are led by their noses down to the café like basset hounds on a hunt. Hello, can I have one of those fresh hot scones, please? (The scones have forty-five grams of fat in them. Each. The manager stopped eating them when the café supervisor let that slip. But do not tell the customers. For the love of God, do not tell the customers. In fact, we never had this conversation.)

Because the good people of Clarence come to Davis and Dean to be happy, not to think about fat grams. To feel good about themselves. To participate in the institutions that make their country great. To fondle books. To have the same retail experience as aunts, third cousins, and long-lost friends around the country. It brings us all a little closer, this chain store business. Right now, everyone in America is smelling cinnamon scones and eyeing staff recommendations marked with red-and-tan 30 percent off stickers. Everyone is drinking fine coffee and enjoying good customer service. And everyone, all over the country, is buying books.

And the manager is a part of it.

After the holiday season, the manager is scheduled for his annual review with the district manager and he has every plan to demand an almost unprecedented raise.

And his employees, his noble and penurious employees, how they toil away, engaging each customer with a friendly smile. Such dedication. The experiment is working. D&D has become a community center. A piazza. Where people gather to discuss the big issues and ponder life's mysteries. What news on the rialto?

There, at the café, sits a college professor sporting tweed and elbow patches sharing a moment with a cherished colleague. And there, in the corner, a young lady with a crop of curly hair sits reading through books from the nursing section, absentmindedly drawing patterns in the foam of her cappuccino. And there sits the pastor's wife, modeling for everyone good commercial behavior. God bless you Clarence. God bless you, and Merry Christmas.

LILITH, THE PERPETUAL café worker, makes lattes in the midst of a dilemma. The manager has offered her a promotion. Management. Responsibility. More money. And, while this particular manager is a bit of a goofball, the job is a good one. She had gone in to give her notice, just this very morning, she was going to go back to the city, back home, they were ready for her to come back. And now she may stay.

Besides, she feels a little proprietary toward the regulars in her café—the professors, the students, the locals, the wanderers. She knows them. The woman who still calls her Brenda who reads the style magazines all the time and looks so unhappy. The man who tries to sneak peeks at pornos underneath newspapers. The college kids who sit there pretending to do homework and just talk and talk. That curly-haired girl in the corner, the one who always flips through magazines, has been in here reading nursing books lately. (Occasionally, she takes a peek through the *Innocence Falls* scrapbook, too. Lilith loves that show—all those toothsome young lads and lasses in the high school hallways. That car accident episode, though, gave her nightmares.) Professor Singer, with that crazy friend of his, what's his name, in that bogus department Mansfield has. These are her people. She would miss them.

LORNA HANSEN SITS in the café with her usual—regular cappuccino, skim milk, and just a splash of sugar-free vanilla flavoring—and pages through the style magazines. She is back in Clarence, where she belongs. She is the pastor's wife and PTA chair and she has a duty to the community. She is alone in the house. Her husband is sleeping on the church floor. She has imposed this exile on him after he told her Certain Things. Now she has some life issues to sort out (after a good bout of plate throwing). Her ghost is gone. After she held open the door to let her husband and his suitcase out, she found a strange quiet settled into the cracks in the walls.

SUSANNAH IS NOT quite concentrating on her nursing books. She has not made any decisions, as of yet. She will not do anything until after she goes home tomorrow. Her family was delighted she was going to stay for so long—even her mother, who seems to be lucid lately. Which is good. Susannah would like to get to know her.

She and Todd have been furnishing the dollhouse. He came home yesterday with a nice bit of wallpaper for the baby's room. She is, frankly, a little surprised by how involved he is in the whole project, but she is learning that there is more about the nature of Todd than she knew.

And he thinks maybe they should get a dog. When she comes back, which she is going to do, right?

Susannah did not know—still does not know—how to thank

Madeline; she went to her in tears, and Madeline hugged her and kissed the top of her forehead.

The nursing school will be mailing all the brochures to her parents' house. For now, she will just sit back and drink her tea and marvel at how good everything smells these days.

BENNIE SITS IN the café with Phil, stirring packets of artificial sweetener into his cup of house blend. He and Phil haven't sat together like this for fourteen chapters. Bennie has dropped Sophie off at Sunny Shadows with a friend for the afternoon; he wanted some time with Phil. They have not even spoken since their encounter in Phil's office, which Bennie remembers grainily, as if the film has begun to erode.

They do not discuss it. An unspoken agreement has passed between them; we move on. Bennie has discussed enough. Phil is about normalcy, about the lighter rhythms of the day, and Bennie is happy sitting just where he is. Still, he is interested that his first instinct after that awful class was to run to see this accidental friend, and this is something he would like to think more about. Later.

But now, they assume their regular postures. Phil is taking the opportunity to break the news. "Listen, no one really knows this, but it was all the deletrium spill. This happened all over town."

Bennie merely arches his eyebrows and says, "Really?"

"Uh-huh. So my sources say. Harris Jones is paying through the nose for damage control. It'll get out, though . . . The potential for scholarship is really, well, something." Phil laughs halfheartedly and Bennie snorts a little bit, thinking of other things.

"So what do you think, Phil? What will the Contemporary Studies people say?"

"Oh, I don't know. I've been going on and on to anyone who will listen about the loss of our pasts in the contemporary age, our own penchant to look forward instead of back, the history-less society, blah blah. But frankly, I'm sure the whole thing will be a lot less interesting than we make it out to be. Best I can do is *The Wizard of Oz*. You know. 'Had this crazy dream. And you were there, and you were there.' And we all watch it, every year, thinking it is a fairy tale about home and courage and stuff, then we grow up and learn that suddenly the whole damn thing is about the gold standard. Do you know what I mean?"

"No." Bennie takes a sip of his house blend, then adds some more sweetener to it.

"Well, I mean, we're all looking for magic and truth and permanence and meaning. It just isn't there. Nothing is ever what we think it means. You know, Bennie, the whole thing made me want to do your line of work. Figuring out what makes people tick and all."

Bennie grins. "I don't know about that. I've been thinking about your job. Down with the past! Long live the perpetual present!"

"I feel sorry for the historians. Poor bastards stuck in the past all the time."

Bennie finishes the last drop of his coffee. "Hold on, I want a refill."

"Don't forget the sweetener," Phil calls after him.

Bennie walks up to the counter and smiles at the dark-haired woman in her red-and-green apron.

"Hello, Lilith. How are you today?"

"Hi, Professor Singer. I'm good!"

"Can I have a refill?"

"Sure."

"Nice apron."

"Thanks."

Bennie throws a dollar in the tip jar, smiles magnanimously, collects his refill, and trips over the leg of the woman at the table behind him, spilling coffee everywhere.

"Oh, I'm so sorry," he says.

Susannah Korbet stands up. "No, it's all right, I'm sorry—"

"I hope I didn't—"

"No, no. I'm dry. Thanks."

Lilith comes over with a mop, and Bennie Singer and Susannah Korbet smile at each other the way that embarrassed strangers do. Something passes between them, and Susannah cocks her head.

"Do I know you?"

"Oh." He blushes. "I teach at Mansfield."

"Ohhhh. Well." And she smiles and sits back down. And in a moment, it occurs to her that this is the man with the little girl that was next to her in the café during the whole siren-spill thing. She thinks of saying something to him, but he has already moved away and she does not want to interrupt. But she finds herself thinking of him and his little girl with sodas as bright as her eyes, wondering about them and what happened to them during the deletrium's reign, thinking about them for a long time, longer than one would expect—even years from now when she is a nurse and she delivers little girls on her own.

Bennie will see this woman again, years from now when she is caring for his mother, and he will think, then, that he has seen her before. But in the meantime, he will have moved away from Clarence, and taken a position at a small liberal arts college in St. Paul because Sophie needs a better high school and the psychology department there seems to be actually interested in people instead of rodents—where father and daughter spend every Friday afternoon at a wonderful bookstore/café right next to campus.

. . .

IN SUNNY SHADOWS Estates, the duck pond has frozen over and the gardens are sleeping under the cover of December. Mildred and her Civil War Guy son have joined the Sunny Shadows groundskeeper as he hangs white lights around the snow-covered pines. Mildred hums, "It's Beginning to Look a Lot Like Christmas."

Sunny Shadows is not entirely back to normal, of course. A few residents have moved away . . . some are staying with their children, some have taken the experience of the past month as evidence of a dwindling mind and gone into the Home. But for the most part things at the Estates are buzzing along the way they always do in winter. In the Sunny Shadows gym, Claire, a female resident with excellent posture, leads five women and one man in a yoga class. (The one man present, Stanley, is not there out of concern for his chi.) In the next room, a retired art history professor sits in on the weekly portrait drawing class. And the library is packed with residents and relatives sitting at the tables or in the overstuffed chairs reading near the fireplace in the sitting room. And near the Madeline Singer shelf, a girl with portentous eyes and a young scruffy-haired boy sit with a pile of books on the floor attempting to whisper.

"And my gramma wrote these," the girl says, beaming, holding a book in her hand.

"Wow." The boy takes a hardcover volume. "These are really big books."

The girl looks around, then leans in. "Yeah. My dad says I'm not allowed to read them until I'm older, but Gramma let me read them. She just told me not to tell dad because he has iss-ues."

"Why can't you read them?"

"Oh. Sometimes the people have sex."

The boy's eyes grow very large. "Really?"

The girl nods solemnly. "Yes."

The boy hunches down and begins to flip through the books. "Do you think I could read them?"

She scrunches her face. "I dunno. You'd have to ask my gramma."

"Oh." He pauses and picks up another book. "Wait. I can't read this one."

"Why not? That's my favorite."

"There's a girl on the cover. I can't read anything with a girl on the cover."

"That's the stupidest thing I've ever heard."

"If it's got a girl on the cover then it's for girls. I'm a boy. I read boys' books."

And they continue to argue in mock whispers as the people at the tables lower their heads into their books and try to hide their smiles.

In Building E in an apartment on the fourth floor, Madeline and Calvin sit in a robin's egg blue living room. Calvin is on the couch. Madeline wonders how long it will take for his eyes to catch fire again, or if they ever will. He has been much more serene since he returned from the hospital—and much more attentive— though he has not made any moves or indeed given any indication at all that his desires go beyond companionship. At night, they sit on Madeline's couch, eat popcorn, and watch Ingrid Bergman movies together. During the day Calvin sits and talks to Madeline. Her tape recorder listens as well.

They are getting there slowly. It will take time.

They begin simply. His tour of duty. His training in Mississippi. His first battle. Being in Belgium during the worst snowstorm in decades.

And slowly they work their way up to who was in his company and what their stories were before the war and what the letters they got were like and who made it out and with what body parts remaining. Calvin talks about what it was like to hold an M-1, fire an M-1, what it was like to kill someone. Calvin talks about what it was really like to take that bridge, in details none of Clarence High School's children past or present have ever heard. He never thought these were the stories they wanted him to tell. This is blood, not heroism. Who is he to destroy the myth?

He and Madeline are slowly working their way up to death and dying and evil and agony and all kinds of killing, and by this time Madeline hopes Calvin will be so used to describing the indescribable that then he will be able to talk about the Thing he has spent his entire life trying to forget ever happened, was ever possible in the world he lived in. She breaks down his carefully reconstructed illusions, all so he can break down hers.

They have a way to go. Calvin grows ashen as he describes the slow death of his sergeant, and Madeline knows it is time for a rest. In the space of the tremendous pause that demarcates the distance between them, Madeline puts down her notebook and lets him be.

After a minute:

"Calvin, are you all right?"

He nods slowly, and half smiles.

"Would you like some wine?"

He nods again.

Madeline gets up from her chair, stops the tape, and brushes his shoulder as she walks into the kitchen.

"Red or white?"

"Red, please."

She uncorks the bottle and gets the glasses down. Calvin stays on the couch.

"You know, one of the things I've decided in my life," Madeline says across the counter, "is that there are a few pleasures one should never deny oneself. Good coffee. Good wine. I'm happy to live a simple life, but there are some instances where you just have to splurge. Life with cheap wine is no life at all."

"An admirable philosophy."

Madeline walks back into the room and stands in front of Calvin and the couch. He looks up at her and smiles slightly. She bends down to meet his eyes. She has to resist the urge to reach out and touch his hatless head. She can feel her hand against his smooth head, and has to remember that that has not happened yet, and she does not know if it ever will.

"Listen, Calvin." Madeline clears her throat. "Are you sure you're all right? Can you keep going?" Madeline hands him his glass and as she leans in, she finds herself kissing him gently on the forehead, not in her imagination, but in real life. Calvin twitches just a little.

And then, there is a pause in which Madeline writes several novels.

Calvin gazes up at her, and smiles slightly. His eyes fill and Madeline leans in again and kisses him on the lips, swiftly but firmly. She leans back. He smiles. Calvin clears his throat and raises his wineglass.

"Madeline Singer, I propose a toast."

Madeline stands in front of him and holds her glass up. Calvin leans in and tugs her arm gently toward him. They sit next to each other on the couch. "That's better," he smiles. Madeline exhales deeply.

Calvin clears his throat again, sneaking a glance at the tape recorder, which rests tensely on the coffee table, pause button depressed, wheels straining to move again. To its right sits a small pile of tapes with dates written on them, the sum total of their work for the last week. To the left stand blank tapes waiting to be filled with his history. Calvin looks up, touches Madeline's cheek, and holds out his glass.

acknowledgments

I don't know how I got so blessed as to have Lisa Bankoff as my agent and Peternelle van Arsdale as my editor; I could not be luckier. Thanks, too, to everyone at Hyperion for providing such a good home for this book, to the inexhaustible, unflappable, ineffable Natalie Kaire, and to Patrick Price at ICM for being his lovely self.

I had the benefit of having two dear former teachers serve as early readers, Linda Lightsey Rice and Tori Haring-Smith. I also owe a debt to Tim Farrell, whose generosity and insight made this a much better book.

Thank you to Brian Costello, Joanna Liao, and Susannah Melone for reading the book early on. To Gretchen Moran Laskas, my comrade-in-arms. To Michael Broich, Matt Muellerleile, and John Addington, who thought of many of the costumes in the

Halloween section. To Jon Van Gieson, Webmaster, and Lisa Tucker, eagle-eyed reader, and Eric "Magnetron Tube" McMaster. To my family—Jane Willis and Dziwe Ntaba, the Broichs, the Jeanblancs, John W. and Suzanne Ursu, and especially to my parents, John J. and Mary Ursu. And, to my husband, John Eric Broich—editor, motivator, peanut butter cup briber, best friend, and most beloved.

If you enjoyed *Spilling Clarence*,
look for *The Disapparation of James*,
also by Anne Ursu and available from Hyperion.

James Woodrow's parents have

never seen him so excited. The boy sits between Hannah and Justin in their orchestra-section seats, bobbing up and down on his springy plush chair and singing some James-like song to himself. His father caresses his thin orange hair and assures him, "The show will start soon, buddy, settle down, okay?" while exchanging puzzled glances with his wife. James's sister, Greta, is rhythmically kicking the chair in front of her, squawking emphatically. Their mother, strategically placed in between the children, whispers, "Shhhh, Greta, sweetie, don't do that."

Hannah and Justin Woodrow are not alone; parents all over the auditorium of the Lindbergh Performing Arts Center are shushing and soothing, cajoling and threatening—a steady murmur underneath the screeches, babbles, and cries of the ten-and-under set. It is two minutes after the Razzlers Circus Stage Show should have begun, and the children are restless.

"Mom, they're *late*," Greta shrieks, pointing at her pink plastic watch. She kicks all the harder and, inspired, James begins to bounce more furiously in rhythm.

There is nothing at all unusual about Greta kicking things and shrieking, but Hannah and Justin do not know what has come over their son. He is usually the quietest boy. Enthusiasm manifests itself as a single syllable, a small smile. James can go hours without making a noise; sometimes his parents half-wonder if he has forgotten how to talk. He spends his days in his own corner of the playroom, solemnly working with his building blocks. At dinner, he sits in his chair assiduously arranging shapes with his slices of hot dog, then he returns to his construction projects until it is time for bath. He is a baby-sitter's dream; "James is so good," they say, "that sometimes you forget he is even there."

But not today. Today, James has been the picture of disobedience. He has been messing, spilling, breaking. He spent the afternoon running laps around the playroom, throwing stuffed animals, gnawing on crayons. For Justin, who has become used to more sedentary afternoons, today was a flashback to when Greta was this age; back then, by the end of the day, Justin would be ready for bed well before his daughter.

When Hannah came home early from work this afternoon, she found Justin on his back in the center of the playroom floor.

"You look as if you could use medical attention," she said. "What happened?"

He sighed theatrically. "Something has possessed your son. Look!"

Justin pointed vaguely in the direction of James's favorite corner, today a mess of broken crayons and scattered blocks, where James was jumping up and down, higher and higher each time, whooping, "Up up up up up!"

Hannah exchanged a glance with her husband, then approached her son carefully. "Hi Jamesie! What are you so excited about, big guy? Is it the circus?"

And, in response, James bent his knees close to the floor, readying himself for the biggest little-boy-jump in the history of the world, and exploded, yelling, "*Circus!*"

Hannah smiled at her son, then turned back to her still-prone husband. "If this is James," she said, "I can't imagine what Greta will be like."

Today is Greta Woodrow's seventh birthday. Seven is, as Greta would be happy to explain to you, a very momentous age indeed. Six is just like Five, and her little brother is just Five, and he's a baby. But Seven is much closer to Ten and that means you are a full-fledged Big Kid.

A momentous occasion requires a momentous celebration: Greta will come home from school to a lavishly decorated house, she will feast on macaroni and cheese and chocolate birthday cake with strawberry ice cream, then the family will head downtown and she will be treated to the best seats in the house for the Razzlers Circus Stage Show. (The tickets are compliments of Stewart Martin, theater writer for the local newspaper and college friend of Justin's. "I got extra," he said. "Take the Munchkins.")

At dinner on her Birthday Eve, Greta cross-examined her father on the exact nature of the entertainment planned for the next evening. Greta has always been skilled at the art of interrogation; she stealthily discomfits the deposed by becoming steadily shriller with each passing question.

"Daddy?" she began, "are there gonna be lions?"

"No. This isn't that kind of circus."

"Daddy, are there gonna be elephants?"

"No."

"Daddy, are there gonna be puppies?"

"Oh, yes, actually, one. And trained birds!"

"Daddy, are there gonna be silly songs?"

"Probably."

"Daddy, are there gonna be jokes?"

"Yes! Lots and lots of jokes!"

"Daddy, are there gonna be clowns?"

"I'm afraid so."

"Are there gonna be tricks?"

"Tricks? Like acrobats?"

Greta's pitch was nearly inhumanly high by then, and Justin had just prepared his answer when James chimed in to ask:

"MAGIC tricks??!"

Justin turned to look at James. "Well I . . . I don't know . . ." he said, shrugging at Hannah.

Now, the show is four minutes late, and Justin and Hannah, for possibly the first time, have to divide their parental attention between their two children. James has stopped bouncing; now he kicks the chair in front of him with a wild giggle, as if to compliment his sister on her most excellent idea for a diversion, and Justin must use his best paternal tone, "James. James, don't do that, I mean it."

In truth, Justin has not exactly been looking forward to the circus. Justin does not like clowns. He says he had a bad experience at his eighth birthday party—he has never elaborated; when pressed, all he will say is, "He just kept coming and coming."

As for Hannah, she would prefer to be in the bath right now with a magazine and a cup of mint tea, but she has no objection to the circus, per se, and seeing James so excited certainly makes her happy. Once the show starts and the children quiet down, she can look forward to one hundred and twenty minutes of sitting—even without a magazine or tea, this is always a good thing. So Hannah Woodrow would be in a reasonably good mood right now, if her evening had not been so handily spoiled in the lobby just moments ago.

A few weeks ago, a chance meeting with Dr. Lewis would have meant nothing—Hannah knows him professionally, of course—but now, things are different, and Hannah could not believe it when he tapped her on the shoulder with a bellowing, "Hello, there, Hannah Woodrow!" And then the doctor looked at James—who was hiding behind Justin's leg—as if he were considering him, inspecting him, diagnosing him right in the lobby. Hannah moved toward her son instinctively—this is not right. Here, here on Greta's birthday, here with the whole family out together, she did not want to be reminded of her son's appointment with the eminent pediatrician next week.

Now, six minutes after the show should have started, Hannah finds herself feeling prickly again, and she wonders where Dr. Lewis is sitting. They have not explained to James that he will be going to a new doctor; he's always hated his physicals and there's no need, yet, to tell him what is about to happen to him. But if he were to find out from Dr. Lewis instead of them, Hannah would never forgive herself—

And now, there!—seven minutes after the show should have started, the lights begin to go down in the auditorium. Three hundred parents let out a sigh of relief, and Hannah whispers to her brood, "Okay, guys, the show is starting, settle down now." At that, Justin lets out a small, "ha"-like noise, and she mutters across James's bouncing head, "You're not helping."

But the instant the lights begin to dance, the music sounds, and the performers explode onto the stage, both children become still. Ten bodies come tumbling onstage, four fly in on trapezes, another storms in on stilts playing the violin, three jump rope, two ride a tandem bike, and a shaggy little puppy jumps up and down in the center of it all. The stage is a flurry of bodies and motion and color and light, and even Greta cannot speak.

The music bounces, bodies flit, and a rubbery man in a tailcoat, clown nose, top hat, and funny pants enters the fracas and tries desperately to command attention. He waves comically and screams and jumps up and down and the children in the audience begin to point and laugh. He takes off his hat and slowly scratches his thick dark brown hair. Finally, the thin man disappears offstage, and then emerges again, slowly pushing a whistle the size of a baby elephant. He stops, looks around, winks at the audience, and blows—a shriek pierces the auditorium, and all the performers stop, start, and hightail it off the stage.

The thin man, now alone amid the chaos the tumblers have left, smiles at the audience, "That's better." Everyone laughs. The man clears his throat. "Hi, I'm Mike the Clown. I'll be your emcee for the evening." He bows dramatically, juggles a few balls, drops them everywhere, then introduces the next act—a woman and her dancing puppy for which Greta lets out a shriek that seems to crack several lighting instruments. Hannah settles back in her chair and James continues to monitor the action onstage intently.

There are acrobats and trapeze artists and bicyclists and jugglers, balance artists and trained birds and, in between each act, Mike the Clown jokes with the audience. At one point he gets a wallet from someone in the front row and turns it into a bouquet of flowers. Justin pats his son on the head and whispers, "See, buddy? There's a magic trick for you."

At intermission, Greta stands up and shouts, "This is the best show EVER!" James is still wide-eyed and quiet—that's the James they know—and Justin squeezes his hand and asks gently, "Are you enjoying the show, big guy?" James looks at his father, he is all eyes, and he nods slowly, seriously.

And the lights come up again, the second half starts, act follows act, and the children begin to get squirrely. They never know how to end things on time for kids, Hannah thinks. Springs squeak and feet kick all over the auditorium. Parents check their programs; one act left, something with the clown—and then the finale. Shh, just a little more, guys, don't you want to see what happens next? The curtain closes and Mike the Clown walks onstage in front of it.

"And now ladies and gentlepeople," he proclaims, "the moment you've been waiting for all evening ... Can I have a drumroll? ... MY ACT!!!"

A spotlight flicks on and appreciative laughter rumbles through the auditorium. This clown is a good entertainer, Justin thinks. He knows how to command a room—even this room.

With ceremony and panache, the clown proceeds to balance a plate, then a broom, then a pool cue, then a folding chair on his chin. And then a bike. The audience cheers. Justin rubs his own chin sympathetically.

"Ohhh, but that's not all!" the clown proclaims, "Mike the Clown has more tricks up his sleeve. Now, I will need a volunteer from the audience."

Children's arms fly up all over the auditorium. Greta's hand shoots up right away; she stands on her seat and shrieks. This is to be expected; Hannah and Justin look at her and smile as parents do. And then something flits in the corner of their eyes. An arm. A hand. They do not believe it: James has raised his hand.

Hannah and Justin exchange a look—what has gotten into their boy tonight? Greta is too busy popping up and down to notice. The clown comes down into the audience—he trips down the stairs and three hundred children squeal. He wades down the aisle—their aisle—he comes closer and closer until, finally, he is next to the Woodrows. His clown nose is very close to Justin's head. Next to Justin, James has his arm up, calmly, stiffly—he seems like an alien among all these screaming "pick me"-ers. The clown leans forward and smiles at James. "How about you, little boy? Do you want to come onstage?"

And James beams and looks up at the clown with his beautiful wide little boy eyes. The clown grabs his hand and pulls him into the aisle.

At this moment, it occurs to Hannah that James could make a fool of himself. This is a clown, not a child psychologist. If James freezes up, panics before the crowd, the clown won't know what to do. He is expecting an outgoing child. He will make jokes at James's expense. The crowd will laugh at James, James will be humiliated, and he will never, ever, ever recover. He will lead his life as a misfit, a recluse, unable to function in public. And then, when he's thirty, after ten years of psychotherapy he will finally be able to confront his mother, "Why did you let me volunteer for the circus, Mom? You're supposed to protect me, Mom. That ruined my life, Mom."

Justin reaches across James's empty chair and strokes her hand a little. "Hannah, it's okay." (Justin always thinks everything is going to be okay; it can be terribly annoying sometimes.)

The clown has James by the hand, and they are heading away from the Woodrows. James follows like a puppy and the clown asks him, just loudly enough for Hannah and Justin to hear, "What's your name, young man?"

There is a pause. The parents watch their son carefully across the rows of heads. Greta, meanwhile, is jumping up and down, shouting her brother's name for the whole auditorium to hear. Justin unconsciously moves into James's seat, channeling all his thoughts toward his son, and Hannah clasps his hand. One breath. Two breaths. Three—and then their son's little voice says, proudly, firmly:

"James."

They exhale.

James and the clown walk down the aisle, chatting and holding hands the whole way, and James is smiling, and the audience is applauding—applauding their son. Greta cannot contain herself, she shrieks, "THAT'S MY BROTHER!" Families turn around to look at them, smiling and pointing. And Justin begins to feel a beneficence toward, not just this clown, but all clowns. "Look at my son!" he wants to shout. "That's my son!"

And there! James is on the stage holding the clown's hand. Greta is still now, enraptured, she doesn't take her eyes off the stage as she tugs on her mom's sleeve, "Mom, do you see him? Do you see James? What are they going to do to him? What do you think he's going to do?"

"Shhh, honey, I don't know . . . Shhhh, watch now."

The clown and James stand side by side, two lone figures on a vast stage. The clown says to the audience, "I'd like you to meet my friend James. James is going to do just what I do, right James?" The clown nods to James.

And then—James nods right back to the clown. The clown smiles. James smiles. The clown waves at the audience. And then, James waves at the audience! The clown grins widely. And then, James grins widely! Everyone laughs and cheers! The clown tips his head toward James, "Look at the kid!" James tips his head to the clown. The clown jumps. James jumps! The clown turns around, grabs the waiting chair, and ceremoniously plops it down in front of him. James turns around, grabs an invisible chair, and mimes plunking it down. The clown giggles. James giggles. The clown mimes sitting down in the chair. James copies him exactly. No, no, the clown seems to say, YOU sit in the chair, and James mimics, YOU sit in the chair. The clown points at him, and at the chair. The boy does the same! The clown slides the chair over to James. James slides it right back!

The audience is nearly in hysterics, laughing and applauding and cheering for their son! For James! Hannah and Justin are mesmerized. Will you look at that? Will you look at our boy? Before his parents' eyes, James grows, James glows, he is energized, electrified. James is brilliant. He's playing the audience! James will be a showman, he will be a star, he will be whatever he wants to be—he will be all right, our son, he will be just fine.

Finally, the clown negotiates James into the chair and gives the audience a triumphant bow. James kicks his legs up in the air and squeals. "He wants more," Justin whispers to Hannah, eyes shining, "He wants to play more."

Greta begins to pull on her mother's arm, "What's he doing, Mom? Huh? What's he doing?!"

The clown then begins to lift James and the chair up into the air. Greta gasps loudly. James lets out a giggling squeal to the heavens. Hannah is too busy watching the expression on her son's face to worry that he might fall and break his neck or otherwise injure his spinal cord. The clown lifts James above his head, and then right above his upward-turned face.

"Wow," says Justin.

"Wow," says Hannah.

"He's gonna put James on his faaaaaaaaace!" explodes Greta.

And that's exactly what the clown does. He sticks his chin up in the air and places the rear chair leg on it. And then, the drumroll starts, he takes his hands away and sticks his arms out to the sides, and there is James, on top of the world. And James—their James—is not scared at all, but delighted, and his glow intensifies; Justin and Hannah can never remember seeing him happier than right now and each tries to grab on to the moment and put it away somewhere where it will be safe forever.

The drumroll continues, the clown staggers back and forth a bit, but James never wobbles, and then, the clown sticks his arms up straight in the air, the drumroll flourishes, and then—

And then, James is gone.

Just gone.

Poof!

The audience is stunned for a moment, silent, and then they get on their feet and begin to yell and cheer. The clown lurches forward, looks up at the chair and blinks.

Hannah and Justin are speechless.

"Wow."

"Wow."

Greta seems to explode next to them, *"He made James disappear!"* she shrieks. After a moment's pause, the clown takes his bows. And again. The applause lasts and lasts. Hannah and Justin mouth the words they will say to their son when he comes back:

James. James, you did well. James, we are so proud of you.

Finally, the applause fades. The lights go down and the curtain opens on the finale—a swinging, swooping, sparkling affair—with no sign of James. And Hannah shifts in her seat and looks around the auditorium and whispers to her husband, "When do you suppose they're going to bring him back?"